THE FRENCH WAY

Betti
Have fun in
France! xox

THE FRENCH WAY

MARY M. WRIGHT

SAPPHIRE BOOKS

SALINAS, CALIFORNIA

The French Way
Copyright © 2017 by Mary M. Wright. All rights reserved.

ISBN - 978-1-943353-83-5

Editor - Nikki Busch
Book Design - LJ Reynolds
Cover Design - Michelle Brodeur

Sapphire Books Publishing, LLC
P.O. Box 8142
Salinas, CA 93912
www.sapphirebooks.com

Printed in the United States of America
First Edition – June 2017

This and other Sapphire Books titles can be found at
www.sapphirebooks.com

Dedication

To my beautiful wife Layne Beckman Wright. She has made this love story come alive and real for me. Without her it would have remained just a story.

Acknowledgment

This book was a long time taking shape. I want to thank Allen and Jane for lovingly reading each chapter of the first draft in 2009. I am very grateful to all my beta readers, and to my editor Nikki. She suggested that the novel needed a major rewrite, and skillfully guided and supported me across that mountain. Finally, I want to acknowledge my lifelong friend I met in Montpellier, Dany Malaval, who helped me with the French.

Chapter One

Please Don't Tell

Paris smelled the same as the first time I'd been there as a teenager three years ago. From our café table, my friend Jade and I inhaled the aroma: croissants and coffee mixed with exhaust, rotten vegetables, and baking bread.

It was a Saturday morning in late August, so customers were dressed casually, most of them just returning from vacations and not back to work yet. A couple and their little boy came through the door and gazed at me in turn as they passed by. Usually, I liked the way people looked straight into your face here. Although we Americans were taught not to stare, I'd always felt comfortable with the open scrutiny I encountered from the Parisians. It made me feel warm and friendly and a part of things instead of like a foreigner. Only right now, I didn't want anyone to look at me. I felt my lip trembling on the edge of my coffee cup.

"What's Natalie like, Sophie?" Jade was asking, oblivious to my change in mood. "I want to know since we're going to be traveling all over Scotland. Do you think I'll like her?"

"Please don't tell her," I blurted out, "about... you know."

"Sophie," Jade said anxiously, "I won't say anything."

I lifted my cup again, this time managing to swallow a mouthful of the delicious, foamy brew.

"Are you all right?" Jade asked.

I shrugged and nodded. Actually, I was like a person who'd just lost their job or had someone break up with them, dangling between shock and shame, not quite ready to talk about it with anyone except, of course, my trusty friend Jade. She'd been with me constantly for the past two weeks and knew everything.

Three days ago

"I'm in France!" Jade cried with a goofy smile. We were sitting outside Café Tout Va Bien, which means Everything's Fine Cafe, on the main square of Montpellier, in the south of France. We had arrived a few hours earlier on a crowded train from Switzerland. It was still night then, so we crashed under the bushes on the Esplanade until piercing sunlight woke us.

"I can't wait to sleep in a real bed again," Jade said. She sipped her coffee.

"I know. Me too."

We'd been backpacking for ten days without much of a plan, falling in with kids at youth hostels, drinking beer, singing at the top of our lungs on hostel steps at night. And it didn't matter that we were from Minneapolis, USA. We could just as well have been from Hamburg, Germany because we were part of a backpacking culture. The only requirements were to be young and footloose with a backpack on your back and a smile on your face, and we definitely qualified for all of those.

True, Jade and I were a little scared that first day stepping off the airport bus in Luxembourg and toiling our way up a steep hill in the summer heat, the sweat rolling down our faces and the straps of our packs digging into our shoulders. We were headed to our very first youth hostel, nervous but propelled by a sense of adventure. It turned out that the travelers we met were friendly and helpful. Our biggest problems became deciding which hostel to head for next, which new friends to meet up with, and which train to board with our Eurail passes.

I gazed around at the old buildings of the square as they caught the morning sun. This was not just another stop in our travels. This was Montpellier, where I was going to attend the Université Paul Valérie for the next year. A woman in a blue smock was spraying the sidewalk in front of her grocery store, getting ready for the day. Gulls wheeled and shrieked, looking for pieces of food to steal. I swiveled my head as though to memorize these sights. This was where I would come after Jade left for home. Here I would find myself alone in a strange country, which was exactly the way I'd planned it. I wanted to see what it was like to live with no one telling me what to do or expecting anything from me. Even so, the prospect seemed daunting. "Jade, I have butterflies," I whispered.

As I turned my head to receive Jade's sympathetic look, I noticed that a woman at the next table was glancing my way. Shyly, I ducked my head but couldn't resist looking back. She was more striking than pretty: large boned with high cheekbones and heavy brows. Her white tailored blouse gave her a businesslike air, along with the briefcase and jacket that lay beside her on the table. She smiled at me. I felt an irresistible urge to start a conversation, my heart hammering, partly with the effort of speaking French, but mostly because of the intelligent gray eyes that were holding mine.

"*Bon*—" I started to say, when my view of the woman was suddenly blocked. A boy of about our age had stopped at our table. Beside him was a man, maybe ten years older. They looked like hippies. I peered around them, trying to regain eye contact with the occupant of the next table, but at that moment, she stood up and gathered her suit jacket and briefcase. With a quick smile and nod at me, the woman made her way out of the café and rounded the corner.

A bit stunned, I sat back, trying to get my head around what had just happened. I didn't have the presence of mind to react to what was going on at my table.

"*Vous permettez?*" the older hippie asked, looking at the empty chairs. Jade smiled invitingly at them, smoothing her chin-length black hair behind her ears and pushing up her glasses. The men sat down. I could hear Jade saying my name and hers. "Jean-Luc," the older one said. "And this is my friend, Bernard."

I was still reeling from the double encounter of the moment before, the woman on one side and the two men on the other. It was one of those moments that opens a window on something that has been in the dark.

Three years earlier, I'd spent six weeks with my Polish-French cousins on their farm near Paris. When I took the train by myself into the great city, I was surprised at first to be approached by young men who, just like these two, tried to make my acquaintance. I didn't think I was especially pretty. My hair was long and thin. I wore a little mascara to enhance my baby face, but basically I felt about as sophisticated as a Chihuahua. Besides that, at home in Saint Paul, in the Midwest of the US, you didn't meet people that way;

you met them in classes, or at parties but not often on the street. I wasn't used to such attention and I always said no.

But I had watched the women of Paris. Who wouldn't? I watched them walk and studied their clothes and hair, trying to understand what made them so elegant. None of them had looked at me the way the woman at the next table just had. None of them smiled at me like that. But maybe if they had...it never occurred to me before that I might not have been very interested in the young men of Paris, and that that was partly why I had always said no.

I sat up straighter. This was something I needed to think about when I had some time to myself..."What?" I said to Jade, who was talking to me.

"Earth to Sophie. I was telling Jean-Luc that you speak good French."

I nodded at Jean-Luc and spoke in that language. "I am here to improve my French and to study at the university."

"*Ah, oui?* At the *fac?*" Jean-Luc's narrow blue eyes showed surprise.

I nodded. "We have to find me a place to live and after that we're going to Paris and London."

I knew from our days in Strasbourg that Jade could understand most of what we were saying, but her high school French was so rusty, she couldn't say much herself. She simply sat there looking bright and eager, the way she had the first day of class when I'd met her at the University of Minnesota. That was why I first spoke to her—she looked like she was up for anything.

We were a study in contrasts: I was petite and blond; Jade was heavier and taller with dark hair. She was an engineering student and I was the artsy type. I was more serious and tended to hang back more. Jade often acted like a kid in a candy store. Yet, despite being different, or maybe because of it, we hit it off that first day of physics class. We'd been getting along pretty well on the road too, but there were moments like now when I wished she would consult me first before jumping into something.

I observed the two hippies as they ordered coffee. Compact and wiry, Jean-Luc had long hair partly hiding a narrow, tanned face. Bernard wore a faded tie-dyed shirt. He had curly brown hair, huge brown eyes, and an urchin-like smile. Jean-Luc's eyes flicked from me to Jade as he spoke to the waiter.

I didn't think Jade was interested in a sexual adventure with these two even though she was crazy about boys. Or men. Whatever. We were at the age when we still used the words "boys" and "girls" although we sometimes spoke of ourselves in a more dignified way as "women." In any case, I thought that these two, one boy, one man, could help us get acquainted with this city and feel less alone, which would be great. We didn't have to do anything else. It was totally up to us. Plus, hanging out with them would give us the chance to practice our French.

My high school French was enough for me to get by on while my cousins Jean-Pierre, Casimir, and Claude introduced me to French life. They took me everywhere, to Paris restaurants, to discos in Pontoise, to local family homes for dinner, and around the farm village. After the first few weeks in France, the little syllables of the language were like bubbles on my lips. I'd felt so proud hearing myself making those sounds and being understood. Knowing the language was like having a pass card to a private club. Once I became a member of that club, I had access to a different way of feeling and thinking and living. By the time I left Paris for home, I knew I had to come back. I had only skimmed the surface of this world and I wanted to get to know it much better.

"*Vous voyagez?*" Jean-Luc asked Jade, with a nod at the backpacks.

"*Voyagez,*" Jade repeated, nodding.

"*Oui.* We are traveling. We're going to Paris then London."

"Ah, *oui?* London?" Jean-Luc gestured toward his little Citroën car. "We also travel. We're artists." He fingered his necklace; its stones were a delicate mixture of colors.

"Did you make that? It's really nice," I said.

Jean-Luc's eyes were so blue they gave off a frosty light like a sunny winter's day as they penetrated mine. I shifted uncomfortably in my seat. "I find a lot of the stones myself, just traveling around," he said. "Bernard helps me. He's very good."

I smiled at Bernard. His bright, childlike face reminded me of my younger brother Joey.

"This is a very bourgeois town, Sophie," Jean-Luc continued. "Students at the medical school come from all over Europe. But you will be in *Lettres*, right?"

"Yes, that's right. French language and literature."

"In the school of Lettres, you'll meet students mostly from this region. They're not thinking about improving the world, just having a comfortable life."

"I'm sure I'll find friends here," I said, annoyed by his intrusive comments. "If I hate it, maybe I can switch to Paris."

"Where have you traveled so far?" Bernard asked, his innocent face defusing the tension I'd started to feel.

"We started out in Luxembourg and then Strasbourg," I said. Jade, recognizing the names, listened more intently. "We took a bus across the Rhine and hitched to where it said Black Forest on the map." I snorted out a laugh. "All we found were some cornfields and woods where you could hear the autobahn. We slept out there and it rained half the night." Bernard laughed, and Jean-Luc's mouth twisted into a smile. "Then we went to Geneva," I finished, "and then here."

"How would you like a tour of Montpellier?" Jean-Luc asked.

Jade understood and looked at me. "You want to?"

"We know a really good restaurant," Bernard added cheerfully. "We can go there for lunch."

"Okay, sure," I said. "Let's take the tour."

Somehow, we fit our backpacks into that already loaded car and sat on top of them, our heads almost touching the ceiling. I stuck my head out the window and felt a rush of cool air on my sweating face. We drove slowly around the old town, stopping to look at sights like the ruins of a Roman-style aqueduct.

Bernard asked, "You want to take a look at the sea?"

"Okay!" Jade and I chorused.

We climbed stone steps to a park permeated by the scent of rosemary. I took a deep breath. We were at the top of the city. Way in the distance, I could see a long gleaming line. "Is that it?" I asked excitedly, pointing.

"*Oui,*" Bernard said. "The Mediterranean has not always been so far away. Since the tenth century when the port of Montpellier was founded, the tides and sand have pushed the shoreline back."

"How far are we from the beach?" I asked.

"About nine kilometers."

Jean-Luc leaned over the railing where we stood, his long hair hanging down. "Would you like to go to the beach after lunch? To Palavas?"

When I translated for Jade she nodded enthusiastically.

"We're going to stay in the university dorms tonight," I said. "Can you drive us back after?"

"No problem," Jean-Luc said. Maybe it was the thought of a plunge into cool water that made me shiver in the warm air or maybe I was afraid for a second he wouldn't really take us back. But even if that did happen, we could always take a bus or hitch back. It wasn't that far.

"Okay," I said.

We went to a Moroccan restaurant for lunch. Then I followed Jade into the back seat again and we roared off toward the beach.

Chapter Two

Saying No

I lifted my feet and floated, shutting my eyes against the salty water as the waves spilled over my head. When I opened my eyes again I saw sailboats bobbing in the distance, and closer by, delicate pink balloons shivering on the surface.

"Jellyfish!" I shouted.

"Do they sting?" Jade asked.

"I don't know."

She quickly went ashore, keeping away from the jellyfish, but I swam and swam through the waves until I was exhausted. It felt so good. Finally, I staggered out and collapsed on a towel next to Jade. Beside her, the two French men lay facedown on beach towels.

Afraid of falling asleep and burning, I sat up to put on suntan lotion then sank back into the sand. We hadn't gotten much sleep last night. The next time I opened my eyes, it was dusk. I sat up feeling chilled. Jade and I went up and changed in the little colorful changing tents at the top of the beach.

"I'm cold. I need to get my sweater," I told Jean-Luc when we returned.

"Me too," said Jade, rubbing her arms.

"Go ahead." He tossed me the car keys. We found the Citroën in the row of small French cars parked along the street. I opened the creaky door. There were so many cases and bags, I had trouble locating our backpacks, which had been wedged down in the pile.

With our sweaters on, we watched the sun disappear along with most of the people on the beach. Families trudged away loaded with colorful beach bags and umbrellas. Jade and I went to buy sandwiches for everyone at a snack place nearby that was just closing down. We sat munching, content with the novelty of being at the seashore. Jade had never seen anything bigger than Lake Superior, and I had only been to the ocean a few times on family vacations, but it had been love at first sight.

Jean-Luc lit up a pipe and passed it around.

"What's that?" I asked.

"Hashish," he answered. I had smoked marijuana, and I knew this was more concentrated, so I only took one hot, acrid pull from the pipe. Jade had never smoked anything before, and after coughing the first time, she didn't want any more. The process of relaxation that had started in my body from swimming deepened now. I didn't want to go anywhere, do anything, at least not for a while.

We sat for a long time talking about French politics. Every so often the hash pipe would come around again. I hadn't felt anything from the first drag, so I continued to take short puffs whenever it was my turn.

The year was 1973, and Jean-Luc and Bernard were part of the Socialist movement. Strikes had become a normal part of life in France: general strikes and specific ones like mail and train, anything connected to the government. The people were demanding change. Bernard became animated as he explained the history of French popular revolts: the Revolution, the Commune, the Paris student riots in '68.

"We've gotten rid of de Gaulle," he said. "But Pompidou isn't much better. François Mitterand's a Socialist. He is going to be our next president."

The men rose to set up their tent before it got too dark. I realized that the hash was much more potent than I had originally thought. "I'm so stoned," I said to Jade with a slight giggle. We stared dreamily out at the foam as it lapped and scalloped the smooth sand.

"Jade," I finally said.

"What?"

"What do you want to do?" I had a strong feeling that we ought to go back to Montpellier, but I didn't feel like moving. I would let Jade decide.

"I don't know," she said, looking down and tracing lines in the sand with her fingers.

We watched the night sky deepen, caught by the rhythm of the waves. *Just a little while longer, and I'll ask for a ride back.* Bernard stood and sauntered down the beach. Jean-Luc sat nearby smoking a cigarette. I stretched out on my back and gazed at the haze of stars. I don't know how much time passed when Jean-Luc spoke, jerking me back into the moment. "So, what are you two going to do? You can stay here tonight if you want."

I turned my head slowly toward Jade. "Do you think we should stay?"

"Sure!" she said.

It had been a long day, and the languid sensation in my body was powerful. I didn't want to get in the car. I didn't want to have to find a room in the dorms. What a crazy idea. Impossible now. I just wanted to curl up in my sleeping bag and go to sleep. Tomorrow, they could drive us back and we'd get a room. "Okay," I replied.

Jade and I retrieved our sleeping bags from the

car. By the time we returned, it was pitch black inside the tent. We spread the bags on the soft, sandy floor. I couldn't see Jade. "Where are you?" I asked.

"Right here," she said softly, apparently already in her sleeping bag. When I stretched my arm out I could just touch her bag. I nestled myself inside mine, still wearing my clothes. The waves produced a dull, soothing roar, over and over. I was starting to fall asleep when I heard Jean-Luc come into the tent.

"Where's Bernard?" I asked.

"He's sleeping in the car." Jean-Luc arranged his bag on one side of me. I could hear Jade beginning to snore beneath the sound of the waves.

Jean-Luc whispered, "Sophie?"

"*Oui,*" I murmured.

"What's it like where you come from? Is it cold?" I didn't reply. He repeated the question.

"Cold? Yes, in the winter."

"What do you do in the winter? Ski?"

"I read a lot." I was floating up through the canvas ceiling as I answered, back out among the stars. A line from T. S. Elliot popped into my head. "*I read much of the night and go south for the winter.*"

I must have recited the line out loud, because he asked, "Do you like poetry? I like Rimbaud."

"Rimbaud." I dreamily repeated the name of one of my favorite French poets.

I felt the slight weight of Jean-Luc's arm across my hip through the sleeping bag. Distant alarm bells started ringing. I struggled up from sleep. He left his arm there and continued talking softly about the way I looked, my blue eyes and blond hair. Through the buzz in my head I tried to think. *He's trying to seduce me! I didn't realize it until now. In the US we could have camped with some guys and been just friends. Apparently not in France.* His hand, still outside the sleeping bag, started traveling slowly down my body.

"Hey, don't do that," I said, twisting away.

"Please," he said, drawing out the word. "I want you! Don't you want me too?" He kissed me on the corner of my mouth and started to unzip the sleeping bag.

"*Mais, non...*"

"Sophie!" He continued to caress me through my clothes, his hard, slight body now hovering above mine.

I was afraid. But my fear was an emotion I couldn't fully own; it seemed to skitter away from me, floating some distance above my head. I tried to talk some sense into myself. *Sophie, this is real! You've got to do something now if you don't want to have sex with this guy!* It had been no accident that Jean-Luc continued to pass the hashish pipe to me. That was why I felt so heavy and passive as though I were sinking into quicksand. Everything I tried to do seemed doomed: ineffectual and pointless. I was so out of it, my attempts to push him off were probably as weak as a baby's. He may not have even noticed them. I struggled weakly beneath him. *Damn, he's strong.* I thought of Jade. I knew once she fell asleep, she slept like the dead, but I called out anyway. "Jade!" The roar of the waves drowned out my voice.

Jean-Luc found the button of my jeans. "*Arrête!*" I managed to whisper hoarsely. "Stop!" I don't know whether he heard me. The men on the streets of Paris had stopped when I said no. But I couldn't seem to figure out a way make Jean-Luc leave me alone.

Holding me down with one arm he managed to push my jeans and underwear past my ankles with the other. On a cushion of hashish, my mind drifted far away from the reality of what was happening. I let my body go limp; I just wanted it to be over so I could go back to sleep and dream about the stars and the sea. I don't know whether I fainted or what, but I seemed to sink into blackness.

Sometime during the night, I came to. My bag was zipped up, and I was, at last, alone.

≈≈≈≈

Above the whooshing of the waves, I heard Bernard's angry voice outside the tent, and Jean-Luc's sharp retort rising above it. I sat up and glanced at Jade beside me, her mouth open as she slept.

The buzz from last night had worn off. I remembered everything: Jean-Luc's hands pressing me down, his penis jabbing into me. Jean-Luc had had sex with me against my will, that much was clear. But it had been my fault too. Why had I let myself get so stoned?

The tent's zipper let in fresh air as I stepped out. Jean-Luc turned away from Bernard to put his hand on my shoulder. I jerked away. Jean-Luc looked surprised and even a little hurt. Really? Did he think we were together now or something? I pulled my cardigan close, buttoning it against the cool morning air. *I've got to play it cool. We're dependent on Jean-Luc to drive us back.* I turned to trek across the sand to the bathrooms. With each footfall, I felt my tears flow faster. I sat, letting the sobs come and when they finally stopped, I wiped the tears away and walked back.

I saw that they had a little blue gas flame burning with a coffeepot on top. Bernard produced half a stick of bread, tore a piece off, and passed the loaf around. I took a deep breath of the pungent sea air. It had helped to cry. I felt a little better. My hands closed gratefully around the mug of fragrant coffee and I sat down in the sand.

Something was going on with the two guys. As they ate, Jean-Luc stared at the sun rising over the waves and Bernard looked down at the ground. They might have been a married couple after a tiff. Jean-Luc lit a cigarette as Jade came stumbling out of the tent. She took the mug of coffee Bernard offered to her.

Jean-Luc said, "We need to take the tent down before people start coming to the beach." So we helped them pack up. Then we piled into the car and drove to a high-rise building in Montpellier.

"Our friends Aimée and Jean live here," said Bernard. "They'll let us use their shower."

Aimée greeted us at the door, kissing the men on both cheeks. She said bonjour to Jade and me.

I tried to shower quickly because I knew the others were waiting. Even so, I tipped my face up to the stream of water and willed it to wash away what had happened last night. But although my face felt clean, my heart was still in no-man's-land. It was as though a part of me was sullenly waiting for me to pay attention to it. But there was no time to do that now; it would have to wait. I put on the same clothes I'd had on from yesterday and waited on the sofa while Jade took her turn in the shower. Jean-Luc sat down beside me and put his arm around my shoulders. I glared at him and moved away from his touch.

"What's wrong?" he said.

I looked at him. *He doesn't even seem to think he's done anything wrong!* "I'm not your girlfriend, that's what," I said. He shrugged as though that was beside the point. "I didn't want to sleep with you last night,"

I tried again.

"I thought you wanted to."

"Yes? Even after I told you I didn't?"

"But by that time, I couldn't stop."

"Couldn't? You mean you didn't want to stop."

"I'm sorry, Sophie." He hung his head.

Was he really sorry? I didn't think so. I was the sorry one.

"We are planning to go to a beautiful cave called Grotte des Demoiselles," he continued. "We are going especially for you and Jade. I think you will like it. Will you come?"

"We have to get back to Montpellier," I said.

"Please, Sophie. I want to do something good for you. After that, I will take you back. But if you don't want to go, I'll take you back now."

"Go where?" Jade asked, plopping down in a chair. Jean-Luc told her about the cave. Naturally, she wanted to go. She never wanted to miss out on anything. So we ended up bumping along in the back seat of Aimée's car with Bernard and Jade. Jean-Luc rode in the front seat. My stomach was suddenly queasy. Sweat pricked my face and I started to cry again. I wanted my mom.

Through my tears, I looked over at Jade's surprised expression. "Arrête!" I said, my voice squeaking. "Stop the car!" The car slowed and stopped by the side of the road. Four faces turned to stare at me as I wiped the tears away. "Take us to the fac," I said, looking into Jean-Luc's piercing blue eyes. I turned to Bernard. "Thank you for yesterday."

Jean-Luc frowned.

For a moment, I actually felt guilty for bailing out. Then abruptly, Aimée started the car and turned the wheel, heading back to Montpellier. We drove in silence.

At the university, the men hauled out our gear and dumped it by the side of the road. Bernard grunted and kissed me and Jade on both cheeks. Jean-Luc grasped my hand, ignoring Jade. "Peace," he said in English.

Chapter Three

Screaming in the Shower

We stood up shakily under the weight of our backpacks.

"Peace," I muttered. "What bullshit."

"Hey," said Jade, peering at me as we walked through the campus. "What's going on?"

"I'll tell you later. Let's find the dorms first, okay?"

After filling out forms in the office, we started up the stairs of the building. "We've got our own rooms!" Jade squealed and I smiled with the first enthusiasm I'd felt all day.

Our rooms were side by side. I had a narrow bed, a desk, a sink, and a braided rug. The sheets smelled sweet as I buried my head in them. Straightening up, I saw I'd left a few grains of sand behind and beat them out vehemently, replacing the spread.

I hadn't had a room to myself since, well, I don't know when. I shared a room with my sister Anne at home. Images entered my mind from over the years: Anne studying late with her lamp on at her desk while I tried to sleep. Mom calling us to come to breakfast, getting dressed for school on dark mornings, the pleasure of sleeping in on Saturdays. Those days were gone forever.

Jade entered through the open door and looked around. "Just like mine. They have sinks in the rooms here." She was well acquainted with dorms since she'd lived in one at school.

"I know. What luxury," I replied from the bed.

"I want to take another shower and change my clothes," she said with a sigh, sinking onto the bed beside me. We looked at each other.

"Sophie," she began, "tell me what's wrong. Are you mad at me?"

"At you? No." I took a deep breath. "Jean-Luc..." The word "rape" was hard to say, but I said it.

"Oh! Oh shit. Sophie!" Alarmed brown eyes looked at me. "I didn't know."

"You were sound asleep—how could you? Hey," I said, raising my hand to forestall her response, "I know what a sound sleeper you are. I don't blame you." My voice cracked. "I let it happen, Jade. I wimped out."

"Sophie, no, it's not your fault. We should never have stayed with them last night."

"I asked you what you wanted to do, and you said we should stay," I replied, my voice taking on an accusing edge.

"I didn't want to spoil it for you if you wanted to."

"You're the one who wanted to meet them so badly," I snapped. "The whole thing started because of you."

Jade awkwardly put her arm around me. "I'm sorry Sophie." She looked up at me sadly over her glasses. "At the airport, your mom asked me to watch out for you. And I didn't."

"Yeah, right. It's like asking a baby to watch a baby."

"We're twenty years old, Sophie," she said solemnly. "We're not babies."

"I know. I didn't mean to yell at you, Jade. It

wasn't your fault. I was pretty out of it last night."

"Yeah, 'cause you smoked that dope."

"I know. I wish I hadn't." I sat in silence for a moment.

Her head still bowed, Jade murmured, "I thought maybe you liked that guy."

"What? Which one? Bernard?"

"Jean-Luc."

"Are you kidding me? No way! God." We sat leaning against each other in silence for a while. There was no possibility of going back, no way to undo what had happened. I knew I was going to have to pull myself together somehow and move on. But first, I wanted a shower, a real shower, and a change of clothes. I stood up. "Jade." I pulled her to her feet. "Come on, girlfriend, why don't we try out those showers?"

"Good idea. Do you mind if I go first? By myself?"

"No, you go ahead."

She left, leaving the door partly open. After a few minutes, I stood up to close the door so I could change into my robe. Pausing in the open doorway, I was startled to hear Jade's voice coming from the bathroom down the hall, starting like a groan and gaining in volume and pitch until it was a full-out scream, though muffled by the sound of the water. Her voice sent a thrill up my spine. I waited until I heard her door click shut and stepped out into the hall.

"Hey, Jade. Can I come in?"

"Sure."

She was still damp, her rounded body wrapped in a towel, her dark hair plastered to her head.

"Are you okay?"

"Actually, yeah. That's what I do when I'm feeling super bad. I wait until no one's around and then I scream as loud as I can." Her face was pink, a bright spot in each of her eyes. "It helps a lot."

"Okay, I'll try it."

It's not easy to scream on purpose. I had some starts and stops, squawking like a chicken before I managed a drawn-out "Aaaaaaaaaagh!" As the shower crashed over me, I felt myself expand, filling the whole room until I was bigger and more powerful than anyone, including Jean-Luc.

I dried off quickly and put on my robe. After all that furious activity in the shower, I felt strangely ghostlike and empty as I wafted down the hall to my room.

❧❧❧❧

Jade and I were pretty good friends back at school, but we'd never spent this much time together before. In the last couple of weeks, I'd noticed things about her that I hadn't before, like her tendency to be too perky and upbeat. In the past, I'd liked the way she was always up for some fun, but lately I'd begun to find it irritating. Not when she was being genuinely enthusiastic; I loved that. But sometimes her voice would take on this fake, squeaky tone as it did last night. In those cases, she was unable to step back and say no even when I was sure she wanted to—as though everything was always fine with her when, in fact, it wasn't.

Now when I passed her room, I detected a subtle change in her. She was relaxing on her bed with the door open. It was something in the way she held her head, in the silent, knowing look we exchanged. Perhaps I could trust her in the future to speak up if something didn't feel right.

I lay down on my bed. I'd been so high last night, I'd only half experienced what happened, so my memory of it was hazy too. But that didn't take away the raw and painful feelings. I felt sleazy and dirty. I had smoked that dope. I had put myself and Jade in jeopardy. No one had made me. Yes, I'd smoked before at parties, but that had been with friends. It's what you did. But these were strange men, friends for the day. And this was France. The drug was hashish, not marijuana. I had chosen to trust Jean-Luc. *Bad choice, Sophie.* I felt like I couldn't rely on my own judgment anymore.

For the next hour or so I drifted in and out of sleep. At one point, I awoke clearheaded enough to start thinking.

Who am I anyway?

The person I used to be was now floating in pieces before my eyes. I couldn't go back to being that girl— the happy backpacker. Nor could I go back to being the daughter I was before I came. She was gone too. Pieces of her were still with me, of course, but I couldn't be her anymore. None of me fit together.

And there was something else, something I'd told myself I was going to think about later. What was it? It was big and important. Oh, yeah! The woman in the café. I had almost forgotten about her. I sat up in bed, remembering the warm and searching way her eyes had connected with mine. She was someone I had seen for a minute and probably never would encounter again, but...it was crazy. That brief moment had done something to me. A quickening of excitement rose up from the center of the chaos and pain. I sat up and swung my legs over the side of the bed. Maybe the woman lived in Montpellier. I might actually run into her again!

In the mirror over the sink I saw I looked like a freak. Having lain down with wet hair, it stuck out all over my head. I grimaced. My eyes were ringed with dark circles. I dug in my backpack for my tiny makeup bag and did my best to fix my face. Wetting my hair down again, I dragged a comb through it severely. Then, after donning my last clean T-shirt over nearly clean jeans, I went next door to Jade's room. She was dressed, lying on her bed, reading a book.

"How are you doing?" she asked.

"Okay. You hungry? You want to go find that student restaurant?" We had gotten meal tickets along with our room keys.

"Sure, I'm starving."

Over lunch I told Jade the gist of what I'd been thinking about in bed—how I couldn't be the same old me anymore.

"Well, you'll find a new way of being you, Sophie."

I felt touched by her simple statement of faith. "Thanks." I looked into her safe brown eyes. "I just can't throw myself in with the youth hostel crowd anymore, Jade. I don't want to even try to be that happy."

Jade laughed. "Me neither. But we're always meeting people. That's how it is when you're on the road. We'll just meet different types from now on."

"You think?"

"I'm sure. Like, wasn't there someone at the café yesterday you wanted to talk to? When the guys showed up?" I nodded, looking shyly away. Jade had noticed.

"Well, she was different, wasn't she?" Jade said.

"Yeah, she sure was." We finished eating in silence, then rose to bus our trays. "Jade," I said, "we have to find me a place to live. How the heck are we going to do that? When I feel like this?"

"Like what?"

"Like crap."

Jade smiled, hooking her elbow into mine. "Don't worry, Sophie. You've got me!"

And I did. I was the walking wounded, but Jade was a force of nature. She energetically forged a path forward as I leaned on her arm. She was the one who found the housing office, eventually asking about housing in her bad French once we got inside. Until then, together we stood in the warm sun at the end of a line of students that snaked outside the door.

The place didn't open until 2:00 p.m. Everything closed down around there during the lunch hour. When it was finally our turn, they gave us a list of addresses and a map. I decided to look first in the new part of town near the university. The first landlady peered at me critically, one of the bourgeois types Jean-Luc had warned me about. Despite my clean T-shirt from when we did laundry in Geneva, my jeans were baggy and slightly gray at the knees.

The room we ultimately found the next afternoon was on rue des Tourterelles, street of the turtledoves, in a two-story house with a little walled-in garden. The houses in that quarter were mostly single-story with red-tile roofs and gardens surrounded by low walls, cypress trees, and aromatic herbs that grew everywhere. I loved the whole neighborhood. Giant pines towered over the houses in the distance. The countryside, with its orchards and vineyards, was not too far down the road.

My new landlord, M. Nguyen, seemed nice. The room was at the end of the corridor and had a sink, a bed, and a desk. Since it was a corner room, I was lucky enough to have two windows. The bare linoleum floor would be cozier after I bought a rug. I'd share the bathroom and kitchen with other students.

Hot and tired, we walked back to the campus. While our clothes tumbled in the dorm's laundry room, I said, "I want to get out of Montpellier as soon as we can. I keep thinking we're going to run into Jean-Luc everywhere we go."

"Yeah, I know what you mean," said Jade. "If there's a train to Paris tonight, let's be on it."

"Sounds good to me."

I pulled out my itinerary from the bottom of my bag. "Let's see. We don't have to meet Natalie in London until..." I read aloud, "Arrive at Luxembourg, August 15. Find housing in Montpellier. Meet Natalie evening August 31, Concorde Hotel, London. Meet Dad September 10, Berkshire Hotel." I stopped reading. "Meet Dad?" I squealed. "Oh my God, I forgot all about that! Things were so crazy before we left. Seems like months ago I wrote this."

My relations with my parents were about as good as that of most people my age, which means kind of up and down. This summer my mom had worried in general about my going to study in Montpellier. I didn't blame her. It was one thing to have your child leave home for college; it was another for her to leave for a different country. And I was the first to go. So of course it was hard for her. Even though I had spent a summer in France already, that had been under the protection of relatives. Now I was determined to live in a city where I knew no one. She'd kept asking me, "Why don't you go to Paris, Sophie? I thought you liked your cousins so much."

"I do, Mom," I'd responded. "But I just want to be on my own. And in the south I'll be near the sea. I think I'll really like it down there."

I was two years older than the age one usually leaves for college, so you might think that I was more mature. In some ways, I probably was. But leaving home was leaving home. I guess Mom knew that better than I did.

In any case, to escape her words of concern, I spent a lot of time over at Jade's before we left the US. She was staying at her brother's house, having given up her dorm room for the summer. We lay around endlessly looking at maps and planning our travels.

My dad, a soil science professor at the University of Minnesota, had been going back to the lab a lot at night. When I did see Dad, we argued about stupid things like how I was going to handle my money. I'd saved that money by working part-time and living at home. I favored taking it in a lump sum and starting a bank account. Dad was worried I might overspend and run out of money before my year was up. I didn't like being dependent on them and the international mail, but in the end, Dad prevailed and I agreed to let them send me a check every month.

"I remember you told me your father was going to be in England at a scientific conference and we were going to meet him in London. I forgot too," said Jade.

"And I was so upset that he didn't come to the airport! He probably figured he'd see me in a few weeks."

"He still should have come to see you off," said Jade staunchly.

"Yeah," I said. "Well, anyway it will be fun to see the sights with him in London. So, let's see: if we leave today, that would give us three days in Paris."

"I just can't wait to see Paris for the first time." Jade was starry-eyed.

I pulled out the train schedule I'd picked up at the

station. "There's a train tonight at twenty-two hours. That's ten o'clock. We could get a sleeper."

That night, we walked along the line of cars until we got to the ones marked *wagon-lits*, and stepped aboard. The porter helped us find a compartment with just two bunks. I took the top berth and was soon gazing out the window, watching as the lights of Montpellier grew dimmer and vanished. Beneath us, a powerful, rumbling vibration was bringing us ever closer to the great city.

Very early the next morning, there was a knock on our door. "Paris, *vingt minutes*." We had twenty minutes to get dressed before rolling to a stop in the great central station, Gare Saint-Lazare.

Chapter Four

Winged Victory

I'll be fine," I told Jade in the café by the station, forcing up the corners of my mouth. "See?" She still looked at me anxiously. "Come on, Jade," I said. "We're going to have fun in Paris. Because if we can't do that, it means Jean-Luc wins."

Jade shook her head vigorously. "That's not gonna happen."

I pulled out the youth hostel guide from my backpack. "Okay, look." We bent over the map. "The hostel is near Porte de Clichy—it's the one Jill told us about." Jill was an American we'd met in Strasbourg.

"Right. It's just five stops on the blue line," Jade said. "Jill said the hostel was pretty big, so they should have openings. After we check in, what do you want to do?" I asked.

"I don't know, Sophie. I want to see the things I've heard about, I guess. Like the Eiffel Tower and the Louvre."

We stopped at a *tabac* on the way to the metro and bought postcards and stamps then leaned against a wall writing to our parents. There was a mailbox outside the shop and we wanted to get them off right away.

"Just got into Paris," I wrote. "Found a nice room in Montpellier near the university." I wrote my new address so they could send the box I'd stuffed with my clothes and belongings before leaving, things I'd need during the school year. As I wrote, I made up my mind never to tell them what happened on the beach. That scenario was one of a parent's worst nightmares, and I was determined to spare them.

Jade was still printing in tiny letters on her postcard of the Eiffel Tower. "Come on, let's get going," I said, dropping my card in the box.

At the hostel, we got a private room. Out the window you could see hilly Montmartre, where a white-domed church appeared through a mixture of sun and wispy clouds. The hostel was nicer than any we'd stayed in. They offered free coffee, rolls, and fruit every morning, so we found the dining room and had a second breakfast.

"Jill said next week," I said, "and that was, what… Monday we left Strasbourg?"

"Tuesday. I got the impression she was arriving this weekend, so maybe we'll run into her."

I stared at a couple of young women at the next table behind Jade. One of them was tomboyish, with short dark hair. The other one had long, curly red hair and wore an embroidered peasant blouse. There was something about them as they leaned close and laughed, a certain tenderness in their postures. I thought of the woman in Montpellier. The redhead moved even closer and kissed the other one briefly on the mouth. I felt my face go hot. The short-haired one caught me gazing at them and smiled. I forced myself to hold her gaze, despite the fact that my heart was pounding and I wanted to look away and run out of the room.

"Hi," I said, and the two young women came over, introducing themselves as Annik and Kari from Holland. The fact that they spoke English made Jade perk up.

"Is this your first day?" Jade asked.

"No, we've been here a week already. Your first day?"

"Yes," I answered. "I've been to Paris before, but Jade hasn't, so I want her to see as much as possible."

We chatted for a while. I noticed a quality about them that I'd seen before in lesbians, a certain direct gaze that was different from the way straight girls looked at me.

"What are you doing tonight?" I asked.

"Well, it's Saturday night," said Annik. "We are going to a club. You want to come with us?"

"I'd love to! Jade?"

Jade nodded eagerly. She was like a sponge soaking up everything that was Paris. We made plans to meet in the lounge at 7:00 p.m. to go out for dinner first and then to the club.

Back in our room, I turned to Jade, my heart again pounding. "You know the club will probably be a gay one. Are you sure this is really something you want to do?"

"Oh, sure! We've gone dancing in gay bars in Minneapolis before," she said blithely. Gay bars were fun because you could go with a group of girls and the men didn't bother you.

"I know. But those were for men. This time, there'll be women and some of them may find you kind of cute," I said with a wink.

"Well, I don't care." She tossed her head. "I don't want to miss it. I'll just dance with you and maybe they'll think we're a couple and leave us alone. Besides, we said we were going to have fun in Paris, right?"

"Of course. But if you change your mind I can go

alone." I wanted to make sure Jade genuinely wanted to go, so even if she had a bad time, it was not going to be somehow my fault for dragging her along.

"I'm a big girl," said Jade. "Now, come on. I want to see the Eiffel Tower."

It was a beautiful summer day. We dressed in sleeveless blouses and jeans and descended back into the metro.

"We have to change at Concorde," I said, consulting the large map on the wall. Inside the metro, I enjoyed reading the ads on the tunnel walls and watching French people, especially the women. They seemed so confident. I wanted to be like them. I wanted to rush out and get a makeover and buy tons of clothes so I could look just like them. Stop it, I told myself. We were apparently having the same thoughts because Jade leaned over and said, "French women are so slim. How do they do that?"

"It's because they all smoke," I said. We laughed. "Plus, they eat a lot of vegetables. And they don't snack between meals like Americans do."

We stood beneath the Eiffel Tower, which straddled the road. As cars went past us, we looked up and saw nothing but black iron lacework covering the sky.

"I can't believe how big it is close up!" Jade marveled. While we stood in line to buy tickets for the elevator, she read from a brochure she'd picked up off the ground.

"The tower was constructed for the 1889 World Exhibition. It is one thousand and fifty feet high. Hmmm...it sways about five inches in high wind. Whew. Makes me dizzy to even read that." She dropped the brochure to the ground.

We passed people climbing steps on our way up in

the elevator. We preferred to ride and save our energy for the rest of the day, although you did have to walk for the last part to the top. It was windy up there and it felt like we were swaying slightly. "Ooh," I said, clutching the railing. "Don't look down."

Back on the ground, we bought sandwiches from a truck and sat on a bench, contentedly people watching as we ate. On a bench across from us, a teenage boy and girl were kissing. A couple of young men strolled toward us, smiling, but I effectively waved them away.

"Hey, they were cute!" protested Jade after they had shrugged and moved on.

I shuddered slightly. "I just can't deal with French guys right now."

"Oh, Sophie, I'm sorry. I didn't think."

That was the trouble with Jade. She didn't often think unless it was about statistics or logarithms, whatever those were. But I didn't mind.

As soon as we finished eating, Jade shot up like a puppy without a leash. She bounced and pounced, her head swiveling to take in everything that she could. I followed her to the end of the park facing the Eiffel Tower and we turned toward the river.

Hanging over the railing on Pont des Invalides, our eyes followed the graceful arch of the next bridge as we watched the river traffic.

"What are those boats called?" asked Jade as the crowded deck of a sightseeing boat passed below us.

I grabbed her arm. "Don't lean over so far. They're called Bateaux Mouches. It means boat of flies." Jade laughed.

We crossed the bridge and walked along the embankment, while traffic whizzed by on our left, before crossing the street to Place de la Concorde.

This gigantic square at the center of Paris held us entranced for a moment, with its circle of gracious old buildings, restaurants, and shops. "This place is just so…incredible," Jade finally said.

"I know. See that obelisk?" I said. "That's from Egypt. It's three thousand years old!"

"How'd they get it here?" she asked

"No idea."

"Isn't this where the guillotine used to be?" she asked.

I nodded. "I prefer to think of it as where Maxim's is. Too bad we can't afford to eat there." We headed toward the iron gates of the adjacent park, weaving our way through the crowd there.

White statues peeked out of the greenery here and there in the Tuileries Gardens. Originally, these were the royal gardens of the Louvre Palace, a haven of pruned shrubs, flower beds, and fountains. We sat on a bench near a statue of Mercury on a winged horse and watched a well-dressed middle-aged woman walk by with her white Standard Poodle. The well-trained pooch didn't even look at us as they passed, although Jade was leaning forward with her hand out, hoping to pet it. Apparently, the canines of Paris were not to be touched.

"So, Sophie," she said. "Why don't you want to tell Natalie about what happened?"

"It's just…I'm ashamed to tell her. It's not like being robbed, I mean. I wouldn't mind telling people I was robbed."

"But if she's your friend…?"

I didn't respond to Jade's question but leaned back on the bench and sighed. How to explain that Natalie had brought light and culture and ideas into my dull little teenage life and part of me still craved her good opinion.

A crew of daycare toddlers was being herded by in front of us. The children were adorable in their tiny dresses and shorts and little white socks and brought a smile to my face. Some of the girls wore bows in their hair. God, I loved Paris.

After they passed, I returned my attention to Jade. "I've known her since high school. We started a school literary magazine with some other kids and we used to do poetry readings. Her dad's on the city council. She has a lot of opinions about everything. You know, I'm not that into politics, but Natalie is very well-informed. She can talk your ear off if you let her."

"Well, she sounds like kind of a bitch."

I looked at Jade incredulously. "What do you mean? She's beautiful. She's tall and slim and has long blond hair and huge blue eyes. She's fun and creative. I've always followed her around like a stray puppy dog. Art is her thing. And she lives in a big Victorian house in Saint Paul."

"You sound like you're in love with her." Jade laughed.

I bristled. "I admire her is all. I'm not in love with her."

"Have you ever thought you might be gay?"

"Well..." I began, my mouth suddenly going dry. It was crazy, but I had never talked to Jade or anyone about this. Here in Europe where we didn't fit in anyway seemed like the right place to finally break my silence. "Sometimes I think I might be," I answered. "I've only dated guys before. But I've actually had some major crushes on girls, especially in high school."

I remembered how there was nothing I could do but wait for those feelings to go away. It was like tumbling into deep water not knowing how to swim. I thought that was because it was forbidden, especially in my Catholic high school. With the boys I'd dated, everything seemed more predictable. That was more like taking swimming lessons in a group with an instructor.

"You could be bi," she said.

"Yeah." I'd assumed that I was at least as interested in boys as I was girls. I had dubbed myself bisexual, conveniently, despite never having even tried out the other half of the equation. I was going to ignore that half of me because everything in my middle-class Midwestern US environment conspired to make me do so. "Anyway," I said, "when it's a boy, at least you can tell your friends and laugh about it. But when it's a girl...I've never told anyone before."

Jade smiled, her brown eyes shining because I'd shared a secret with her. Then she frowned and asked, "So is that why you broke up with Ted?"

"Oh, Ted." I waved my hand dismissively at the mention of my college boyfriend.

"Does breaking up with him have anything to do with liking girls?"

"Not really. I wasn't in love with him. I think I was more attracted to his sister than to Ted."

"Huh. Does she feel like that about you too?"

"No, no." I laughed, then sobered up. "I've always wanted to get married and have kids and everything. But...I'd hate to get married without ever finding out what it's like with a girl, Jade." I grimaced. "I'm almost afraid to find out though, in case it turns out I like them better."

There, I'd told her what was really messing with my head right now. If I preferred girls, then my dream of marriage and kids would remain just that, a dream, not to mention the fact that I might feel like a pariah among the people I knew back home. The solid ground beneath my feet would truly shift away.

"Well, as long as you really love someone, I think that's all that matters," Jade said.

๛๛๛๛

The first thing that greeted us inside the Louvre was the Winged Victory statue, standing gloriously tall on the landing above the front hall. A tingle ran from my head to my toes. The Greek goddess Victory had one leg thrust forward, her body arched, her wings wide open, ready to fly. She was so bold and strong and beautiful. She had once graced the prow of an ancient Greek ship. I may have admired Natalie as a teenager, but Natalie had nothing on this lady.

We walked through the galleries until we stood at last in front of the *Mona Lisa*. Peering between people's shoulders, I viewed a very different feminine image from Victory, but there was something seductive in her smile that I liked just as much.

"Wow," Jade said, "now I know what all the fuss is about. It's like she's alive, isn't it?"

I nodded as I checked the plaque next to another Renaissance painting, a crowded party scene topped by fluffy clouds. It was called, the *Marriage at Cana*, by Veronese. Suddenly, I thought of my parents. *Lucky them: they're still together and I guess still in love.* In fact, I thought with surprise, *It's their wedding anniversary today, isn't it?* August 28. *When Mom was my age, she was just getting married. And here I am not even sure about my sexuality, much less ready for marriage. Oh well.* I looked fondly at Jade who was leaping ahead to the next gallery. *At least now I've told someone.*

Chapter Five

Not Officially Crazy

Jade and I decided to go back to the hostel. We collapsed on our beds and soon fell asleep. I had a dream that I was in the tent with Jean-Luc and had floated up to the ceiling where he couldn't reach me. I wanted to get out of the tent, but the only way out was through the door and I would have had to come down and risk being grabbed by him. "Jade!" I yelled.

Her head appeared upside down from the upper mattress. "What's the matter?" When I told her the dream, she said, "Oh, that's awful, Sophie." She looked at her watch. "We ought to get ready for dinner." Climbing down from her bunk, she put her hand comfortingly on my shoulder. "Are you okay?"

"Oh, sure," I mumbled, determined for it to be true.

Jade and I dug in our backpacks for something to wear, pulling out our dresses from the bottom. They were short, pretty synthetic numbers; easy-care types, but mine was wrinkled and it smelled funny. I sprinkled the dress with water and some cologne of Jade's then waved it around out the window.

"That's where I want to go for dinner," I pointed. "Up that hill. See? That's Sacré-Coeur."

"What does that mean? Sacred cow?"

"No, you ding-dong. They wouldn't name a church that. It means Sacred Heart."

"Oh."

We put on colored knee socks that matched our dresses. We even applied some makeup and put on our platform shoes. I could only find one earring. Anyway, my hair had grown out over my ears by then so I decided to skip earrings. It seemed ages ago when I'd gotten a haircut back home. I brushed my blond hair until it shone, deciding I'd rather wait to get it cut when it was long enough for me to try something different. We took sweaters in case it got cool. I was nervous when we thumped down the stairs to meet Kari and Annik, wondering whether we were dressed right or if we had to wear jeans and flannel shirts to go to a lesbian club.

Annik was wearing pants, but she looked dressed up in a long-sleeved lacy top and dangly earrings, so I relaxed about how we looked. Kari looked nice too in a white shirt with a large pointed collar, a pearl on a chain around her neck, and dark flared pants. She sported earrings too but not the dangly kind.

We didn't talk much on the subway, but I stole glances at the two women, who were holding hands discreetly. They seemed a few years older than us. I bet they had jobs. I liked Annik's red tangly hair, the way it changed color and glowed with the shifting light. I have always been riveted by red hair and the translucent skin that often goes with it. Kari sat beside her and smiled as she caught my eye as though she knew I'd been admiring her girlfriend. I couldn't help but grin back. Excitement bubbled through my body. Here I was with lesbians, on my way to who knows where? It was the start of a great adventure, I just knew it, and I could hardly believe that something like this was really happening to me.

We climbed the stone steps toward the top of Montmartre where the Sacré-Coeur Basilica glowed above us in the floodlights. On the left, across a stretch of grass, were dark woods. We could have been in the country instead of the middle of Paris, except when I glanced back over Jade and Kari's heads I could see the city spread out. On one side was the Étoile—its lighted streets radiated from the Arc de Triomphe to form a star. And beyond the black curve of the river glittered the Eiffel Tower. "Look, Jade," I said pointing.

I remembered the night Natalie ran down a stairway just like this from Linden Park in Saint Paul toward the river. It was winter and her long sealskin coat flew dramatically behind her. I turned back to the steps and continued trudging up them as the wind whipped around my face. I hugged myself against the chill and when we finally reached the top, I pulled my sweater on. Our eyes were drawn to the satin blanket of light that spread around us on all sides. No wonder Paris was called "the city of light." Our eyes turned back to the church with its lighted dome.

"How old is it?" asked Jade.

"Oh, it's new." Annik laughed. "Finished in the early part of this century. But that little church over there"—she pointed down a nearby lane—"that one is one of the oldest in Paris, maybe eight hundred years old."

"Do you know why this hill is called Montmartre?" I asked.

"Sure," said Kari. "Something to do with some martyrs. When was that? When were there Christian martyrs? Close to two thousand years ago, I think."

"It was Saint Denis and a couple others," said Annik. "They were beheaded on this hill."

"Gross," said Jade.

"This hill used to be a peaceful little country

village," Annik continued, "with windmills. There is still a little vineyard up here somewhere. And they dug out plaster of Paris here, too."

"It's the mineral gypsum, actually," Jade said, catching and holding her hair away from her face.

"Oh, yes," said Annik. "They used the windmills to grind it up. Then the windmills became cabarets like the Moulin Rouge. And famous artists lived up here, like Renoir and Picasso."

We followed Kari down a narrow, cobbled lane past the old church. Cars were parked halfway up on the sidewalk so we had to walk single file. Ahead, I glimpsed a large square from which drifted snatches of music. Several small restaurants on this side street had tables set out on the sidewalk, but no diners were out because of the wind. We checked menus posted in the windows and entered a tiny place called les Grands Amis. The large owner greeted us with a big smile, called us *mesdemoiselles*, and seated us near the window. All the empty tables had wineglasses turned upside down.

We ordered a bottle of red and, as an appetizer, some snails in garlic sauce with medallions of fried bread. I'd never had snails. Despite my initial distaste, they were delicious. But then, almost everything tastes good in France. When the waiter came back, I ordered the more familiar *Boef Bourguignon* as my entrée.

"So, you are going to study in France, Sophie?" said Annik.

"Yes, I'm majoring in French," I said. "Jade's in engineering."

"You are going to build bridges, eh?" said Kari.

"I'll build something," said Jade.

"Where have you been on your travels?" asked Kari, leaning her elbows on the table with the air of a good listener.

We told them where we had been, finishing with Montpellier.

"We met these French guys in Montpellier," Jade blurted out.

I am going to kill her.

"They seemed nice," Jade continued, oblivious to my mood. "We went to the beach and camped with them."

"Oh?" said Kari. She looked at my glowering face. "Did something happen?"

Annik said, "Stop it, Kari. This is none of our business."

I took a long drink of my wine, recovering my poise as the liquid seeped through my veins. After all, we had told no one so far. Who better to confide in than these kind strangers? I finally said truthfully, "I don't mind talking about it. One of them thought I wanted to have sex with him," I said.

"Why did he think that?" Kari asked.

"I don't know. Maybe because we decided to camp with them."

"That is not a reason," Kari replied sternly.

"For a French person it might be," I replied.

"Are you saying you were raped, Sophie?" Annik asked.

I nodded. I took a deep breath to explain, but just then the waiter arrived with our meals. When he left, I said, "Actually, I learned a big lesson."

"What is that?" Annik asked.

"That I need to learn to trust myself." They nodded, seeming to understand what I meant. "I'm getting better at it." I grinned. "When I met you two I didn't let my shyness stop me like I normally would have."

"That's wonderful," said Annik. "I'm so glad we met."

"We thought at first you two were a couple," said Kari, changing the subject. I relaxed, concentrating again on my delicious meal.

"Oh no, we're just friends," Jade said.

"I am usually not wrong," Kari said, looking at me. "I had a feeling maybe you are one who likes girls."

"I guess I am," I said. "But I don't know—I have no experience."

Kari said, "Do you need experience to know what you like?"

I laughed nervously. "No. But tell us about you. Are you students, too?"

"I am a nurse," said Annik, "and Kari is a medical student."

"Where are you from in Holland?" I asked.

"Amsterdam," she said. "We live together now, since just before we came on this trip." They exchanged a happy glance.

"Oh," said Jade. "Congratulations."

"Thank you. We plan to get married," said Kari.

I gasped. "Really?"

"Are you surprised?" asked Kari.

"Well, I always thought marriage had to be between a man and a woman."

"Why?"

"I guess it doesn't," I said, my voice faltering.

"Is it legal in Holland?" Jade asked, a step ahead of me.

"No, not yet," said Annik with a smile. "We'll have a ceremony with our family and friends."

"But someday we'll have the real thing," said Kari. "It will happen in the Netherlands. Things are changing so fast. Two years ago, they lowered the age of consent. It used to be twenty-one for gays and sixteen for everyone else."

"That wasn't fair," Jade said.

"No, it wasn't. And now, just this year," said Annik excitedly, "the military has decided to accept homosexuals, and also we are no longer officially considered crazy by the mental health association." She laughed. "That's something, eh? Anyway, our country has always had a liberal attitude, like France. A lot of people are coming out in the Netherlands now."

"I guess a lot are in the US too," I said, "but you're miles ahead of us. Our country is so conservative."

"And yet, because of you we have the gay liberation movement around the world, because of Stonewall," Kari said.

"What's that?" asked Jade. I hadn't heard of it either.

"You don't know about Stonewall? It's a famous bar in Greenwich Village in New York," she answered. "I can't believe it was just four years ago. The police used to raid gay bars. But this time, the people fought back. There was a riot and the police lost control. After that, there were protests around the world. This was a very big story, Sophie."

"I was in high school," I said defensively, "and there were so many riots and protests going on."

"Well, now you know about it," Kari said.

"Are there lesbian bars in Amsterdam?" I asked.

"A few, yes."

Jade said, "I see lots of androgynous-looking women on campus."

"I can't see myself dressing that way," I said. "I like pretty clothes."

Annik said, "The women the police went after, they were butches, dressed just like men. But now, it's not considered feminist to want to look like a man. You have to be androgynous."

"Not everywhere," said Kari. "There are still some bars in Paris where you walk in and think you are looking at men and women, but they're actually all women. A lot of women in the past wanted to pass as men just for their own protection on the streets."

"You two don't dress androgynously," Jade observed.

"No, we don't," said Annik.

Our food came and we became absorbed in eating. After a while, Jade asked, "What club are we going to tonight?"

"It's called Club 18," said Kari. "It's mixed. We sometimes go to women's clubs here too, like Frida— Annik likes that one—and Moune. But at Club 18 the music is really good. Saturday is ladies' night, which just means there are more women. It is near Palais Royale. I think we can take a bus from here. Would you like that? You can see more of Paris."

"You guys seem to know Paris pretty well," I said.

"We do," Kari said, taking Annik's hand. "We love Paris. It's so free here. You can kiss on the street, and no one cares!"

We paid and walked out again into the breezy night. On the way back down the stairs, I held onto the railing. Two glasses of wine for me was a lot, but by the time we got to the bottom and were waiting at the bus stop, my head had cleared. On the bus sitting next to Jade, I looked at buildings and watched the traffic, I felt nervous about what lay ahead.

Finally, we got off and walked a couple of blocks

to rue Beaujolais, stopping at a door where people were milling around. The number over the door was "18." I could hear music inside. As we went through and paid the cover charge, I saw an ordinary club. The walls were painted gold. There were tables and red vinyl booths along the sides of the room and a dance floor with a mirrored globe light above.

"This place is usually packed," said Kari. "We are lucky. I think many people are still on vacation. So we won't have to wait for a table."

We sat down and ordered drinks. I feasted my eyes on the crowd. There were many women sitting in pairs or in groups or walking between tables. Some had their arms draped around each other; some were holding hands.

This being Paris, I shouldn't have worried that anyone would be dressed too casually. I saw women in stylish jackets and pants and also in dresses or long, flowered skirts. Jade and I did not stand out as I'd feared.

The music started again. It was a good thing that staring was allowed in France because I could not stop doing it. Men danced with men and women with women. Everyone looked happy with the arrangement.

What's the big deal? Why do people want everyone to be the same? Nature doesn't make us all the same. Only I guess people like to be with others like themselves. Now I'm the one who feels different. All these people seem so sure of who they are.

I sipped my drink as my eyes continued to dart around the room. Everyone I knew seemed to fall into a slot, including Jade and Kari and Annik. I felt a huge hunger to have what they had, to know where I belonged the way they did.

Chapter Six

Slow Dance

A woman was standing squarely beside me on the dance floor, her face framed by springy brown hair. She seemed familiar somehow. Tanned, well-muscled arms showed from beneath the short sleeves of her cowboy shirt. Her fitted jeans showed off full hips and shapely legs. She bowed her head slightly with a gallant smile and asked me to dance. There was something about this woman…I felt safe near her and at the same time more disturbed than I could begin to make sense of. I took her hand and she turned me in steps that I was able to follow.

Jade glided by, giggling. Being with a female partner did not seem to bother her, or maybe she was still in shock. Apparently, our strategy of dancing with each other to avoid being hit on was not too successful. Anyway, this was France. Why would the women here be any less forward than the men?

My own partner looked at me with warm gray eyes. We hadn't exchanged a word yet; she probably didn't even know I was American. She pulled me close for a moment as we turned together, her spongy breasts resting above mine for a moment. The contact sent bolts of desire to all parts of my body. What was happening? It's not as though I'd never hugged a girl before, but this was different from anything I'd ever experienced with anyone, boy or girl. There was no slow buildup. These feelings were hitting me hard and all at once. We danced separately to the next song, a French one. I tried to keep a safe distance, but kept catching her eye, and whenever I did, my knees turned into soft wax. I had to look away again to restore my sense of balance. There was no mistaking the signs; I was wildly attracted to this woman. I knew it even though I'd never felt anything quite like this before.

As the song ended, the woman took my hand and bowed her head in thanks for the dance. As she did, her layered hair framed her face like a curtain. I liked the firm clasp of her hand. "*Merci,*" I said breathlessly, grinning up at her like an idiot. I knew I needed to sit down and gather my wits. I nodded to the woman and wobbled back toward our table.

Jade was there sitting alone. "Don't leave me!" she cried, grabbing my arm.

"What?" I pretended ignorance. "It looked like you were having a good time."

"I was, but how can I enjoy the dancing when they think I'm gay? I'm here under false pretenses."

I laughed. "Is there such a thing as true pretenses?" Jade grinned. "Maybe I could make a sign to pin to your front that says: 'I am not gay.'"

"I don't think that would work." She was clearly having a good time and enjoying the attention.

For myself, I didn't want to talk about that last dance. Even though I had already told Jade about my attraction to women, I was afraid to admit I had stepped over that line. There was a great difference between what I had just done and felt and the secret crushes I'd had on girls in my school, girls who didn't dance with me or touch me or return my feelings. There was a stigma attached to being gay. And yet I knew it was too late. I had done it—it had happened. I had danced with a lesbian and felt everything that I was supposed to feel with a man, except that I never felt like that with a man.

So I hid my feelings. I teased Jade by putting my arm around her waist as if I were her date. I puckered my lips and stuck them out at her as she laughed and dodged me.

Just then, the woman Jade had been dancing with in the beginning came by with a friend and asked Jade to dance again. Jade blushed. I said, "She doesn't speak much French. She wants me to tell you that she'd like to dance, but you should know that she is not gay." The woman said it didn't matter. I translated for Jade and she smiled and stood up. Her friend held out a hand to me and the four of us went off together. We danced to several Abba tunes. I smiled politely but couldn't help looking around for my previous partner. She seemed to have disappeared. Had she gone home? I was disappointed, but after a moment, I tried to put her out of my mind and just concentrate on the music.

Then a slow song started—"Color My World"— one I loved and had danced to with boys at home. I nodded to the woman I'd been dancing with and started back to the table, but before I got there, I saw the woman in the cowboy shirt again. She approached and looked questioningly at me. I felt a flutter of nerves. I never slow danced with someone I'd just met. I started to shake my head, but maybe it was the hypnotic piano introduction that made me move closer and place my arms lightly over hers.

We swayed slowly to the music. *This isn't real. This isn't happening.* Every time I glanced up, she looked back steadily. Hers was a solid face with large, deep-set gray eyes that tilted slightly downward. It was a face you could trust, or so it seemed to me. I felt a shiver of excitement flow slowly from my spine down to my knees as I leaned into her, my face resting just below her shoulder. I closed my eyes and drifted along in a happy daze. During the flute part near the end of the song, I opened them again and saw Kari and Annik kissing.

The music ended. I looked up at her. "Would you like to sit down?" She smiled and nodded. We made our way slowly back to the table. *I don't think I want to dance anymore. I don't think I could.*

The woman sat down next to me and shook hands with Kari and Annik. "*Je m'appelle Geneviève,*" she said. She had a deep, full voice. I liked the French pronunciation of the name, Zhun-vee-yev. We each introduced ourselves.

"Sophie," said Geneviève. "Where are you from?" I told her and explained the now routine story about what I was doing here in France.

"Montpellier," she said when I mentioned the city. "I sometimes travel there for my job. I'm a buyer for an interior decorator firm. I often go to the south. I buy beautiful things for clients." Suddenly I thought of the woman at the café.

"You weren't in Montpellier a few days ago, were you?" I asked, my voice shaky.

Geneviève nodded. "I just came back from there yesterday."

I stared at her. A shock went through me. "I might have seen you. Were you sitting outside a café on the central square early in the morning on Wednesday?" *It can't be. Things like this don't happen.*

"Oh! Was that you two with the backpacks? You're different now, dressed up. I remember you. You were with two men. I thought you were going to speak to me, and then your friends showed up."

I shook my head. "They weren't our friends. But that was you? I...I can't believe it."

"Well, these things happen," Geneviève said, smiling that same smile that had attracted me in Montpellier. "It means we were meant to meet."

I could only stare at her, still in shock. This was the woman in Montpellier? But she looked completely different! In her cowboy shirt, Geneviève didn't resemble the woman in the business suit I'd seen. And yet, I had to admit that the smile was the same. And so was my reaction to her.

The waiter came over and we ordered more drinks. Having recovered my power of speech, I asked the Dutch women, "Have you seen Jade?"

"Oh, yes," said Kari. "She seems to be having a good time."

"Jade loves to dance." I explained what I'd told her partner about Jade being straight, and everyone laughed. Geneviève looked questioningly at me.

"What about you?" she asked with a glint in her eyes.

I smiled but did not answer.

"She is!" Kari laughed. "I knew it as soon as I saw her at the hostel. If not, I wouldn't have invited them here."

"And you?" Geneviève looked back at me. "What do you have to say?"

I put up my hand and rocked it in the gesture for a little of this, a little of that. "You are the first girl I have ever danced with," I pronounced gravely.

Geneviève's face broke into a grin. "I am very honored," she said. "I had no idea. You seemed so natural." She turned toward me and leaned an elbow on the back of her chair.

I grinned back, delighted with the praise. "You're a good dancer—maybe that's why."

Jade returned and sat down, her faced flushed and her eyes bright.

"Geneviève, this is Jade, my friend from home."

"You are enjoying?" asked Geneviève, waving her hand around the room. I was glad to hear she spoke some English.

"Yes," said Jade.

"Nobody tries to, you know," Geneviève curved her arms together and puckered her lips comically as we all laughed.

"No. I can take care of myself. Besides, Sophie talked to her."

Geneviève signaled the waiter and asked, "Are you hungry?" We nodded. She ordered some *pomme frîtes* and steak strips. "I pay," she said. "How do you say?"

"My treat," I said.

She's nice. I wonder if I'll see her again after tonight. I hope so. She said she came to Montpellier sometimes.

As we ate, Kari entertained us with funny stories about her internship at her hospital in Amsterdam. Geneviève excused herself politely to Jade and started a story in French. *She's not from Paris.* Something about her vowels and the speed of her speech told me she was from a smaller place, maybe in the north. Kari and Annik seemed to understand the story better than I did. There was plenty of slang mixed in, which added flavor to her speech. We laughed hard at Geneviève's expressions and gestures. *The woman is naturally funny.* I translated for Jade the best I could, but she had started to get a forlorn expression on her face.

"Speak English," I said when the flow of French had stopped. I yawned. It had been another incredibly long day. All I wanted suddenly was to crawl into my bed. So much had happened today. I closed my eyes and leaned back.

"She is tired," Geneviève said in English, her soft, deep voice caressing my ears. In fact, every word she spoke seemed to stir something deep inside me. "How long do you two stay in Paris?" she asked.

Jade answered, "We leave on Monday. We have to meet a friend in England."

"Oh, it is too bad," said Geneviève. "I go to Reims tomorrow. It is my mother's birthday. But maybe...I meet you tomorrow morning for coffee, yes? Then we don't say good-bye now."

"Not too early, I hope," said Jade. "I think I'm going to sleep in."

I opened my eyes. "Yes," I said, "that would be nice." I pulled out a piece of paper from my bag and wrote the address of our hostel.

"Also, please, write your address in Montpellier," she said, "and I will give you mine. I live close to here." She handed me the napkin she'd been writing on with a pen from her pocket. *Never go to a club without a pen.*

"I have no telephone, but this belongs to my friend and neighbor," she said.

"See you tomorrow then. What time?" I said.

"Oh, maybe nine thirty, but I will wait for you."

I nodded and looked at our friends. "Are you ready to go?" The Dutch women nodded. We stood up and wove our way through the now crowded room and out the door. A light drizzle greeted us outside. "Until tomorrow," we said to Geneviève and hurried away after Kari, who said the metro was the quickest way back.

On the train I said, "Jade, did you have a good time?"

She nodded sleepily and asked, "You, too?"

"Yeah."

"Weird, isn't it? You just told me about liking girls today, and then you go and meet someone the same night."

I leaned toward her. "Jade, do you know, we've seen her before?" Jade had been on the floor dancing when Geneviève told us about Montpellier. "Remember the woman at the café?"

"No way! Are you telling me that was her?"

"Yeah. Isn't that totally bizarre? She remembered us, too." We were silent as the train rumbled along. Jade kept glancing at me, and I knew she too was contemplating the strangeness of that coincidence. "I wonder if she'll really show up for breakfast?" I said.

"Oh, I'm sure she will."

"How do you know?"

"I can just tell. She likes you."

"Really?"

"Sophie, come on. Can't you tell she likes you?"

"Yes." I inhaled deeply and let out my breath in a rush. "But maybe she just wants to be friends. Maybe she'll come see me in Montpellier when she's there on business."

"Uh-huh. If you're just friends, why were you slow dancing with her?"

I shrugged, grinning idiotically.

We disembarked at the Porte Clichy stop; then the group of us trudged the two blocks to our hostel. Hugging the Dutch girls in turn, we said good night and at last Jade and I were alone in our room.

"I'm too tired to shower." I stripped off my dress

and pulled on a robe. "I'll do it tomorrow," I said.

I went down the hall to do my hasty ablutions in the bathroom before crawling into bed. Jade returned from her trip to the bathroom and the springs creaked above me as she settled down. In the darkness, images crowded into my overstimulated mind. I could see the *Mona Lisa* smiling coyly at me, and then I saw my parents coming down the steps of the church where they'd just been married. I saw Jade and me climbing the stairway to Montmartre and Annik and Kari kissing in the club amid all the dancers. Then I heard again Geneviève's deep, velvety voice saying, "She is tired." The phrase repeated like soothing music in my ears as I fell asleep.

Chapter Seven

Radiance

A giant eraser had rubbed everything out by the next morning. I opened my eyes, not knowing where I was. Gradually it started coming back. *I'm in Paris.* I snuggled down again. *Oh, no.* I sat up in bed. *Someone's coming this morning. What was her name? Geneviève.* Adrenaline started pumping through me. *Will she really show up?*

I looked down at my watch on the floor and shot out of bed. 9:15 a.m.! I had to get ready. Jade was still fast asleep in the bunk above me. *Let her sleep. I didn't shower last night.* I stumbled over my backpack, which lay by the bunk, and grabbed Jade's leg to steady myself. Jade groaned. *No, don't wake up.* Having Jade awake would make it worse. There was my robe, where I'd flung it last night, along with my towel. I put it on and tiptoed out of the room.

Someone was showering already. After using the toilet, I lunged into a free shower stall. I usually take baths at home. "Ahhh!" I shrunk back from the stream of cold water as I tried to adjust it. *That's better. I have to meet someone, have to hurry.* Stop, I commanded myself. *She said she'd wait.* I ignored my command and continued frantically soaping myself, washing my hair. The shampoo slipped out of my hand. The bottle was so tiny; I couldn't see it in the shadowy stall. *Oh, there it is.* I stopped the water and stepped out on the cold tile. *Just get dry. It doesn't matter if someone sees you naked. This is France.*

Finally dry, and clad in my robe again, I brushed my teeth without toothpaste, surrounded by the blast of another bathroom occupant's hair dryer. *I can't eat breakfast with the taste of toothpaste in my mouth, but I can't meet a strange woman without brushing my teeth.*

I dressed in jeans and a pullover and combed my damp hair. I didn't have a hairdryer. Maybe if I stuck my head out the window it would dry. I wrenched open the window clasp and a fresh breeze hit my face. *Everything is fine. If she shows, it's fine. If she doesn't, it's also fine. I'll go for a walk by myself and explore this neighborhood. A nice long walk would feel good.*

Geneviève's head was bent over a magazine when I came down the stairs. She stood up and grinned, running her hand through her springy brown hair. I beamed back.

"Bonjour, Sophie."

"Bonjour." She kissed me quickly on both cheeks, as people who are friends or hope to become friends do in France. It was one of the customs I had to learn three years ago. "Do you want to have coffee?" I asked. "Come on." Full of suppressed excitement, I led her to the dining room. "We may as well eat here. It's free." We got our coffee and plain rolls and I took a banana. Geneviève took one too. We sat facing each other in the otherwise empty room, everyone else apparently sleeping in along with Jade.

"I wasn't sure you would come," I said, sipping my coffee and eyeing her nervously.

"Yes, I felt the same way. I was afraid that maybe I'd get here and I'd wait and no Sophie."

I smiled. "I have to have my coffee in the morning. If you waited long enough, I would have come down."

"Ah, but my mother is expecting me for Sunday lunch. I would have missed you if you came down much later." She looked at me with a steady smile.

I studied her face as bright gray eyes watched me. I thought her handsome with her broad cheekbones, down-slanting gray eyes, and well-defined brows. "I still can't really connect you with that woman in Montpellier," I said.

"Well, that was me," she replied with a twinkle in her eyes. I felt my stomach lurch as though I was meeting a celebrity on the street.

"I know," I said. But..." I shook my head. It was hard to talk about feelings in another language.

"What?" she asked gently.

"Well. Last night on the metro, Jade and I were talking. She thought it was a coincidence that...well, I'd just told her about liking girls yesterday, for the first time. Then she said I went and met someone the same night." I paused. "But, you see, it was no coincidence. She didn't know I'd met you before. It was because of you that..." I couldn't say anymore. I ducked my head, embarrassed.

"I think I understand," Geneviève said. I raised my eyes to meet hers. "Of course it was a coincidence that we met twice like that. Unless it was destiny, of course." She grinned and tilted her head back, her eyes half-closed as she continued talking. "But what you are saying is that telling your friend about liking girls and meeting me are not random events, yes? That they are connected?"

"Something like that." Boldly, I explained further, "It was because of meeting you in Montpellier that I told her that."

"Ah! Yes. Well, me too—even in Montpellier, I couldn't stop thinking about you."

"Really?"

She nodded. "Then last night, I didn't recognize you either. But my reaction was the same as the first time." Her eyes twinkled. "I thought, Geneviève, you have to dance with that girl. Whoever she is, you have to get to her before someone else does. She is so…radiant." Geneviève extended her arms expressively.

"Oh!" I laughed, flattered. "It reminds me of one of my favorite children's books: *Charlotte's Web*. It's about a spider called Charlotte who is supposed to be radiant."

With mock seriousness, she teased, "Yes, exactly, you are like a spider, just waiting for someone like me to catch in your web."

I could feel myself getting embarrassed again. Did she always talk to women like this? But even as I asked myself that, I knew she was just trying to get me to laugh and relax a little.

"I almost didn't go to the club last night," Geneviève said. "But I'm very glad I did." More people had begun coming in, filling up the tables as we sat looking at each other. "I wish we could spend more time together today," she said wistfully.

"Did you say you are driving to Reims?"

"Yes, for my mom's birthday. What are you and your friend doing today?" she asked.

"I don't know. Maybe Annik and Kari will come with us to see more of the sights. I really like them. We only met yesterday." I babbled on, as Geneviève listened intently. "I have never gotten to know any lesbians before. But lately, on this trip, it seems like my whole life is turning upside down. When I first saw Kari and Annik—normally I would have been too shy to speak to them. But I did it! And last night, I had a good time. I've been in gay clubs before, but never ones with women."

Geneviève raised her eyebrows and asked, "Then what is the point? *Les lesbiennes*," she said. "We are not so bad. Perhaps you will become one of us."

My cheeks warmed and I felt like a raw teenager. She must know from last night that I had no experience with women.

But what she didn't know was how messed up I really was. How to explain in French that I shouldn't even be allowed out without Jade, my keeper? That I was in no condition to start a relationship? But I couldn't tell her about the rape. Maybe if we met again in the future I would. But now—I wanted to make her understand without having to bring up that subject. "I am not very…" I began, searching for a word in French to express what I meant. "I am not very solid at the moment." "*Solide*." I waved my hands around. "I am all over the place." I laughed nervously. "You know? Not together," I said, bringing my palms parallel. Did the French have a word for that?

She looked years older than me, with the confidence that comes with a lot of experience. "You are older. I am just…" I shrugged.

She nodded calmly, not seeming disturbed by what I was saying. "You are charming," she said, smiling. *Charmante*. Again my fears were diffused by French flattery. "Don't worry about this," she continued. "You are okay the way you are. I like you," she added. "*Je t'aime bien*."

I nodded dumbly. I wanted to ask her why she liked me but was afraid she would reply with more flattery.

Not that I minded flattery, but...I tried one more time to make her understand. "I am like an adolescent. Even though I'm not," I quickly amended, lest she think I was even younger than I was. "And you are an adult. You see what I mean? We are too different maybe..."

"*Mais, pas du tout,*" she replied soothingly. "Not at all." She slid her hand across the table and tentatively took mine in hers. It wasn't a romantic gesture. It was more like what Jade would do. She didn't try to persuade me with words. She just sat there looking at me in an encouraging way, and I looked back and finally relaxed. I liked the way her mouth turned slightly up at the corners even when she wasn't smiling. I thought that was called a cupid's bow mouth. It looked soft and friendly, and the thought of kissing it made me look down quickly, my face heating up.

"Tell me about your travels." Geneviève propped her head on her hand to listen. So I told her about the castle where we stayed in Luxembourg, and how we slept out in the Black Forest. I didn't mention how soaked our sleeping bags got after being out in the rain all night. And of course, I didn't tell her what fools Jade and I had been in Montpellier.

At that moment, Kari and Annik entered the room, laughing. They saw me and Geneviève, and their smiles grew bigger. "Hello, you two," said Annik, waving. "Come on, Kari." They moved off toward the food.

Geneviève looked at her watch. "I'm sorry, Sophie. I must get started soon. I'm sorry I can't spend more time with you. But, will you be coming back through Paris on your way to Montpellier?"

"Yes."

"Well, then, you have my address. Can we see

each other then?"

"Okay," I said, pleased. "My cousins live near here, on a farm. I'm planning to stop and see them."

"Ah, you have cousins! Are they French?"

"Yes, half French, half Polish."

"No wonder you speak French so well. I noticed you have a Polish name," she said. "Wolnak."

"*Oui*. It means free person," I said and smiled at her approving expression. "Probably my ancestors were serfs originally and then became free."

"You seem like a free spirit."

I laughed wryly. "You think?" I thought of how Jade and I had begun our travels with a carefully planned itinerary, then started deviating from it the first day and after three days, we threw it away completely.

"So we can meet on your way back?" she asked.

I paused, calculating times and dates. "I should be back this way in about two weeks. I need to see my cousins, but I'd like to see you, too," I said shyly. "I'll write you from England."

"That will be great." We both stood up and walked toward the door.

"We'll see each other again, eh?" she said.

"Yes, soon," I replied.

"I like you, Sophie," she said again softly in my ear as we embraced. I felt the way I did when we were dancing the night before. Light-headed, a little off-balance.

Just then, I saw a familiar face come through the doorway: it was our backpacking buddy, Jill. "Hey, Jill!" I said, breaking apart from Geneviève. Jill looked surprised, said hello, and passed us on her way into the reception area.

From the door, I watched Geneviève get into her

bright blue van. The lettering on the side was hard to read because of the glare, but I saw an address on rue Saint-Antoine. Sunday morning church bells began hollowly clanging. As the van pulled out, her head emerged and she waved.

I turned in a bit of a daze and went back into the hostel. Kari and Annik both gave me thumbs up when I sat down with them. "So, what's going on?" asked Annik. "Do you like her? Will you go out with her?"

I could feel my face growing warm. "I'm supposed to see her on my way back from England."

I saw them exchange glances. "Well, that's good," said Kari.

"Do you two have any big plans for today?" I asked, to change the subject. "Do you want to hang out with us?"

"Sure." We agreed to meet in half an hour. Jade was in the room getting dressed when I entered.

"I saw Jill," I said.

"You did?"

"Yeah. I saw her coming in the door. I was saying good-bye to Geneviève."

"Oh, did Geneviève come? Great! I slept right through it. So did you talk to Jill?"

"No, she walked right by, although she did say hello. I was hugging Geneviève good-bye. Jill acted kind of weird."

"Did she?" said Jade. "Maybe she thinks you're gay. What kind of hug was it?"

I felt myself blushing again. "It's probably more the way Geneviève looks. She is kind of butch, don't you think?"

"Yeah. I didn't think Jill would care about that."

"Screw her," I said, but it hurt. She had been our

friend in Strasbourg. "Things like this always get to me. Why?" I said. "Why is she like that?"

"Well, in some circles, I suppose being homosexual is considered a vice or a perversion."

"It's not a vice. You mean like smoking?"

Jade laughed. "Who knows? People are stupid. It's funny, we came here to meet Jill and now we've made other friends."

"That's right. I came up to tell you that Kari and Annik are waiting for us downstairs."

"Cool."

When we met them in the dining room, Kari asked, "What about Geneviève? Can't she join us?"

"She's gone to Reims for her mom's birthday," I said.

"What about tomorrow?"

"She didn't say. I suppose she's staying over."

The four of us stood up and sailed out the door into the streets of Paris. After the rain last night, the world looked bright and new. It seemed to me that everything was smiling at us: the people, the buildings, the trees, and the dogs as they passed by at the heels of their owners.

We explored the wooden bookstalls on the wall bordering the river that sold old books, postcards, pictures, and postage stamps. I bought some cheap prints of Paris scenes to send to my siblings for their birthdays.

We walked across the bridge to the cathedral of Notre Dame and visited the Luxembourg Palace. Despite her being a student, Kari seemed to have money and she was generous with it, inviting us to lunch and dinner in restaurants. "Someday, you will invite us," she said. "Maybe we will visit you in the US, eh? And while you are in Europe, you are welcome to come to Amsterdam."

"Yes, that would be nice," I said.

That evening we walked along the Champs Élysées, a busy street, meaning Elysian Fields, or heaven on earth. The phrase matched my mood that day. I felt happy and unhurried, enjoying everything: the balconied buildings, the rows of brasseries and cafés, and the people sitting on the sidewalks outside restaurants looking chic, smoking cigarettes. I didn't even mind how I looked in my ordinary American clothes. I absorbed all the elegance around me instead of comparing myself to it. I watched the cars drive by under the canopy of big-leafed trees with mottled trunks.

I knew that the way I was feeling had everything to do with Geneviève.

Chapter Eight

I'm Fat and Ugly

My euphoria faded by the next morning. On the train to the northern coast of France, the events of Montpellier settled back over me like a cold, damp blanket. Aware of my mood, Jade took my hand and held it as we rolled along.

Jade could tell you what the north of France looked like because she kept her eyes focused out the window. She counted the number of French towns we passed and later could remember most of the names. If I had looked, I would have noticed different things: the wind through the trees and whether the people I saw in the stations seemed happy or sad. But I didn't look. I kept my eyes closed most of the time and fingered the napkin that Geneviève had given me with her address and her friend's phone number.

Away from her persuasive charm, my doubts came back. *Why is she even interested in me? We are so different. If she only knew how immature I really am, how stupid I was in Montpellier, she would not be so interested.*

When our train stopped, not far from the shoreline, we disembarked and waited for the ferry. "They're going to build a tunnel under the Channel," Jade informed me. "The undersea portion will be twenty-three and a half miles long. I read about it in *Newsweek*."

That would be like a really long subway ride. You'd have that eerie feeling of being in no-man's land, of being neither in one place nor the other, like on a long bridge. *My life is sort of like that right now.*

On the boat, Jade ran around like a little kid, dragging me with her until I finally begged off and grabbed a seat near the snack bar. I was feeling a little bit queasy, so I bought a bottle of English fizzy water. Everything on the boat was either French or English. The man behind the bar was definitely French, dark and somber. The stewards were British, with their roses-and-cream skin and jaunty smiles. British voices pierced through the low murmur of French conversation like birdsong.

I watched the coast of France shrink into the churning water as I said good-bye to a land that was intriguing but a little dangerous for me, just like the attraction I felt for Geneviève.

When the shore disappeared, I turned around to look through the front windows of the boat toward England. Soon, we would be meeting my old friend Natalie there. She was a planner and I knew our travels would be relatively predictable and comfortable while she was around. Jade and I wouldn't have to decide what to do all the time; we'd be able to tag along after Natalie. That was good. I needed the rest. I needed to heal my raw emotions and this would be a good way to do it.

I sighed and slumped down in my seat. I was glad that after England and Scotland I would be returning across the Channel because I knew that France was where I needed to be. *England is a temporary safe haven. But after that, even if things don't work out in the long run with Geneviève, I think she is the kind of danger I need in my life right now.*

ぶ.ぶぶぶ

"Is anyone sitting here?" a young man said with an English accent.

I scooted over. "No." I turned my attention back to *The Second Sex*, by Simone de Beauvoir. He pushed his blond hair out of his eyes and smiled. "Thanks." He slipped his bulky backpack off his slim shoulders and let it hit the deck.

"You know you can check your backpack, right?"

"Good to know. Ben," he said, sticking his hand out.

"Sophie," I said, hesitantly, remembering what happened the last time I met a strange man. And yet, as I looked into Ben's fair-skinned, open face, I knew I could trust him and could trust my instincts about the people I met. Whether they were male or female really didn't matter. With that thought, I left my depression of the morning behind.

We stashed his backpack and toured the ship, ending up on the upper deck watching the boat's wake. As the wind whipped my hair back, I realized that my stomach felt better now. A few minutes later, we saw Jade laughing heartily, surrounded by what looked like a family of English boys, four different ages, the oldest one with his arm around her. He seemed about seventeen. Jade looked ecstatic.

"There's my friend over there," I exclaimed, and we went over and joined the giddy group.

"Hi!" said Jade. "This is Colin. He and his brothers were just telling me about their vacation in France. These boys got into a serious amount of trouble over there. Their parents are mad at them, so they're hiding up here."

"Yeah, the parents can't stand the stiff air up top," said the boy who was cuddling Jade. "They're down below smoking and making plans to kill us when we get home."

"What did you do?"

"Nothing much, really," said the smallest one. "Just a lot of little things. Like last night in the restaurant in Paris, I petted the lady's dog at the next table. She said I could. She said I was adorable. That's French, you know."

"But then he knocked over her wineglass and it spilled all over the lady's dress. It was a white dress, too!" The boys howled again with laughter.

Finally, we all stood at the prow and watched as the car ferry approached land. The pale cliffs of Dover got bigger then disappeared as the boat slid into port at Folkestone. The boys' parents found them and took them off. Ben stayed with Jade and me. He was only going as far as Canterbury, where he lived.

No one bothered about our passports and we waited around in the drizzle for the train, eating sandwiches and drinking paper cups of tea full of milk and sugar. Then we shared a compartment on the train headed toward London until Ben had to get off.

"Too bad we finally meet some nice guys and they have to leave," Jade said gloomily.

That boy on the boat was just a kid. "Well, it's a transitory life we're leading, what do you expect?" I said, in a world-weary voice.

"Yeah." She stared moodily out the window. It was rare that her enthusiasm waned like that but I knew her good humor would likely bounce back soon.

We grabbed some Wimpy burgers in a corner

of Victoria Station, where announcements for trains echoed amid the babble of passengers' voices.

"Natalie made the arrangements," I said, "so naturally we're staying in a hotel, not a hostel. It's nice to have someone else do the planning for once. I hope it's not too expensive. I'm not rich like some people."

"Well, it's only for one night, right?"

"Or two, I can't remember. Then we're going to help her move to Coventry where she'll be going to school. If you want to see more of London, remember we'll be back after Scotland to meet my dad. He'll probably get a double room for us to share. I hope you don't mind. We can change in the bathroom. He really can't afford to put us in our own room."

"That's okay. I'm glad we're staying in a real hotel tonight. It feels more grown-up than a hostel," she said.

"I guess if I run out of money I can always ask my dad for some," I said.

"I'm sure if you really need it, your dad will help you out," said Jade. "My parents said they'd wire me some money if I need it."

"Come on," I said as we shouldered our backpacks. "Let's go find the tube."

We walked on London streets with unbroken rows of brick and stone houses, iron fences, and tiny gardens. The Concorde Hotel was in one of these rows on Great Cumberland, near Hyde Park. We registered in a small reception area carpeted in red shag. The receptionist was a young Indian woman with very white teeth. It was about 6:00 p.m. and Natalie hadn't arrived yet, but we had two single rooms next door to each other reserved in her name.

"You don't mind sharing a double bed, do you, Jade?"

"No, I don't mind."

The room overlooked the street and felt like the height of luxury after our travels, with a bathroom and a real bed, not a thin hostel mattress.

"Look, there are clean towels!" I cried. "I feel like throwing away my old one and stealing one of these."

"Oh, Sophie."

"Don't worry, I'm kidding."

"I'm going to take a bath," said Jade. She sounded tired. Jade never got tired. I heard water running and an occasional splash. Being considerate, she didn't take too long and then it was my turn. I prayed there was not some problem with hot water in England or maybe just in this economy hotel. But it was fine and, as I sank into the hot water, I felt grateful to Natalie for getting us this temporary refuge. When I came out of the bathroom, clad in my light travel robe, Jade was in bed, under the covers, her face covered too.

"Jade, are you asleep?" She grunted and turned toward me. "Have you been crying?" I could tell she had unless she'd suddenly developed a cold. I sat on the bed, which creaked. "What?" I put my hand on her shoulder. No answer. "Jade, come on. Move over. Don't hog the bed," I said, trying to make her smile. I got in and wondered what to do to help her. I am not very good at this sort of thing, especially if someone won't tell me what's wrong. For me, comfort equals being held or touched. I know it's not the same for everyone, but I put my arms around Jade and snuggled up to her. She didn't seem to mind; I felt her shoulders shaking silently.

I tried again, my mouth close to her ear. "Is it because of the boy on the boat?"

No answer for a while. Then she said, "I was so happy on the boat. Just for a little while, I believed someone could actually find me attractive and even love me."

"Jade!"

"I've never been in love. I've never even had sex. I'm a virgin. I'm fat and ugly, and you don't know what it's like because you're so attractive."

"Me? The French guys who tried to pick us up in Paris were always looking at you, too, not just me. And what about in the club, all the women wanted to dance with you, plus there was the boy on the boat."

"I know. I don't really count the women, though. And Colin just made everything worse because he was so nice and then he had to go. I'm glad it happened, but it kind of got to me."

"Well, you're not fat or ugly," I said, running my hand over her glossy hair.

"Do you find me attractive?" she asked.

As soon as she said that I started feeling confused. What was going on? Jade was my best friend. But I was lying in bed holding her, something I had never done before, and it felt very strange. "Sure, I do," I said carefully. "But I don't have those kinds of feelings for you." Jade turned over to face me, breaking into a sly smile. Her robe was undone and I could see more than I wanted to at the moment. Then she kissed me on the mouth. Hardly knowing what was happening, I kissed her back. I had never kissed a girl before! Her lips were soft, her face smooth. Then I pulled away. I got off the bed and strode across the room.

"This is not being very mature," I said, clutching my robe around me and looking out the window. "I thought you said you were straight."

"I am. I just wanted to see what it would feel like. Don't be mad."

"You had a new experience. Are you happy now?"

"Sorry," she said in a small voice.

I walked back toward the bed and saw her dark, contrite eyes. Was there a hint of a guilty smile, like a child who'd gotten away with something? I laughed. "Don't be," I said. "I finally got to kiss a girl."

"Me, too," she said. "It's different than kissing a boy, less prickly. And I didn't realize how much tougher a boy's lips are."

"Okay. Just remember you're not gay. Or even bi, according to you."

"I read in *Ms.* magazine that everyone is bisexual to some degree."

"I'm sure that's true." I grabbed some clothes from my backpack. "You know, Jade, you're really nice looking. Too bad you don't know that."

"No, I do really. I was just having a crisis. I'll be okay."

I went into the bathroom and dressed. I added a sweater then grabbed the key. "I think I'll go for a walk by myself. You planning on going anywhere?" She shook her head. "Good, because we have only one key and I'm locking you in. You're dangerous."

As I walked briskly down the street I realized I was full of nervous energy. *I love Jade, but sometimes she drives me crazy. It feels good to get away by myself. I'm going to do it at least once a day from now on.* After a couple of blocks, I found myself crossing the busy street over to Hyde Park. The sun was getting lower, casting shadows on the lawn. As I strode through the wide-open space along the path, I tingled at the memory of those lips touching mine, only it wasn't Jade's lips I was thinking of. Just for a moment, I imagined they belonged to Geneviève.

People were sitting around the fountain and I joined a young mother with an old-fashioned baby buggy. Her eyes looked a bit puffy and her yellow cardigan was buttoned crookedly. We exchanged a friendly glance and I saw that the baby must be very young, bundled as it was, sleeping. The wind shifted and a fine spray reached our faces.

I sat there contentedly, holding the memory of Geneviève close to me. The sun slipped behind the trees, turning everything into one big shadow. When it began to get darker, I got up and headed back. Rounding the corner to our hotel, I saw headlights glowing down the street. A taxi was parked in front of the hotel, and sure enough, that was Natalie getting out! Natalie, my old friend. One by one she and the driver pulled six pieces of luggage—I counted them—out of the back seat and trunk until finally, a backpack toppled onto the sidewalk. "Natalie!" I screamed.

Chapter Nine

Natalie

Wolnak!" Natalie hugged me ferociously. "Am I glad to see you."

All my latent homesickness surfaced. Natalie felt so familiar, even in the way she liked to call me by my last name, a vestige from high school.

I started helping her carry in her luggage. After she checked in, we wrestled all her bags and suitcases into the elevator. Then Natalie sagged against the wall, her eyelids drooping, her blue eyes shot with red. "I came straight from the airport," she said in a tremulous voice. "I'm so tired and I'm starving. I couldn't eat anything on the plane. I felt too sick." Natalie wiped away the tears escaping from her eyes. "You're lucky you had your friend with you. I'm not usually afraid of flying. It was just…Christ, I'm going to be here for a whole year! I feel like I've landed on another planet. And I was afraid you wouldn't show up." She sniffled. This disintegrating Natalie was one I had never seen before.

"Hey, Cummings, don't worry," I said. "I'm here. We're going to be fine." *If she only knew how "fine" I've been lately.*

Natalie looked up as the elevator stopped. I shoved a suitcase in the door to keep it open. She gazed at me with swollen eyes. "Wolnak," she cried dramatically, "do you realize? We're all we've got!" Then one corner of her mouth turned up. I didn't know if she was going to laugh or start crying again, but then she snorted, which got me going. Soon we were both doubled over with laughter, as the door kept banging into her suitcase. I laughed helplessly at the thought of either of us having to rely on the other until my stomach hurt.

Jade appeared in the hallway in her robe and stood there watching us. The elevator door was still propped open and Jade began purposefully dragging everything out. That sobered us up and we helped her.

"Natalie, this is Jade."

"Nice to meet you," said Jade. She looked sort of stunned. "I was sleeping," she said. "I'm kind of out of it."

"That makes three of us." Natalie grinned as she unlocked her room door. "Come to my room when you're ready. We'll go find someplace to eat. And hurry, okay? I'm starving."

In our room, Jade said, "What was that all about?"

It was impossible to explain, but I tried. "It was scary for her to travel alone. And now here she is by herself except for me. And you, of course. It's just that Natalie is used to having people around."

Jade shrugged. "My cousin's like that. She has to be the center of attention all the time. I think it's just insecurity." Jade began rummaging in her backpack.

"Oh, for God's sake," I said. "Like you and I aren't insecure, too. You're just envious because she's beautiful."

"Maybe I am. Do you still want me not to mention certain things to her?"

"No, that's okay. I've thought about it. She's my friend. I'll tell her everything. Except the part when you kissed me."

She blushed. "That's personal, but it wasn't a bad thing, was it?"

I grimaced. "No. It's like we had to try it. Or you had to, I guess," I said teasingly.

"Yeah."

"But, did you like it?" I asked, curious.

"Kind of, but as you said, we're friends. And I think I'll stick with boys. I'm going to get dressed." She took her clothes into the bathroom. We'd always undressed in front of each other before. I felt a little sad. Was our friendship changed forever now?

❧❧❧❧

Sitting across the table from us, Natalie looked lovely despite her long journey. She was dressed in a bright print skirt and white T-shirt under an orange jacket, her long wavy blond hair completing the picture. I gazed at her with fond admiration and she gazed back. We were both floating high, so grateful to have found each other again in a strange country. I wondered whether I would feel the same way when I saw my father.

After we'd ordered, Natalie said sheepishly, "Sorry for falling to pieces back there."

"That's okay," I said, "I haven't laughed like that in forever. And I get it. I felt the same way when we first landed in Luxembourg. It just suddenly hit me that I was here for a year and it was too late to turn back. I mean, it didn't seem real before that."

Natalie nodded, "Yeah. But it really does help to have you guys here. We'll travel and by the time school starts I'll be sort of used to it. And we won't be so far away from each other. We can visit."

"Yeah, maybe we can go somewhere together at

Christmas," I said.

"I might go home for Christmas."

"Really? I don't think I could do that. I couldn't face leaving home a second time. Not that I could afford it anyway."

"Well, by then I'll be settled. I'll have friends, I suppose. It'll be different."

"How's Max?" I asked.

"Oh God. I miss him already. That's part of why I got into such a state. Can't talk about him yet."

Natalie turned to Jade and politely asked what she studied and whether she was having a good time.

"We've had some glitches, but still, I'm having the time of my life," stated Jade.

"Really?" said Natalie. "I want to hear all about it. How about tomorrow when I'm rested? I have to go to bed early tonight. It's the middle of the night to me."

The Indian food was delicious and spicy. After she'd sated the worst of her hunger, Natalie said, "Sophie, I have messages from your mother."

"You do?" I was instantly on alert.

"Yeah, she's freaking out." Natalie laughed. "She even called my mom, and they don't really even know each other. I listened on the extension."

"Cripes. Do you know if they got my postcards?"

"I think the last one was from Strasbourg."

"So she didn't get the Paris one yet?"

"She's complaining you don't write enough."

"Of course. She'd like to have a camera on me twenty-four hours a day."

"Oh, I don't know. She's not that bad. Just the normal mom stuff, I think. She wants to know if you found a room and what's your address." Natalie imitated my mother's voice. "I worry about those two girls traveling alone like that. Sophie can be so naïve at times."

Even though I knew Natalie was kidding, the words hurt. The worst part was that I knew my mother was right. "She says I don't live in the real world," I said gloomily.

"What does that mean, anyway?" said Jade, patting my arm. "Reality is different for each person." Jade was always coming up with these wise little sayings.

"I think we should live in the reality that's true for us," I said with a sigh. "Whatever that might be."

"Right on," said Jade. We were silent for a moment.

"Well, anyway," Natalie continued, "your mom said it's good you'll be seeing your dad soon. He can check up on you. Then he can give her the report."

"She knows what he's like on trips," I said. "He'll be too excited to remember anything. I'll have to give him a letter for her."

"Actually, she suggested that," said Natalie.

We paid and hurried through light rain back to the hotel. "Tomorrow, I want to go shopping for some clothes for school. You want to come along?" asked Natalie. "And maybe we could look at some art or something. Then I figure we could get an early start for my school and maybe still get to Edinburgh by evening." She yawned. "I have to hit the hay."

≈≈≈≈

In the morning, I lay there beside Jade, her face still crumpled into the pillow. It seemed like I was always the one who woke up first. Outside, I could hear the windy rain rattling the glass. My cold nose poked out of the covers. I don't think the room was heated. I wanted to burrow down and go back to sleep, but I couldn't.

Natalie was here, with her combination of madness and practicality. There were messages from home, and Dad was coming. Lately I'd been feeling that my life was in pieces. Well, here were more pieces from my past mixing in with the present, making even more of a mess. I hoped my newly hatched self would be up to the task of dealing with it all. Now, Natalie was going to learn about my fuckups. But there was no help for it because she was my friend and I wanted her to know. I sat up in bed, hoping I wasn't getting a cold. Where was that vitamin C I'd packed?

Jade and I took turns again in the bathroom to get dressed, but I dared hope that our new modesty might pass soon.

My bad mood continued through the morning as we trailed Natalie through Selfridges, Harrods, and Marks & Spencer's. It wasn't fair that Natalie had a clothes allowance. Jade and I rifled through all the beautiful fall clothes in our ugly rain ponchos, the same ones we'd worn in the rain in Germany. The salesgirls watched us warily, or so I thought. Natalie bought a shiny black, belted raincoat that emphasized her small waist and willowy figure, warm pants, a few turtlenecks, and underwear. I was acutely aware of how new clothes could make you feel confident and independent and how old clothes left you exposed; you had to work harder to feel good about yourself.

In a fit of pique, I tore off my poncho in Marks & Spencer's and thrust it into the trash bin in the ladies' bathroom and bought a raincoat: a cheaper, unlined version of Natalie's in kelly green. It was roomy enough to wear a sweater underneath, and I thought I looked good in it. Jade bought one too. Then, we went back out into the misty morning wearing our new purchases.

The pub where we went for lunch was full of the business crowd: lots of tweed and sweaters and dark suits. I listened to the bright rise and fall of British inflections. Sun streamed through the window and some boys played darts in the next room; you could hear a thwack every few seconds.

"So, tell me about your trip," said Natalie.

"All right," I said. I took a sip of Guinness, swirling the rich, heavy taste in my mouth. "We had some adventures."

"I can already tell the word is misadventures," said Natalie wryly.

"Well, every time you do anything, there is the potential for misadventure," I said.

"Or disaster," agreed Natalie. "But good planning helps." Sometimes Natalie sounded like a Girl Scout.

"Yes, but sometimes in order to have an adventure, you have to throw away your plan," I replied.

"Right," said Natalie, her eyes glittering. "Now tell me everything."

Between bites of fish and chips, we told her about Luxembourg and Strasbourg. "Go on," said Natalie, "I don't sense real adventure there."

We told her about discovering the Black Forest and sleeping under trees. "Ah, yes," she said approvingly, "you're getting warmer."

We told her about Montpellier.

"Hippies?" Natalie raised an eyebrow.

"They showed us all the sights in Montpellier and we went to the beach and went swimming," I said. "We talked a lot about French politics. They seemed very intelligent."

"Such nice girls cavorting on the beach with

French hippies? What should Auntie Natalie think?"

"Auntie Natalie should shut up," I said dryly. "So then we smoked some weed. Hashish, actually."

"Except I didn't," said Jade.

"And?" said Natalie.

"Well, and then we decided to camp on the beach with them."

"Who decided this?"

Jade and I looked at each other. "We both did," I said.

Natalie looked at me and asked, "Did you want to?"

"Well, yes, in a way. I didn't want to *sleep* with them. I thought it would be nice to camp on the beach. I might not have been thinking too clearly."

"Yeah? So, what happened? Did you sleep with them?"

"Well, that's the thing. One of them raped me." I added, "Sort of."

"Oh God. Sort of? How can you be sort of raped?" she cried. "Are you okay?" She peered in my eyes as if to check for signs of injury.

"I'm fine," I said.

"Jesus, Wolnak. Backpacking in Europe. That's why I want to just stick to the British Isles. It's safer. Really, though, smoking dope with hippies you just met! I never would have been in that situation to begin with."

"I know. I know you wouldn't," I said. But suppose you'd just had a nice time together, and then they'd invited you to the beach? Wouldn't you have been tempted?"

"No, I wouldn't," said Natalie. "I'm sorry, I don't think I would. But especially not if they were hippies. Or French."

"It's easy enough to sit here and say that," Jade said indignantly. "You don't know what you'd do in the situation. It could happen to anyone."

"Sophie, I don't believe you really like hippies anyway," said Natalie.

"What about Ted?" I said.

"Ted? Your recent boyfriend? He's got long hair, that's all. He's a medical student, for God's sake. Did you actually trust this guy on the beach?"

"Well, I wasn't sure about him, but it wasn't because he was a hippie. I don't just judge people like that," I said heatedly.

"Well, maybe you should. Maybe you'd be safer if you did."

"I'll keep it in mind for next time," I said dryly. *There is only so much maturity I can take, especially from someone my own age.*

"Sorry." Natalie smiled her beautiful smile. "Don't be mad. I am sympathetic. I admit it could have happened to me, okay? But I'm not as adventurous as you. I'm very careful—it's the way I am."

"You can't tell anyone," I warned her. "Especially not your parents."

"No, I won't. I promise. So what else did you do?"

"We had an incredible time in Paris, didn't we Sophie?" Jade said. I nodded, still sulking.

"Come on, Sophie, I really want to hear about this. What did you do in Paris?"

"If you really want to know, we met a lesbian couple at our hostel."

"Oh, really?" said Natalie.

"Yeah, they were great," said Jade. "They're from Holland. We spent the whole weekend with them."

"They're going to get married," I said

enthusiastically. "They're the most darling couple. They invited us to visit them in Amsterdam."

"And they took us to a gay nightclub," said Jade.

"No kidding," said Natalie. "You guys amaze me. So how was it? Did you have a good time? Did you dance with any women?"

"Oh, yeah," Jade grinned.

"I danced with a couple girls, and Jade? Who knows how many—?" I said extravagantly.

"Three, four...I lost count," said Jade modestly.

"But the point is, I sort of met somebody," I said.

Natalie stared at me. "A woman?"

"Well, it was a gay club."

"Oh my God," she cried incredulously. "Does that mean you're gay?"

"I don't really know, but I need to find out. I've had these feelings for a long time, but I never told anyone."

"Wow," said Natalie. "You just never know what secrets quiet little Wolnak may have hidden inside her. Did you kiss her?" she asked teasingly.

"No," I grinned, not glancing at Jade, "but I did kiss a girl once. It was a pivotal experience."

"When? In high school?"

"No," I said enigmatically.

"So? What's her name?"

"I'm not telling," I said.

"No, no. Not the one you kissed. The one you met at the club."

"Geneviève Fournier."

"What's she like?" Natalie asked.

"She's this gorgeous, sophisticated French woman." I sighed. "And look at me."

Natalie said, "Maybe she likes scruffy little

American girls."

I laughed. "Maybe so."

"Come on, Sophie," Jade said, "tell her what she's like."

"Well, I don't know. She seems nice. She works for an interior decorating firm in Paris."

"Not a hippie, then?" I shook my head. "Are you going to see her again?" asked Natalie.

"I think so. She came to our hostel the next day for breakfast. We're planning to meet on my way back south."

Natalie grinned and shook her head. "You just made my day, Wolnak. Be warned, I want to hear more about this. I bet you had crushes on girls at school. Anyone I know? And to think you never said anything."

"Well, would you?"

"Never having been in the situation, I don't know. But you know what a blabbermouth I am, so probably I'd have told our gang at least."

"Yeah, maybe," I replied. It was easy enough for Natalie to say that. But given the climate at our all-girls Catholic high school, I don't know what any of us would have done. The liberal Catholics of my upbringing did not condemn homosexuality or say it came from the devil, nothing like that. They just didn't talk about it much. The nuns, after all, were open-minded. They simply said, or passed the word along, that we were not to be caught with another girl. Because it happened, although my friends and I didn't know the details. We knew that it had happened once behind the curtain on the stage. The parents wouldn't like it. They might pull their girls out; that was the practical tone the nuns took with us.

At school, we talked about it in occasional whispers

and giggles, but no one was really comfortable with the topic. So I doubt Natalie would have told, as she said. I don't think she would have known what to say any more than I did. Most of the time, except when I was in the throes of a crush, I pretended that side of things didn't exist. So now that I was away from that whole environment, it didn't surprise me in the least that everything that had been pressed and folded up inside me was now bursting at the seams. It just made sense.

Chapter Ten

Far North

When we left the pub, the rain started up again. "Typical English weather," said Natalie, as though she'd been living there for years. "Let's go to the National Gallery. We can look at art and then have tea."

At the museum, we trailed after Natalie as she lectured us on various paintings. She had recently switched her major from art history to theater. The University of Warwick, where she was going to study, was known for its theater department. At one point, when Natalie was out of earshot, Jade said, "Sorry I said what I did about her. She's not so bad."

"She's got a certain charm." I nodded affectionately.

Natalie had bought a copy of *Time Out* at the airport and had circled a poetry reading in a pub in the West End. We arrived early so we could eat before the reading. I listened distractedly to the music and looked at Jade and Natalie talking and at all the other people eating and chattering. I leaned back and let the hubbub wash over me. At moments like this when I wasn't required to talk or to do anything, my awareness of Geneviève increased. It was as though my insides had been hollowed out and replaced by her presence, which pushed on me from the inside, creating a mixture of pain, pleasure, and longing. Had I felt this way in high school when I was first going out with Sam? I didn't know. I didn't think so. Not like this. I hoped the feelings got more mellow after a while. Otherwise I didn't know how I could bear this for the next two weeks. At least it was distracting me from my trauma on the beach.

ᨎᨎᨎᨎ

We got Natalie and her suitcases off the train at Kenilworth and helped her move into her room at the top of a large brick house on a quiet, well-kept street. There were roses crowding the brick walkway and the streets were lined with trees full of chattering birds. Up the block was the village green. Everything was indeed intensely green because of the intermittent rain, which we were starting to get used to.

Edinburgh was crammed with tea shops. I had a slight cold, and it seemed a good excuse to lapse into hot cups of tea and indulge in cream scones and jam every chance we got. The castle was grim and full of specters, kings, and queens who had suffered and died and stories of Mary Queen of Scots imprisoned up a stairway. We stayed in a hostel and tried to economize as Jade and I had in France, buying food to cook in the hostel kitchen.

At night lying in bed, I longed to see Geneviève, to touch her, to talk to her again. She didn't have a telephone. What was wrong with France? It would be nice to be able to call her and hear that deep, sexy voice again. My mind reeled at the thought. When she'd spoken softly in my ear just before she left, I'd shivered all over. What was it she had said? "I like you, Sophie." I wanted to hear her say that again.

The three of us traveled far north into the county

of Inverness, high into the hills whose rounded shapes merged with fog and clouds. At the tiny bus station at Loch Garry, Natalie came out of a phone booth and told us our hosts at the farm would be there shortly to pick us up. When they arrived, we dashed through the rain into an old station wagon, to lurch and rock over a rutted road deeper into the hills to sheep country.

The two-story stone farmhouse was a bed and breakfast in addition to being the hub of a working farm. The family had two younger children and a teenage boy. Everyone was always stomping in from outdoors in their high rubber boots, bits of hay sticking to their clothing. We ate together as a family. In the bathroom, novels and letters were left around; a cat was curled by the fireplace. We went for long, wet walks on tracks through sheep and mud and returned to steam ourselves by the fire. I would sit staring at the flames, picturing Geneviève's rounded cheeks, her clear gray eyes and heavy brows, the way her lips curved slightly up at the corners, making her look as though she was about to smile all the time.

I wondered whether she had taken my words to heart about how ill-suited we were. I hoped not. I never meant for her to agree with me; I just wanted to warn her. Better for her to find out sooner rather than later. In any case, she didn't pay much attention to my warning. Unless she thought about it on the drive to her mom's that Sunday and realized I was right. But I didn't actually believe that.

Scotland was having the effect I'd hoped it would. More and more often I was able to sleep deeply and wake up in the morning without any remnants in my head of what had happened in Montpellier.

We stayed at Loch Ness in another bed and

breakfast. I spent a lot of time sauntering along the lake shore throwing rocks and scanning the water for a long neck and puny head emerging from the choppy surface of the water.

Jade and Natalie bought plaid woolen coats and tweedy sweaters that were made to repel the frequent showers. I didn't buy anything because of my meager funds, but I enjoyed seeing them in their Scottish finery.

Natalie and I bickered at times. Sometimes our arguments were interesting and sometimes pointless and irritating, but we always made up sooner or later over hot tea or pints of beer. That was the way it was when you traveled with someone. Even Jade and I had our dicey moments.

At times, in the pubs, we tried and failed to understand a word of the local dialect. "Are they speaking English?" Jade asked. We knew they were, a version of it anyways, but it might as well have been Norwegian.

At one of the pubs in Loch Lomond, we picked up a Japanese student, who became our travel companion. He took photos of us against the backdrop of hills and the lake and dutifully sent them to me later. Natalie was flushed from the cool air, her hair curling from the moisture, holding a bouquet of wildflowers. Jade looked lovely, too, with her dark hair now down to her shoulders and her body robust. We sat on the shore of the famous lake and sang the song, as much as we knew of it: *You take the high road and I'll take the low road.*

In our bed and breakfast one evening, I wrote to Geneviève at the little desk in our room. My written French was not too good, so I kept it short.

Chère Geneviève,

I am having a good time here in Scotland with my friend Natalie from high school and Jade. Next week, I will see my father in London. I expect to be in Paris September 15. I will go directly to your place from the train. It will be easy to find because I know it is near the club.

I hesitated. I wanted to find words that might show something of how I'd been feeling about her. But I couldn't think of what to say about any of that, so I just wrote, *Thinking of you, Sophie.*

Natalie sat gloomily one afternoon sipping her beer as we listened to the rain outside. Our clothes were steaming from the warm pub fire. We were comfortable for the moment and in no hurry to leave. "I miss Max so much," Natalie said. "I wonder what he's doing right now. Sleeping, maybe." She'd met Max in theater class. He was a clown and a magician. "I wonder if he'll wait for me? He's probably going to start dating somebody else; it's inevitable. He's so handsome. That's really why I want to go home for Christmas. He promised he'd tell me if he started seeing someone else. If he does, maybe I won't go home."

"Natalie, you're obsessed. He'll wait for you if he really loves you."

"Yeah, if. Don't you ever miss Ted? Have you really broken up for good?"

"Yeah, that one's down the drain."

"Too busy thinking about your lesbian girlfriend?"

"She's not my girlfriend," I said testily. I was getting tired of her teasing. To change the subject, I said, "I wonder what it will be like seeing my dad next week. I'm kind of looking forward to it."

"Tell us about your parents, Sophie," said Jade. "How did they meet?" It was as good a topic as any for a rainy day. I took a sip of my beer and swiveled my chair to toast the other side of my back at the fire.

"They met in grade school," I said. "My mother always had a mad crush on my dad. She used to go watch him play baseball when she was just a little girl. It's kind of romantic, isn't it? She dated a couple other boys, but she never loved anyone but my dad. So she says. Anyhow, when he was in the marines, after ignoring her all those years, he got hold of her address from some other guy who was writing her and started writing her himself. Anyway, Dad went on to college and graduate school and became a professor."

"Good for him," said Jade.

"You must be proud of him," Natalie concurred. "What about him and your mom?"

"Well, when Dad got out of the service, they got married. They were our age! That's what I can't get over. What's cool is my parents still love each other," I said. "But there's been a lot of yelling at home lately. I guess Dad's under a strain at work."

"My dad's the same way," said Natalie. "He comes home late from work, practically foaming at the mouth. Mom treats him like she's his geisha girl or something, like, 'Oh, let me give you a massage, dear' and 'I saved some supper for you, dear.' Never mind that he's crabby and the kids are all hiding in their rooms."

"It's not that easy being married," said Jade. "You have to be nice to each other."

"That's right," Natalie said. "It works both ways. Why does the woman always have to be the nice one? Mom works, too. She owns her own business, but she's always the one who comes home and makes dinner."

"I've always had this fantasy of my wedding," I said dreamily, hardly listening to Natalie's feminist rhetoric.

"Me too," agreed Jade.

"It's a cultural ideal," said Natalie. "I have it, too. I'm wearing a white floaty dress and walking down the aisle toward my prince charming."

"Well," I said gloomily, "If I'm going to be a lesbian I might as well kiss that fantasy good-bye."

"Not necessarily," said Jade. "What about Kari and Annik? Didn't they say they were going to get married or something?"

"Yeah," I answered, glancing out the window. Darkness had filled the panes and the rain had started hammering down again.

Chapter Eleven

Dad

"Think they'll let us in?" I joked when our taxi stopped in front of the Berkshire Hotel in Bloomsbury.

"I don't know." Jade frowned, glancing down. We still had streaks of Scottish mud on our jeans and sneakers. The doorman opened the door for us, giving us a once-over.

We walked across a plush carpet to the desk. "Has Dr. Wolnak checked in yet?" I asked.

"Yes, miss," said the young receptionist, with the hint of a smile. "He said his daughter would be arriving. Shall I call his room?"

"Yes, please."

The man spoke into the phone and said, "He'll be right down."

We waited, our backpacks at our feet. Even though my father and I hadn't been getting along so well before I left, now I'd hardly ever wanted to see anyone as much as him. And there he was, hugging me and pulling back to look at me. His reddish-brown hair was slightly longer than when I left, and he had long sideburns, which I didn't remember. He was dressed in a suit with wide lapels, a red shirt underneath, and a flamboyant tie. "You look good, Sophie," he said. "How are you?"

"Great, Dad. I'm so glad to see you." I could feel

tears leaking out the corners of my eyes as I stood there grinning stupidly.

Dad turned to Jade, who was waiting shyly beside me. He gave her a hug, too. "How are you, Jade? What have you two been doing?"

"Oh, you know. Traipsing all over Scotland," Jade said.

"We said good-bye to Natalie this morning," I said.

"Oh, Natalie. Such a smart girl. I wasn't sure when you would be arriving, but I made a late reservation for dinner. Do you want to go up to the room?" His blue eyes brimmed with excitement.

"Yeah!" we both said, catching his enthusiasm.

We went up to the fifth floor to a room with two queen-sized beds and sweeping velvet curtains overlooking Bloomsbury Street and the lights of London.

"This is a lot nicer than what we've been used to lately, Dad."

"Good. Why don't I let you girls get changed?" He handed me his key. "Wash up and put on nice clothes. I'll be back in fifteen minutes or so. Is that enough time?"

"Sure," I said, and he was gone. "He's on a high," I said.

"I feel like a queen," said Jade, stretching out on the bed. "Let's go check out the bathroom."

We were scrubbed, at least superficially, and changed when Dad reappeared. I basked in his familiar presence as we walked out into the clear, cool London night, passing the dark mass of the British Museum and the University of London, where Dad had his conference. I linked my elbow in his and grabbed Jade's arm, too. I felt so safe walking with him. *Don't get used to it; it's only for two days.*

The Queen's Larder was painted bright green with little latticed windows. We were shown to a table near the bar, which was made of dark wood with twinkling rows of glasses overhead. There was something very cozy about London pubs and restaurants.

"Good thing I made a reservation," Dad said.

"How are things at home?" I asked.

"Fine. You should write more often. Your mother looks for your postcards every day."

"Well, they take a long time to get there," I said defensively. "I wrote her from Paris. Did you get that one?"

"Yes, I think so."

"And one from Scotland. I'm working on a letter for you to take home with you for Mom."

"That's good. We all miss you, Sophie. Anne and Stan talk about you every day."

"What about Joey? Has he forgotten me?"

"Are you kidding? He still cries for you to read him stories before bed."

I listened as Dad related more news from home then asked, "So how's your trip going?" I took a deep breath. I wanted to be honest with him, but I knew I couldn't tell him about the beach. It was nice to see him so happy; I didn't want to upset him. And my mother was anxious enough as it was.

Instead, I gave him a detailed version of our time in Scotland. I told a little about Montpellier but let him assume we'd stayed at the dorm both nights. I even told him about the lesbians in Paris.

"Oh," he said. "Well, they sound nice."

"Yeah, Dad, Annik and Kari are great! We had the best time with them." Dad beamed at me. *He has no clue. Why should he since I've never talked about it?*

"It's good you're doing this, Sophie. Travel is a great education." He smiled hesitantly. "We pray for you every night."

"What do you pray for?"

"Mostly that you're safe. So what would you like to do now?"

"Aren't you tired, Daddy? Didn't you just get in today?"

"Yesterday. I'm fine. Maybe you'd like a night-time tour of London?" he asked eagerly.

"Sure, we'd love it."

We took the taxi tour all over London that night, getting out briefly at a few places: Trafalgar Square, London Bridge, Saint Paul's. We crossed the bridge toward Big Ben and the houses of Parliament, which were all lit up, reflecting in the inky Thames. Lighted fountains and monuments passed in the taxi window until they all became a blur.

I awoke several times to Dad's familiar snores, feeling like a girl sleeping safe and protected in her little room at home.

☙ ☙ ❧ ❧

I was surprised the next morning to see that Jade was already up. How late was it? Dad had left already for his conference, and the sun shone through a crack in the heavy draperies. I could hear her in the bathroom, splashing around. I didn't want to move, as though jet lag had finally claimed me. I felt more like cocooning than sightseeing. Jade came out and bounced around the room, fresh and eager. One thing about Jade was her robust energy and enthusiasm for life. This was not always good, from my point of view, especially first thing in the morning.

"I'm tired of being a tourist," I moaned, over our breakfast in the dining room. Jade looked up from her London guidebook in surprise. "I think I have PMS," I said.

"I thought you wanted to see the tower today."

"I don't want to see anything today. I'd rather go back to bed."

Jade looked shocked. "But, Sophie. I'm really looking forward to it."

"Well, you're a big girl. Why can't you go by yourself?"

Jade frowned. "But I want you to come. It won't be much fun seeing all those spooky rooms by myself!"

"Okay, fine. I'll go to the tower, but then I'm coming back here to rest and maybe catch up on my correspondence."

"Okay. I can go to the other places by myself. I know how to use the tube. Do you still want to go dancing tonight?"

"I guess."

"You don't have to." Jade pouted.

"No, I'll be into it by tonight."

The gloomy Tower of London did nothing to improve my mood. I left Jade on her way to London Bridge and Madame Tussauds wax museum. I needed some time to myself. I decided to walk part of the way to Bloomsbury, getting off the Bakerloo line at Piccadilly. I knew the oldest bookstore in London was supposed to be near there.

It was a cool fall day, more like home than any day so far. I found Hatchards bookstore and browsed around. It seemed silly to buy French books in London.

There would be so much more choice in Paris. But I needed to start reading for school, even if it was just books I picked out for fun. Besides, Dad had slipped me twenty pounds last night. I bought a book of poetry: *Les Fleurs du Mal* by Baudelaire, a mystery by Mauriac, and the novel *Bonjour Tristesse*, by Françoise Sagan.

Passing through the lobby back at the hotel, I almost hurried past my father, who was sitting and laughing raucously with some other dark-suited men and one woman. His face was pink and he was smoking a cigarette! I couldn't believe it. Dad had quit smoking years ago, or so I'd thought. I'd seen only prim photos of him and his colleagues standing in line with their conference badges or having dinners in dim restaurants. Occasionally Mom was with him. What would she say if she saw him now?

I waved. After he had introduced me and the conversation resumed, I leaned close. "Why don't you come dancing with us tonight, Dad? Please?"

"Oh, I'm too old for the kind of places you go."

"No, you're not. You look very hip."

"Oh, well, maybe I will," he said, taking a drag. "This is just between us, right?" He waved his cigarette. "I always quit as soon as I get home."

I laughed. "Your secret is safe with me, Dad."

Up in our room, I forced myself to start on my letter to Mom about Paris and Scotland. I wrote that she shouldn't worry and repeated my school address for her to send me the money.

After that, I took a long bath. I could get used to this, I thought, lying full length in the roomy tub, viewing the room through steam. There were thick towels and bathrobes, all white. I loved the color white. The snow at home was soft and pristine when it first fell. It reminded me of the conversation about weddings and veils we'd had in the pub.

I climbed out of the tub, dried off, and wrapped the white robe around me. Under the covers, I imagined myself in a long white dress and veil, falling into a huge drift of snow. The snow was as soft as a feather pillow and as I snuggled down, Geneviève's arms encircled and held me. I drifted into sleep.

The door opened and I heard a thump of something landing on the desk. "Hi, honey," Dad said. "I'm done with my session. How are you feeling?"

"Okay." I smiled from my pillow. I slowly sat up and slid my legs over the side of the bed.

"I wondered why you came back so soon," he said. "I'm glad you're okay."

"I'm just tired." Looking at his cheery face, I remembered that this was our last day together. "Maybe I'm kind of down because you're leaving tomorrow and Jade's going home the day after. I'll be all alone." My father reached down and held me. I could smell a whiff of tobacco along with his spicy cologne. "I don't know if I can really do this, Dad." He looked at me, his brow furrowed. "I mean it, Dad. I don't think I can do it."

He gave me another squeeze. "You can, Sophie. You're my daughter. I know you can do it with flying colors."

🙠🙠🙢🙢

At the club that evening, the strobe made people look like they were moving twice as fast as they were. Dad's movements were more deliberate than Jade's or mine, but he was clearly having a good time. I thought of that night at Club 18 and slow dancing with Geneviève.

What will it be like seeing her again? Will I still be attracted to her? I thought so, the way she kept dropping into my mind, startling my heart each time. *But will she still want me? No way to know that until I see her in Paris.*

I felt a little dizzy and sat down. What in the world was wrong with me? I was tired, despite my nap this afternoon. I was about to get my period, that's what. A terrifying dagger of a thought shot through me. *When was my period due, anyway? I think it should have come sometime while we were in Scotland.*

Chapter Twelve

Good-bye, Jade

As the cab with Dad in it disappeared down the road, Jade and I hurried toward the nearby hostel where we would spend our last night in England, bowing our heads under the pattering rain. The weekend had sped by too fast. Tomorrow, we would head south so Jade could catch her plane home and I would go on to Paris and Montpellier.

The British Museum was as good a place as any to spend the rainy afternoon, looking at Egyptian mummies and suits of armor. When we left the museum, the lighted windows of a nearby pub beckoned to us.

"I wouldn't mind getting a bit tanked," I said.

"Me neither," said Jade. "We don't have to leave too early tomorrow, do we?" she asked as we settled ourselves on stools.

"No. Are you going to stay at the Luxembourg hostel again?"

"Uh-huh. That seems like forever ago, doesn't it? I feel like a different person now."

"Me, too." I looked around the lively pub, knowing that by tomorrow this familiar sight would be gone. "Last chance to have fish and chips."

After we'd ordered, I asked her, "Why do you feel different do you think?"

"I don't know," said Jade thoughtfully. We sat

sipping our beers and gazing around the pub. A raucous group in the corner was singing "Happy Birthday" and swaying back and forth. I thought that the French, while more emotionally direct than the English, were also more serious, less jolly in public.

Finally, Jade said, "I've done all these things I've never done before. And also, when you travel with someone, they end up seeing you at your worst, which you'd really rather they didn't." She giggled nervously, watching my face.

"Yeah?" I prompted, with a smile.

"But the good thing is if they don't think you're a total loser...I mean, if by some miracle they like you anyway, well, that's really cool."

"Yeah, by some miracle," I said fondly. "So what didn't you want me to know about you?"

"Oh, you know. That I'm kind of a dork. I don't always do or say the right thing."

"But you're a lovable dork! And besides, you've gotten much more sophisticated on this trip."

Jade giggled. "Sophisticated, oh yeah. Remember when we yelled in the shower?"

I smiled. "That was one of your better ideas. So, was there anything else I wasn't supposed to know?"

"I don't know. When I saw Natalie, I knew she was the type who would see right through me and reject me."

"But, she didn't!"

"No. But she would never have hung out with someone like me if it weren't for you."

"I don't know. You two sure spent a lot of time bullshitting together."

"Yeah, she did seem to like me, didn't she? So I thought, wow, maybe I have changed. Maybe I've gotten more, you know, likable and normal."

"You always were likable. I don't know about normal."

Jade grinned. "Well, you've changed too, Sophie."

I smiled back. "Me? Like how?"

"You're just different. I'll never forget first seeing you dancing with that Geneviève. I thought, 'Uh-oh, what's going on here?' And ever since then...you've had this sort of dazed look on your face. You've been thinking about her, right?"

I nodded nervously. "Daydreaming is one thing. But now I'm going to see her again for real. Jade, have you ever felt like your life was sort of going out of control? Like too much was happening at once?"

She sat thoughtfully drinking her Guinness. "When I left Michigan for college I felt that way. But you get over it."

Our second round of beers came. "I don't know what I'm gonna do without you, Jade." I sniffled.

"I know, me too. I'll have no one to do crazy things with like sleeping out in the woods and singing in the rain and having no clue what we're going to do the next day."

"I know," I said.

Jade wiped her eyes on a napkin. "Guess I'll just have to adjust to normal life again. But I've gotten used to living this way. You don't have to think so much. And all our crazy ideas kind of worked out, didn't they?"

"Yeah, most of them."

Jade cast me a concerned look. "You haven't talked about you-know-what lately."

"No." In fact, it *had* been a few days since the trauma on the beach had even entered my mind. "Thank you for helping me through that, Jade. I don't know what I would have done without you."

"Hey, no problem. Do you still feel like it was your fault?" she asked.

"Kind of."

"Because it wasn't, Sophie. He set you up. You've got to let that go… "

"It's not just that. I mean, everything was going so great, you and me, backpacking around. I felt kind of invincible. And then it happened, and it was like a sign that I couldn't really take care of myself. So how was I ever going to make it on my own this year?"

"I get it," she said. "But you'll be fine, Sophie. I know you will."

"That's what my dad said. But he didn't know what happened."

"But he knows you."

"I guess."

"Anyway, we're not as clueless as we used to be."

It was dark outside and raining harder. We watched the water sloshing down the window pane. "Jade," I said, "I think I might be pregnant!"

"What?" We stared at each other. "You can't be. Just from that one time?"

I shrugged.

"That's bad," she said.

"No kidding. I'm on my junior year abroad, knocked up before school even starts. Talk about a bad trip."

"What are the odds of that happening? Like a hundred to one? How late are you?"

"I don't know. A week? I've been so tired lately. I just haven't felt right, Jade. But it's probably just PMS."

"You can't let your mother be right, after all her worrying," she whispered.

We sat there in rigid silence for a while. I felt like

everything I'd been fighting to escape, my dependence on home, my undefined sexuality, my vulnerability as a female, all were closing in on me, immobilizing me.

"Hey," Jade shook my shoulder gently. "I think those mummies have had an effect on us. Come on. Let's get back to the hostel."

"Okay." I pushed my fears to the back of my mind, promising myself not to think about them until I returned to Montpellier for school.

The next day, at Folkestone, Jade was going to take a different ship from mine, one that went to Ostende in Belgium. I bought a ticket for the hovercraft to Calais, a faster alternative to the car ferry. We waited, silently huddled together on top of our backpacks until it was time for her to board.

After all the time we'd been together almost constantly, there didn't seem to be much left to say. The boat's horn blasted as a signal to board and people began slowly moving forward. Tears were trickling down my cheeks; I hugged Jade, then stepped back to let her go.

Chapter Thirteen

Rue Vivienne

On the boat, I cheered myself up by studying my Paris map, planning the route I'd take to Geneviève's apartment. I liked the name of her little street, rue Vivienne. It had the same root as the word for "life" in French, which was *vie*. Also akin to the words, "vivid" and "vivacious" in English. I liked that her street had a woman's name that sounded pretty and feminine.

When I stepped off the metro that evening, a little corner of my heart still buzzed with the anticipation of seeing Geneviève. The rest of me was just tired—emotionally from losing Jade and physically from the long day of travel. All I really wanted was to come to a stop somewhere, no matter where, and not have to move again for the night. I was counting on Geneviève letting me sleep on her sofa.

Fortunately, her street was easy to find, even in the dark. A ceramic plaque on the building right at the top of the metro steps said "rue Vivienne." I exhaled with relief. Sand-colored buildings rose up on both sides of the old and narrow street. I found her number above a weathered gate standing open and leading into a large courtyard. I rapped on the concierge's window. She came forward at once, a tiny woman with tight gray curls, wearing an apron. She seemed to be expecting me. "Mlle Fournier, please," I said.

The woman nodded. "You are the American? First floor, doorway to the left." I knew that the first floor in France was one flight up. The doorway off the courtyard was black inside. "Push the button!" came a shout behind me. She had come out of her lair to make sure I was all right, showing me the knob with a button you pushed. Thanking her, I began to trudge up the well-worn stone stairs, my backpack weighing me down, my pulse racing. I was at the end of the day's journey at last, but what would I find? How would it be? Geneviève had become almost made up in my imagination. I could not even summon her features to mind right now. I felt almost as if I had dreamed her or made her up and that I would get to the door and some stranger would answer and tell me I had the wrong address.

An inviting smell wafted from under Geneviève's door. When I knocked, I heard movement inside then was startled to see a strange face appear in the doorway, just as I had feared. It was a narrow face that belonged to a woman with shoulder-length, fine dark hair and bright, excited eyes. She waved me in. "Sophie, *excusez-moi*, Geneviève is not here! Sit down, put that down," she said, as, bewildered, I shrugged my backpack onto the floor and heaved myself onto a wooden chair next to an ancient-looking kitchen table. *She's not here?* The apartment was small and crowded with furniture. "I am Sylvie, a friend of Genny's. I live close by." The woman held out her hand for me to shake.

"Oh, are you the friend with the telephone?"

"Yes, that's right. Genny is very sorry—she had to travel for her job. She will be back tomorrow. She asked me to be here. She left a note." She gestured toward an envelope on the sideboard. "You will sleep here tonight, yes? I have cooked something for you." She sat down. "I used to live here with my brother. We are all from Reims. Then I got married, and later, my brother moved in with his girlfriend. Geneviève was a student at les Beaux-Arts and she came with her roommates. She's lived here ever since, although alone now. She still sublets it from my brother. Come, let me show you."

She stood and I numbly followed her around the kitchen. "Here are the dishes, the cutlery. Here is where you make coffee. She gestured toward a small bedroom off the kitchen with an antique-looking bed. "She asked me to change the sheets. She had to leave quickly this morning." I stood there in a daze. Sylvie looked at me, flustered. "I am so sorry, Sophie. She wanted so much to be here."

I did not want to be left alone in this place. Every bit of space was neatly crowded with a stranger's things.

Back in the kitchen, Sylvie said, "Did you have a good voyage?"

"Yes, everything went well," I said woodenly, sitting down again.

"I would like to stay to get acquainted, but that will have to be another time, Sophie. I have a child; my husband is not home and I left her with a neighbor. Here is a key. What are your plans for tomorrow? Will you wait for Genny?"

"I...No, I have to go see my cousins," I said, feeling confused. "They are expecting me. They live on a farm near Pontoise."

"Yes, of course. You are French-American, then? That is why you speak so well?"

"No, I'm not French, but my cousins are part French. I spent some time with them a few summers ago. And I am studying French at the university."

"I see. Listen. Will you return to see Genny? She

won't forgive me if I let you get away." Sylvie smiled.
Her teeth were crooked in a charming way.

"I'll leave my cousins' phone number," I said.
"Tomorrow or the next day, I'll return."

Sylvie said, her eyes twinkling, "Genny is a woman
of business with the heart of a poet." She laughed.
"I don't understand half the things she talks about
sometimes. I have to go. You can push the key under the
door when you leave. You will be all right?" I nodded.
"Feel free to make breakfast. I know Americans like eggs
in the morning." She waved at the tiny fridge.

"No, I usually just have coffee and bread, French-
style."

"The bread is yesterday's, I'm afraid, but there's a
boulangerie on rue de la Banque if you like."

"Thank you."

Sylvie opened the door, looking at me doubtfully.
"You're sure you're all right?" I assured her I would be
fine. Still, she eyed me like she wanted to warn me—be
nice to my friend or else—but politeness kept her mute.
I stared back. With a shrug, she said, "See you soon."
The door closed.

I stood as though paralyzed for a moment in
Geneviève's kitchen. Then I lifted the lid on the pan on
the stove to see what Sylvie had cooked. Sliced potatoes
and bits of ham in a white sauce. It looked delicious. I lit
the gas to heat it up for a minute, stirring with the spoon
that had been left in the pan. The loaf of bread was not
stale. Other French essentials were on the small counter;
a half bottle of red wine, a bowl of fruit, several pieces
of cheese under a stone-lidded plate. Never refrigerate
cheese, another French rule. Only after I had my meal
arranged on the table did I open the envelope with my
name on it. The handwriting was the same as the address

and phone number she'd given me on a napkin at Club 18. Only this message was more carefully set down in her squared-off printing. It looked like she had taken time to write it. I began reading as I ate.

> *Ma chère, Sophie,*
> *Please feel at home. I will see you very soon, I hope.*
> *I had to go to Dijon to buy some furniture. My boss is very*
> *understanding, but the clients are not. I implore you, give*
> *me a chance to redeem myself after tomorrow. Please,*
> *leave me your cousins' phone number. You said you will*
> *go there. I will call you there. Until later, Geneviève.*

I liked the formal language: the words "implore" and "redeem myself" were very effective on me. I smiled. She must have known they would charm me. The woman had a way with words, for sure. I was feeling better. The food helped too. This Sylvie was some kind of wizard in the kitchen.

It was kind of amazing that Geneviève trusted me enough to let me stay here alone, someone she barely knew. I would have done the same for her, but I am not French, and I tend to be trusting by nature. The French, I knew, were not. For them, everyone is a criminal until you get to know them unless vouched for by someone in their circle of friends.

I had figured out some of this after my summer in France. Everything French people did fascinated me. Even the way they used a knife and fork was different, holding the fork in the left hand and knife in the right, not switching the way we do. I could never eat naturally after that. Never having gotten the hang of doing it the French way, I couldn't do it the old way anymore either.

I didn't think Geneviève's trust had anything to

do with sexual attraction. Why was it that although one meets so many people in the course of daily life, one person penetrates one's inner sanctum, a room where only close friends may enter? Sometimes it's someone you've only known for five seconds. This was a source of endless mystery to me.

Having drunk a glass of Geneviève's red wine, I relaxed enough to venture into the other rooms. There was a cramped bathroom with an ancient-looking sink, a toilet, and a claw-foot tub. I peeked into the living room overlooking the courtyard. It was dark and I did not turn on the light. I made out the outlines of a sofa and a couple of chairs, pictures on the wall, a table covered in small objects, a cabinet with a small television.

I wondered how Sylvie had lived here with her brother. Which of them slept on the couch? I staggered into the bedroom and exhaustion quickly took over. Deciding to skip pajamas, brushing teeth and the like, I tore off my clothes and crawled into bed. I regretted my nudity immediately as the sheets were cold, but I soon stopped shivering under the down comforter. Little sounds floated from the courtyard and the building: music, faint voices, a thump or two.

⚜⚜⚜⚜

The next morning, over coffee in her kitchen, I realized that this was the first night in my whole life that I had slept alone, really alone, with no family or friends nearby. No Jade. I closed my eyes and breathed it in. *Freedom. I think I like it.*

I wandered into the living room and raised the blinds. With the light from the courtyard, I could see the original oil paintings on the walls, which were in different styles, mostly bright abstracts and figure studies.

My pulse quickened at the sight of all the art. Sylvie said that Geneviève had attended the Beaux-Arts academy. I was impressed, because the school, housed in a palace across the river from the Louvre, was part of the French system of *grandes écoles*, which admitted only the very top students. Those strange lumpy objects on the table by the window turned out to be little clay sculptures. Some of the pieces were covered in plastic to keep moist; others on the shelf were fired and finished. They looked like landscapes. One of the hills had a woman's face. *Wow. I had no idea Geneviève was an artist!*

I looked around the room for photographs and saw only one: a family group with Geneviève in the front row. She looked younger and thinner in the picture, her hair waving around her shoulders, longer than it was now. She stood straight and tall, looking right at the camera. "I like you, Sophie." That was the last thing she'd said to me. "Je t'aime bien." I wondered whether she'd still feel the same when we met again.

Chapter Fourteen

You'll Never Get a Husband

My *cousine* Anna dumped a pile of clothes on the kitchen table for me to iron. Despite my mother's training at home, I seemed to lack all domestic skills in her eyes, I guess because her standards were even higher than my mother's. Once, when I was here three years ago, Anna had teased me, "You'll never get a husband, Sophie." On that point, she might have been right.

Anna wandered by, her large, solid body completely in control. Now, she picked up a pair of folded pants and shook it out. "Not like this, Sophie," she said, pointing out wrinkles. Patiently, she showed me how a pair of pants is supposed to be folded. "I'll have to do these over," she said with a sigh.

"No, please," I begged. "Let me try again." I worked on the pile again, this time spraying with water and paying complete attention. Well, almost. True, my mind had a tendency to wander. I would never be the perfect homemaker, not by Anna's old-world standards. Though born in Poland, she had lived in France since her teens, married two French men, and produced two families of boys. No wonder she had to work so hard.

Anna's rosy grin had greeted me on my arrival, her warm embrace enfolding me. "Three years, Sophie! You look just the same." Of course she wasn't going to tell me that I looked more grown-up, although that was what I wanted to hear. But to be fair, my backpacking persona was not very sophisticated.

Her mild-mannered husband Georges came in from the dairy for dinner and was now sitting in his favorite corner smoking a cigar and watching me iron, an understanding smile on his face.

All day I had been listening for Geneviève's phone call. Now, glancing at Anna's broad back as she cooked at the stove, at her dyed red-blond hair, I shook my head and smiled. I wondered what she'd say if I told her about meeting Geneviève. She probably thought lesbians were something nice people didn't talk about. That was an outdated view. I was beginning to understand that there was great variety in human sexual expression. Being gay was the most natural thing in the world, but few people seemed to know that. Still, I could hardly blame Anna for not understanding when I hadn't caught on myself for so long.

My second try at ironing was grudgingly accepted and I began setting the table. Another thing I appreciated around there was that no one treated me as a guest. That was why I liked doing chores. I could relax, more or less, and be a part of the family.

We sat around the supper table in the kitchen; the dining room was reserved for Sundays and holidays. There to see me were Jean-Pierre, Casimir, and Claude: three blue-eyed, mischievous male creatures, the oldest two in their thirties. Jean-Pierre, just a couple years older than me, was a pharmacy student in Paris. It was because of them, three years ago, that I had experienced French life so fully, had frequented cafés and clubs in Paris and nearby Pontoise, and had learned to converse and joke in French and eat and dress the French way.

"Where's Yvonne?" I asked Casimir, "and the baby? I wanted to see the baby."

"Yvonne said to say hello and sorry she couldn't come. Claudine is only five months old, you know. You'll meet her the next time you come." He pulled a picture out of his wallet and showed me a bundled infant in pink.

After dinner, the four of us sat in the living room watching the news on television. I could hear the clink of dishes in the kitchen and was feeling guilty for not helping Anna when the phone rang. It was in the kitchen, just through the doorway, and Jean-Pierre answered it. His eyebrows shot up and he called, "Sophie! For you."

I sprang up as all eyes followed me, and I grabbed the phone.

"Sophie," said Geneviève, "*Ça va?*"

I grinned and felt myself beginning to melt at the sound of her rich voice. "I'm fine," I managed to say.

"I am the guilty one," she said. "Were you comfortable last night?"

"Yes, of course. I love your place. Sylvie fed me. I was fine. I really needed some time to myself anyway."

"Okay, good. Can I see you tomorrow for dinner?"

"Yes. Should I meet you at your apartment? About seven o'clock?"

"Sounds good, Thank you, Sophie."

"Au revoir," I finished, breathlessly.

Then my cousins pounced on me. "Who was that woman? A Parisian?" My face was hot; I didn't know how to reply.

"That's Geneviève. She's a friend," I said lamely.

"A French friend?" All their faces were questions marks. How could I have a Parisian friend they didn't know about? It takes time to make friends and I had only just arrived in this country.

"I met her when I was in Paris two weeks ago."

"Oh, yes, playing tourist with your American friend," said Casimir.

"So where did you meet this girl?"

"In a club."

"What club?" demanded Claude.

"Club 18." Surely they wouldn't have heard of it.

"Ahhh!" they said in unison. They seemed both shocked and delighted with this information.

"Who knew? You don't seem the type, Sophie."

"What's she like, this *lesbienne,* eh Sophie?"

"What does she look like?"

I sensed, despite the teasing, that they really wanted to know. I sat down and, in a lowered voice, I described Geneviève as best I could. "She's taller than me. She has hair to here"—I pointed to halfway down my neck—"and gray eyes, and she is very smart. And nice, very *sympa,*" I finished. They all three sat eyeing me, digesting this information like a good meal as the television news went on unheard.

"Don't tell," I jerked my head toward the kitchen.

"Oh, no, of course not," they assured me. And the subject was dropped as we turned back to the television.

Finally, I told everyone, "bonsoir," and went up the stairs to my room from three summers ago. A fresh breeze laden with the smell of hay meandered in the window, billowing the curtain. Everything was the same as before. I got ready for bed and snuggled down under the covers.

It didn't seem possible that I was now on my own and planning to go on a date with a woman tomorrow. The last time I was here, I'd been a high school student, still dating Sam. I was a different person now, more grown-up, despite what Anna thought. Alone in that familiar room, I could hear dogs barking at a distant farm and an owl rhythmically hooting.

The next day, I was awakened by the drone of the milking machines, so familiar from mornings past.

❧ ❧ ❧ ❧

All the words I'd prepared on the train ride flew out of my head when I stood at her door. Geneviève's welcoming grin disarmed me as she kissed both my cheeks French-style. Then she pulled me in the door and we hugged American style. When we broke apart, I gazed into her gray eyes wonderingly. What had happened in the last two weeks to bring this sense of intimacy?

"I'd forgotten what you looked like," I said, my voice weak.

"Not me. I have a photographic memory. You are so beautiful." There it was again, the French charm that came so easily from her lips.

"Like Charlotte the spider?" I asked, smiling.

"What?" She laughed. "Oh yes. Radiant."

Geneviève led me over to the table and we sat opposite each other. I examined her curvy lips; her high, round cheekbones; the downward tilt of her eyes. It was obvious that she tanned in the summer instead of collecting freckles like me, and beneath the tan her cheeks were rosy. I admired her sturdy shoulders. She carried a little extra weight. On her it looked good.

Ever since that first day in Montpellier, there was something about this woman, something I didn't understand that drew me, that shortened my breath and made me feel things I'd never felt before. I remembered my sharp pang of regret when she walked away in

Montpellier. Yet despite the tumult of emotions she evoked in me, her easy smile and the way she sat there so solidly gave me confidence. It seemed as though I could lean on her and count on her to hold me up if I started to fall. She was watching me look at her. I dropped my eyes, despite the fact that I knew the French didn't mind being scrutinized.

Touching the scarred, dark-varnished table I'd dined on the other night, I asked, "What's this table? It looks like it's a hundred years old."

"It came from my family's antique store in Reims. It's at least two hundred years old. My dad gave it to me when I moved to Paris. It came from a farmhouse in Normandy. He gave me my bed, too."

I nodded, impressed. "Your family is in antiques? Did you learn a lot about that growing up?"

"*Mais, oui.* I know old things and what they're worth. But I'm more interested in their history. I love history. Like this table—I like to imagine the farmers in Normandy who owned it and what their lives were like two hundred years ago." I looked into her deep-set eyes and nodded.

"But why didn't you go into the antiques business?"

"Well, one reason is I would have had to stay in Reims and work with my family like my brother did. He went back after university." She made a face. "I love my family, but it's better like this. And anyway, I like decorating better…I like to be creative, put things together. In antiques, you don't do that so much."

"How many brothers and sisters do you have?"

"One brother and one sister. We're pretty close, but my sister and I are very different. She's the feminine type. She is married and has a daughter." Geneviève suddenly broke into a smile. "That's my Minette. She's four now."

"Yes, I think I saw them on the photo in the living room." I smiled shyly. "My cousin's wife Yvonne has a new baby, but they didn't come last night. She wasn't feeling well."

"Oh, too bad. So how was your visit with your cousins?"

I told her about how my male cousins had found out about her and me.

She laughed. "You don't mind that they know about you?"

I shrugged. "No, I don't care."

She nodded approvingly and changed the subject. "Are you hungry, Sophie?"

"*Oui.*"

"I thought we could go below to the wine bar where Sylvie works. You can't get a full meal there, but they have very good *apéritifs* and wonderful cheeses, all kinds, and wine. Would that be all right?"

I nodded. "That sounds perfect. I bet you bring all your girlfriends there, right?"

"Of course." She shrugged and pressed her lips in an ironic French smile. "I feel comfortable there, that's why. I can be myself." She came around the table, taking my arm as she pulled out my chair and helped me up in an effortless way that came from long practice. I sucked in my breath. I was not used to such attentions even from the boys I'd dated.

"How old are you, Geneviève?" I blurted out.

"Twenty-five," she replied.

"I'm only twenty." I smiled nervously up at her.

"Does that bother you?"

"Yes," I answered honestly. I shook my head. "I feel...so young."

"You told me in the club that I was the first woman you'd danced with. But I don't mind. You are like clay. I get to watch you mold yourself and maybe I can help a little. But you're the artist."

My eyes filled with tears. She knew how to say just the things I needed to hear. "Thanks," I mumbled. "I think what I am most afraid of is letting someone else decide my life for me." I sniffled, wiping my eyes with my sleeve.

"I don't want to do that, Sophie. I remember what it felt like when I first came to Paris. I had never been with a woman—or a man either. I was a monster, the girl who didn't fit in anywhere. I needed to get away from Reims where I knew everyone. My mother wanted me to be more like my sister. She expected me to get married. I knew from a very young age that marriage was not my scene, at least not with a man. But I just wanted to fit in, and I couldn't do that in Reims with my family around. Papa understood me, though. I was always closer to him. Then when I got to Paris it took me forever to meet any lesbians. My first lover took advantage of me. I don't want to do the same thing to anyone else."

"No, I didn't think you would," I said. "It's just… you've had so much experience and I haven't." She looked at me, her brow furrowed. I smiled, hoping to erase her frown. "But never mind. All I want to know," I said teasingly, "is whether you have a girlfriend. I hope you don't."

She smiled back. "No. Just a few women I see from time to time, that's all."

I sighed. Of course she had other women in her life. She was way too attractive not to. But at least she didn't have a girlfriend. Taking Geneviève's arm, I descended with her down to the street.

Chapter Fifteen

Saint Geneviève

Sylvie is a *sous-chef* here," she told me as we stood outside le Vieux Sabot. The sign in the window said *degustation—specialités Provences.* Like the rest of the street, the place looked as though it had been there forever. We opened the creaky door and Geneviève spoke to the waiter as we sat down at a table by the window. Sylvie soon came out in her white apron with a little chef's hat perched on her straight dark hair. She kissed Geneviève on both cheeks and did the same to me. She politely asked how I'd slept. I thanked her for the dinner. Sylvie nodded and recommended the quiche chèvre and pâté champignon before nipping back into the kitchen. We ordered those and a red Côtes-du-rhône wine. The room began to fill up.

"Sylvie called you 'Genny' the other night," I said, leaning back in my chair. "Is that what your friends call you?"

"Just my friends from home. I don't mind, but I prefer my full name. I always have since I was a little girl and I learned that Saint Geneviève is the patron saint of Paris."

"Oh, is she?"

"Do you know the story?" Geneviève asked after savoring a bite of quiche. I shook my head. "She was born in 422 in Nanterre, then a small village and now a suburb of Paris. In fact, Nanterre is where the events started in '68. A student from that campus blew up the American embassy. Anyway, Geneviève was a young nun who had lots of visions. No one believed her at first, but then she predicted that the Huns were coming to sack Paris, which it turned out they were. She saved the city. Everyone trusted her after that. Another time she collected a lot of food and kept the city from starving. So anyway, because of my name, I always thought I was meant to come and live here. When I came to school, I never intended to go back."

"Were you in the student riots?"

"Yes I marched in the riots," she answered. Our food came and I was hoping she wouldn't notice that I wasn't entirely comfortable using my knife and fork the French way. But I was damned if I was going to do it the American way either in front of her.

"It was mostly university students protesting their own conditions. Things were much better for Beaux-Arts students, but we believed in the general cause, too. We were against the Vietnam War and the Gaullist regime. It was my last year there and I marched." She frowned. "But those are not good memories for me. I don't like violence. Still, I'm glad I was there. This is a great time to live, you know, with all the changes, with gay liberation and everything. My friends call it the joyous seventies."

"Yes, I'm just learning about it."

"Just? Where have you been?"

"In high school."

She laughed. "Well, you should have paid more attention. It was in the US that it all started. I am very interested in the US. I think there are a lot of possibilities for change there, maybe more than in Europe."

"But the US is so conservative."

"In some ways not. The French are willing to live and let live, but they also can make you feel invisible if you're different. I mean the women here don't want anything to do with feminism, for the most part. The French woman has to be chic and feminine, a good wife, and all that. So someone like me who doesn't fit the mold, well, I just feel that in the US you can be accepted more, be more free in the way you dress and live."

"Hmm, you may be right." I laughed. "So in some ways, we are better? I never thought I'd hear *une Française* say that."

"You just don't know enough French people. Some of us really like Americans. Maybe not the government."

"Lucky for me." I smiled into her eyes. We sat there sipping wine, eating, and looking at each other as the dusk turned into night outside the window.

"When do you return to Montpellier?" she asked.

"Tomorrow night, I'm afraid. My travels are over. I have to take a placement exam the day after tomorrow and register for my classes. School starts in two weeks."

"What will you be studying?"

"Well, French mostly. I'm registered in the Institute for Foreign Students, but I may switch to regular classes. They said I could do that. I think my French is better than that of most foreign students."

"I think you would do fine in regular classes."

"Except my reading and writing are not too good, but we'll see. That's why I'm anxious to get down there."

"I just wish we could have spent more time together." She sighed. "I'm still sorry about the other night. I had to accompany some clients to an auction."

"It's all right. I was disappointed too, but it was good for me to spend a night alone. It's a new experience.

I'm on my own for the first time, you know."

Geneviève smiled. "*La petite* Sophie," she said gently.

My skin warmed. The French like to use the word "petite" a lot and I know it's an endearment and not really about size or age, but it tended to embarrass me. Although, I think this time she *was* referring to my age. We talked as we finished the bottle of wine. As I told her about my recent travels, she reached across the table and took my hand. I felt a prickling on my scalp and down my spine. It was the first time I'd held hands with a woman, and here we were in public. I glanced around the room and back to Geneviève's warm gaze. Nobody seemed to care, but I was still a little self-conscious. Many of the other patrons trickled out as we still sat there, clasping hands.

On the dark street, we walked with our arms circled around each other. My hand pressed into the soft folds around her waist, feeling the warmth through her sweater. It wasn't that different from touching a boy, except that most boys were bonier and more muscular. I liked Geneviève's softness, the way I could just sink into her. At the same time, I could feel the muscles in her arms as she held me against her side. She was strong... and feminine, too. As we walked along, I kept almost losing my balance, only it wasn't my outer balance as much as my inner equilibrium. *I am walking in public with another woman as though we were lovers.*

Geneviève showed me the local landmarks: the Exchange with its dome, the huge gated library that used to be some rich people's palace. We crossed a busy street and she pointed out Club 18 as we continued toward the Palais Royale.

"Inside is a beautiful garden," she said. "We'll

go in there sometime. You wouldn't believe it—that's where the French Revolution started."

"Really?" *We'll go in there sometime. So she wants to see me again?*

"There used to be all kinds of shops and cafés in there under the arches. That's where the revolutionaries met and talked." We stopped and faced each other for a moment. Geneviève briefly touched my face. I thought with a slight shock that she was going to kiss me, but instead, she said, "You are very pretty."

She smoothed my jaw-length shock of blond hair behind me ear, making my scalp tingle. I resisted saying thank you for the compliment because I wasn't sure the French did that.

"You too—you are beautiful," I whispered. "*Tu es belle.*"

She pulled me to her, so that I was pillowed against her for a moment, and we walked on.

"This is the way I went to school every day," she said. "Under this arch through the Louvre, and over Pont des Arts."

The Louvre looked completely different at night. Its arcades cast black shadows against the lighted façade. We crossed the bridge, admiring the glittering river, and entered the Latin Quarter.

"I spent my student days in this *quartier*," she said, smiling. "I'm afraid I wasted a lot of time sitting around in these cafés."

The population did seem to be younger here than on the other side of the river. I saw another female couple strolling by, holding hands, although it was hard to tell for sure because a lot of the women in Paris held hands or linked arms. The men did it too. *It's nice the way people touch each other here. I wish we did that more at home*. We continued along the Seine, turned onto Boulevard Saint-Michel, otherwise known as Boule-Miche. Then we turned onto Boulevard Saint-Germain. The street was lively, with many brightly lit cafés. It was an unseasonably mild night. People were eating at tables outside, wearing sweaters, military-style jackets, and colorful crocheted hats.

"Saint Germain was the bishop at the time of Saint Geneviève," she said, turning back to me as my steps lagged. "Are you tired, Sophie?"

"No!" I said, although I was.

"I want to show you something," she said mysteriously. We turned at Place Maubert and went up a gentle hill.

"The Romans used to live here on this hill, way back in the third century. That way they could keep an eye on the Gauls living down on the islands in the Seine. I came here a lot when I was a student, especially late at night. This is her street, Montagne de Saint-Geneviève. On the top is where she built a church—well, she got Clovis to build it."

"Did Geneviève always get what she wanted?" I teased.

"Usually."

We climbed the narrow street full of cafés and shops, an ordinary street in Paris and at the same time, I felt like we were passing through centuries past. "You sure know a lot about history," I said admiringly.

"I told you, I have a mania for history. I used to come up here when I was feeling down. It was my cure. She pointed up the street. "I used to sit in that café."

"Do you still come here?"

"Hardly ever. Tonight is special." We stopped at a small church at the top of the street. "Here is Saint

Étienne's. It's on the site where Saint Geneviève's original church was. There's a shrine to her inside with her relics. It's not open now. If you'd like we could go and visit another time."

Another time? She has been doing this all night, implying that we will continue to see each other. We stood by the church in silence, our arms around each other. I imagined a future visit. Geneviève and I would kneel in front of the altar before a statue of Saint Geneviève that stood amid flickering candles. I felt my scalp prickle.

"I feel her here sometimes," she said, smiling down at me. "I never told anyone else about that before, although I came by here many times with friends. I was afraid they would make fun of me."

I tucked my hand into her larger one and felt a thrill when she gave it a warm squeeze. "You're not afraid I'll make fun of you?" I asked.

A tender light played in her gray eyes. "Mais, non." She pointed. "Down that way is the rue Mouffetard. It's famous because of the poets and artists who used to go there."

"I've heard of it. I'd like to see it sometime," I said, purposely alluding to the future too. We crossed the street to the little café at the top of the street and sat at a table outside, ordering herbal tea. I sipped the hot liquid and stole looks at her face as she sat beside me. "Did you bring all your girlfriends up here?"

"Sometimes. They thought it was cute. Geneviève's street."

"Has there been anyone since her, that first woman you dated who hurt you?"

"Brigitte? Yes, I had a girlfriend since her. That relationship lasted two years."

"Was it serious?"

"I thought so, but we were not so well suited, now when I look back. But who knows those things at the time?"

"When did it end?"

"About a year ago. But what about you, Sophie? We talk too much about me. You have had boyfriends, haven't you?"

I nodded. I wasn't like Jade, who had dated a lot of boys but never had a real boyfriend. I sipped my hot tea and closed my eyes. I knew what was coming; I was going to have to talk about myself. I was afraid that would break the spell that Geneviève and this enchanted city had woven over me.

"So you are not a complete innocent," she concluded.

I laughed shyly. "No. Just with women."

"But don't the boys count for something? You say I have had so much experience and you have had none. I don't think that is really true."

I looked up for a moment into the intelligent gray eyes that were watching me. I tried to think how to answer her. Her question had dug a hole under the surface calm I'd carried with me this evening, exposing the mixture of desire, terror, and amazement that was underneath. Amazement that I was here in this place with this woman. Terror because of everything that might happen if I continued to follow the path I was on with her.

I remembered what I'd told Jade a few days before, how too much was happening at once. I felt that way now. It was like standing out in the surf at the ocean as a wave hit you, knocking you off your feet. Yet somehow your instinct for survival made you get back up on your feet again, either to retreat to the shore, or to stay where you were and learn how to dodge the waves. In my case, I wanted to stay where I was. I was about to speak when she moved her chair closer to me so our legs were touching.

I paused, pulling my attention away from my nearly overwhelming attraction to her. I shifted slightly away, so our knees were just touching.

"*Oui.* Of course the boys do count," I said slowly, trying to pull my mind back to what my life was like a few years ago. I took a deep breath. "I began my '*Sentimental Education,*' (I was quoting the title of a famous novel by Flaubert) when I met my boyfriend Sam in high school. I was fifteen, almost sixteen. He changed my life. Like when you first came to Paris, I suppose. My childhood ended and my adulthood began. I mean, I wasn't really an adult yet, but that's how I felt. Like a door had opened and he pulled me through it, away from who I'd been with my family. I used to see myself mostly through their eyes, but now I saw myself through his."

"So you were in love?"

"Yes, for the first time." I laughed. "Lucky for me, it was a good experience. He was a nice guy. But I don't really want to talk about Sam."

She nodded, encouraging me to keep on talking anyway. I knew there was more I wanted to say, but I wasn't sure exactly what it was or how to say it. I sipped my tea. It was deliciously spicy and sugar-sweet. The night still felt like late summer although we were well into September. I had on the cashmere cardigan my mother had given me as a going-away present. Perfect for backpacking: lightweight and warm. This was the kind of night where you could sit out on the sidewalk and talk for hours in the soft breeze. More young patrons filled up the tables around us, their laughter and muffled voices providing an encouraging background. The white-coated waiter came by and we ordered glasses of vermouth along with some pastries.

"Well, there was a girl I liked around that time too," I said.

"Yes?" Geneviève prompted me.

"She was a good friend of mine. She was beautiful. Her parents were Mexican; something to do with the government. She and I hung around a lot with the artsy crowd and my friend Natalie."

"The one you traveled with in Scotland?"

"Yes." I took a bite of a small apple tart. Delicious. "Anyway, this girl was incredibly bright, much smarter than me, but I loved talking to her; we used to sit and talk about everything, you know, books, politics, whatever. I loved being with her. I still remember how I felt about her in high school, around the time I started dating Sam. She was in my homeroom. I used to wait to see her in the morning and at the end of the day. On the days when she didn't come to school, I felt like the day had lost its light, like everything was drab and ordinary."

"You were in love with her?"

"Not exactly." I wanted to say I did not have a crush on her like I did some other girls. *What's the word for "crush" in French?* "She was my friend," I said. "And she had a boyfriend. I guess I just loved her. But now that I think about it, she was someone I could have been in love with if she'd felt the same way about me. And I wonder what would have happened if I'd dated her instead of Sam. Or, you know, maybe not instead. But later, after we broke up, someone like her." I sipped my sweet wine. I didn't know all the French for what I wanted to say. I was making it up the best I could.

Alcohol helped. Someday it would be easier to talk about these things when I'd been here awhile and knew the language better. French was supposed to be the language of love. There were more words and phrases for feelings in French than in English, but I didn't know very many of them yet.

"It wasn't just her," I continued. "This had been going on for years."

All those feelings were associated with locales near my home, because I was so often in those places when those soaring sensations appeared. They zipped around the top of the Grandstand in the empty fairgrounds near my house in the spring. They zinged across the shining surface of Como Lake where I walked, and filled my heart as I rode my best friend's horse through the snowy fields where she boarded it outside the city. The feelings lived all over the place because I could rarely be with whoever inspired them. That was the way it was.

I shrugged. "I didn't know if anyone else felt the way I did. They never talked about it, so I thought not. Anyway, I liked boys too, so..." Geneviève moved closer to me again. I reached under the table and took her hand, sucking in my breath at the inevitable jolt of electricity that hit my stomach. "Did you ever like boys?" I asked, looking up at her mouth, wanting to kiss her.

She smiled. "Yes, a little bit. Not really. I tried, but they were more like friends."

"Well, you said you didn't fit in. You said you felt like a monster."

"More or less."

"Not me," I said. "The point is, I did fit in. No one knew. I thought I could have gone either way, but the problem was I felt like I had no choice. There was really no other choice for me but to go with boys. I didn't know any lesbians. I heard a couple of friends talking about it once at a sleepover, how they wished one of them was a boy. You know, that kind of thing. But I didn't know anyone who was really out. I just wish..." I sighed.

"What, *chérie?*"

I squeezed her hand. "All those lost opportunities, you know? All that lost time!"

"But you are still so young, Sophie. It is not too late." She beamed at me as she sipped her wine.

I smiled back, no doubt blushing. "Well, I know, but..." For a moment I felt foolish complaining about my lack of opportunities when here was one as big as life sitting next to me. But I wanted to make her understand. I frowned. "You'd think I could have found someone else like me. Where were they back then? I remember once, one summer, I spent a lot time at the Catholic Youth Center. One time I was in the ladies' room. It was an old building, so the room was large, with a lounge area on one end. I was sitting there facing the window, sun pouring in, and this older girl started talking to another girl. She smiled at me, including me in the conversation. She talked about a group of them. Girls with girls. She was all happy and excited about it, like it was a wonderful thing and she wanted me to be a part of it. I listened with my ears wide open. Then they said good-bye and left. I thought I might see them around again, but I never did. Anyway, I was already going out with Sam then."

"And when you went to the university?"

"I don't know where the lesbians were all hiding."

"Under bushes. In dark alleys. You just didn't look in the right places," Geneviève laughed.

"Well, I should have. I found Ted instead. Ted

should have been a girl. Like when you first came to Paris. I needed that. Even if I got hurt, I wouldn't have cared. Then I wouldn't feel so..." I blushed again.

"Feel like what, *chérie?*"

"Like *une petite idiote!*" I half shouted. "Like I'm fifteen years old again! Starting all over. I mean okay, I have had experience with boys and that does count for something. But still, with a woman it's different."

"Yes, it's different." She grinned. "But you seem okay, Sophie. You seem *bien dans la peau.*" This was an important French phrase which meant literally, feeling good in your skin or being comfortable with yourself. It was a state that I aspired to, but rarely felt I achieved.

"Well, I'm not," I answered. "That's just the point, I'm not." I grimaced and shook my head. "I'm just..." I was running out of French. I might have burst into tears of frustration, but Geneviève rescued me with a suggestion.

"Afraid?" she asked gently.

"*Oui, c'est ça!* That's it."

"I do understand, you know. I am scared too." Geneviève cocked an eyebrow at me, making me smile.

"You? What do you have to be scared of?

"Every time I find you, you disappear!"

"Oh, but I come back. Anyway, you are the one who disappeared the other night."

"True, and I was afraid you would slip through my fingers that time. I never know for sure if I will see you again." The waiter returned and Geneviève settled the bill. Then she turned to me. "You are departing again tomorrow, right?" she said, as if to underscore her point that I was always leaving.

I shrugged and nodded. "I have to get ready for school."

"But of course." She stood up and took my hand. "Of course you do." Her next words echoed the phrase she'd used that first night. "You look tired, Sophie. Let's get you home. I'm sure you will fit just right on my sofa."

I laughed. "I was hoping you wouldn't turn me out onto the street."

"You? Never." We left the café and descended the hill in the warm night air. A star winked at us through the haze of city lights. *It's so bright, it has to be Venus, named for the Roman goddess of love.*

On the way to the bridge, Geneviève pointed out an old palace near the Louvre. "My school," she said. The plaque read, "Académie des Beaux-Arts." A photograph came to mind, one I'd seen by Brassai in a book about Paris in the '30s. The students from the Beaux-Arts school had a ball in the spring, *le Bal des Quatres Arts*, dance of the four arts. What were they—painting, sculpture, music, theater? The students were naked or nearly so except for their costumes. Did that still go on? I couldn't help picturing Geneviève, wearing some kind of Roman toga, dancing energetically in a group through the streets. I laughed silently to myself.

"What?" she said, squeezing me against her side.

"Nothing. Just imagining you at the *Bal*."

"Ah," she said. "You have heard about that?" I nodded, still laughing, this time out loud.

Finally, we reached rue Vivienne and climbed wearily up the stairs. Once inside, Geneviève was all business, fixing me a bed on the large sofa, with sheets, pillows, and a fluffy quilt. As she did this, I sat looking at her table of little clay sculptures.

"What are they about?" I asked.

"Oh, they're places I like, Paris and other sites. I form them like parts of the body, you know? That hill we went to tonight, that is the heart of Paris for me."

I wanted to ask more about her work, but I was tired. "And the paintings?"

"Those are by my classmates. We used to trade for each other's work."

After I got ready for bed, Geneviève came to the sofa to say good night. She sat down beside me, her weight shifting me closer. I put my arms around her as hers slid around me. I moved my hand to the nape of her neck, to the fine hair there. She pulled her fingers down my cheek, looking into my eyes and leaned forward and kissed me softly. Our arms tightened around each other and our lips pressed together. From the moment I'd started dancing with her at Club 18 that first night, this was what I'd wanted to do.

A tiny army of sensations marched through my body. I pulled back to look at her and she gazed at me with darkened eyes. She leaned forward abruptly and kissed me again. I kissed her back. A flood of held-back emotion went into that kiss. I didn't want to stop, but before I knew it Geneviève had pulled away again. With tender regret in her voice, she stood up and said, "I'm going to let you sleep now, *ma petite.*"

Chapter Sixteen

You Are Not Married?

Geneviève and I had made no specific plans to get together again, just that she would visit me soon or I would come back up to Paris before my Eurail pass expired in three weeks. We would write. The fact that neither of us had a phone certainly didn't help. Geneviève said she was on a waiting list. The old sections of Paris were far behind the modern world. She expected to get one soon, however.

On the train I tried to read one of the new books I'd bought in London, *Le Mystère Frontenac*, by François Mauriac, but I kept losing my place. Instead, I replayed our kiss as the train rumbled south and the miles increased between us.

I thought about Jade too. I missed her exuberance and her funny monkey face. And I was dying to tell her about my date last night. I wanted to tell her that I liked Geneviève's feminine qualities, the soft parts of her body, her gentleness, her nurturance, as well as her hearty intelligence. I wanted to tell her that it really was different with a woman. It didn't matter about the body parts so much. What mattered was the feelings.

I wanted to tell Jade that I was falling in love. I wasn't obeying the rules, any of the rules I grew up with. I was doing something irrevocable like walking a tightrope between the two towers of Notre Dame as

Philippe Petit had done, risking everything.

I'd read about Petit a couple years ago in a news magazine. Anything about France used to catch my eye. He was a high-wire artist, circus trained, who became a street performer. He did his own thing, performing more and more original and daring feats to the amazement of the Parisians. He made the news when he strung his wires between the towers of Notre Dame without permission. That phrase reverberated in my mind: "without permission." It perfectly described the way I felt about my affair with Geneviève. Like Petit, I was going against the rules without a safety net. He became a true artist in my eyes when he stopped obeying the rules.

I am the artist of my life. Geneviève had told me that. If she hadn't, I might not have talked to her last night as freely as I did. But she made it seem okay. I would be the artist of myself. I liked that phrase. I would carry it with me to Montpellier. I would form myself like clay the way she did with her sculptures. Maybe it was fine that I was nowhere near a finished product yet.

I pulled out a small spiral notebook I kept in my bag. If I couldn't talk to Jade, at least I could write her a letter. I began to summarize everything that had happened since we parted. I asked how she felt about going back home. To me, Minnesota seemed like another planet and I imagined she might be feeling the same way.

I stared out the window and remembered what I had promised myself not to think about until I got to Montpellier. "Please, God, don't let me be pregnant. Please God." *No, no, erase that.* Every time I prayed like that, it backfired. It almost seemed like the prayer itself caused the thing I didn't want to happen. No, no. That was not the way to pray. It should be something positive and more general. That worked much better.

That brought better results. Besides, I was probably not pregnant, anyway.

What should I pray for, then? That I get through this time of my life without going crazy? But "crazy" is negative too. Try again. Please help me to get my feet on the ground. Help me adjust to my new life. Please let me be okay.

⁂

That evening on rue des Tourterelles I was thrilled to find a large box addressed to me in my room, as well as a letter from Kari and Annik. I opened that first. They wanted to know about my trip and how it went with Geneviève. They invited me to visit them during the Christmas break. Putting the letter aside, I unpacked familiar items from home: my fluffy yellow robe and slippers, a favorite blanket and pillow, clothes and books, a tape player and tapes, a framed photo of my family, my stuffed penguin. It was like getting bits of myself back. While I arranged these things, attempting to soften the starkness of my room, I could hear strange voices echoing around the place.

There was a girl, Gerti from Germany, and her visiting boyfriend, Wolfie. Two very cute Vietnamese students were always around; they were the son and daughter of the landlord. And there was Charles, a French medical student with incredibly white teeth who smiled a lot even though the French aren't taught to smile. I guess he didn't want to waste teeth like that. He had a girlfriend who turned out to be in one of my classes. And there was a Chinese student who had the room across from me. We became friendly even though he wore smoky-colored glasses all the time and was a bit weird. We all walked together to the university restaurant, or *restau-U*. The one we went to that was closest was called Vert Bois, which means Green Wood.

The student eating hole seemed like a good place to meet people. I encountered a very friendly, freckly red-haired girl who was sitting alone in the lounge, Roz from Texas. She gave me her address and said to stop by anytime; she was living with a French family.

The first night in my new room, I huddled in my bed and thought of Geneviève. Doubts assailed me. What was I doing here in Montpellier, after all? Putting down roots where I knew no one? I could be going to school in Paris instead. Besides Geneviève, I had my cousins there. They would no doubt be happy to see more of me. But…the whole reason I was here in this southern French city was because I didn't want to depend on my cousins or anyone. That was the decision I made before coming here, and it hadn't changed. If anything, my need for independence was even stronger now.

Feelings and thoughts about Geneviève were with me everywhere I went. If I could see her anytime I wanted, I was afraid those feelings would take over my life. Thinking about her, being with her would be all I could do. I would have nothing else to fall back on, no one else to be. No, it was better this way, with a little space for me to breathe in, to grow in. Surely Geneviève could appreciate that. I would go up there; she would come here. Maybe sometimes we could meet in one of the French cities where she traveled for work. And during the in-between times, I would see what it felt like to live my own life. It seemed to me like the perfect arrangement. I thought it was more romantic this way too.

If I got all my school arrangements made by the end of the week, I could even go up to Paris this very weekend. School didn't start for another week after that. We could continue that amazing kiss!

The next day, when I went to the Institute for Foreign Students and took my placement exam, I noticed that all the Americans were speaking English to each other; how was I going to improve my French in that environment? I decided I wanted to attend the regular university and do what I'd come to do: immerse myself in French life and language. I went the same day to register. I signed up for a French lit class, art history, and Russian language, which I'd been taking at home. University tuition was free, but I had to spend almost the last of my money on the registration fee.

To my great frustration, the first installment of my money still hadn't arrived from home because there was a mail strike on. It was a good thing that my box had made it there before that started. It turned out no one had been getting any mail. This had been going on for a week or so. In addition to the mail problem, I found out there was also a railroad strike, although a few trains still ran.

So maybe it hadn't been such a great idea after all to have my mother send me checks through the mail. Apparently we didn't understand the way things worked in France. But of all the times for there to be a strike! Besides compulsively checking my panties for stains, I took to checking the empty mailbox and asking my roommates how long they thought the strike might last. Their theories ranged from a few days to a month. A month! I was getting desperate. I needed to buy books and supplies. I had my packet of meal tickets and a few francs left. I couldn't even buy Tampax should the need arise. It never occurred to me at the time that I might call my parents and have them wire the money to a bank. I didn't really understand about those things then.

The next day in the bathroom while checking again for blood, I snapped. I marched to Vert Bois, dialed the number for a local clinic that my roommate Charles's girlfriend had given me, and got an appointment at Clinique Saint-Eloi for tomorrow, Friday. That was lucky. I had worked myself up to such a frenzy of nervous apprehension that I didn't think I could stand to wait the whole weekend.

Strolling through the warm, fragrant campus and down a quiet street to the clinic the next day, I relished my last moments of not knowing. The scent of rosemary wafted out from behind vine-covered garden walls. With a sigh, I opened the door to the fluorescent, linoleum-floored lobby and was handed a jar to collect my urine specimen. After turning it in, I sat in the waiting room, my hands knotted between my knees, awaiting the verdict. I kept telling myself to keep breathing.

When my name was called, I went into the doctor's office, not an exam room, and sat on a comfortable chair opposite his desk. He was a middle-aged man with dark hair combed across a bald spot and large kindly eyes. On his desk were pictures of children and a pretty dark-haired woman I supposed was his wife.

He smiled at me and said, *"C'est positif."* Immediately my composure left me and I began to cry.

"Excuse me," I choked. "I was hoping…"

"I take it this is not welcome news," he said sympathetically. "You are not married?"

"No," I choked, "I'm starting school. I'm far from home. I can't have a baby! In other circumstances…but it's not possible." I paused, my thoughts in fast motion.

"I'm going to have an abortion," I said. The decision was almost instantaneous and I didn't believe I would change my mind.

"Ah, mademoiselle," the doctor said gently. "I sympathize with your situation, but abortion is not legal in France—you know that?"

"Then I will go to England." I knew it was legal there.

"I cannot condone abortion."

"But I was raped! *Violé.*"

"*Violé?*" he repeated.

"*Oui.*" Violated. "Don't you think from the moral point of view that changes things, Doctor?"

"From the moral point of view, yes. But from my personal point of view, no. Only to save the life of the mother. He stood up to shake my hand. "I am sorry. I wish you luck, mademoiselle, but don't come back here."

"No, I understand," I said, choking back my resentment.

I walked out the door in a daze, continuing until I was out of sight of the clinic. I sat on a low wall and let the rest of my tears flow. *It's easy enough to disapprove of abortion when you are a man, a married doctor in a comfortable office. I doubt he's ever been raped.* My thoughts turned away from the doctor toward the baby, the beginnings of which I was carrying. Maybe it was an innocent boy or a girl with Jean-Luc's eyes and my own artistic nature. *Damn you, Jean-Luc!*

The worst had dropped out of the sky upon me. Yet I could still move around, could still decide what to do, where to go. I had options. I cried the last of my tears and pulled out my map of the city, crumpled in the bottom of my bag, checking the address Roz had given me. *I have to talk to someone.* Walking fast in the hot sun, I got dizzy spots before my eyes and had to sit down again before arriving at her house. When I rang the doorbell, a middle-aged woman came to the door. "Roz is not here. Sorry, mademoiselle."

I felt crushed. "Tell her Sophie stopped by," I murmured. The woman looked at me sympathetically. It was obvious something was wrong, but she didn't ask what. I said good-bye and walked home in shock. All I could think to do was lie on my bed and wait for it to be time for dinner.

I didn't see Roz at Vert Bois, and I avoided talking to anyone else. In the evening, around the kitchen table with my housemates, I smiled and took part in the conversation like a robot while my mind whirred. *How can I go to England for an abortion? I'm broke! A Eurail pass will not get me across the Channel or buy me food. And an abortion costs money. I suppose I should call my parents. But, no! I don't want them to know! I don't want them to worry! And I feel like I need to leave as soon as possible. I don't know how long an abortion takes to set up. School is starting in ten days and I want to be back in time. I'll borrow money from someone to get to England. I'll look for a nice American girl here if I can't find Roz. Then once I'm in England, I can borrow the rest from Natalie.*

Now that I had a plan, I crawled into bed that night with my tape player. To the soft music of Simon and Garfunkel, I lay curled around the new life inside me. I couldn't believe it. I was a mother! For just a brief period of time, I was the nurturer of a human life. "I love you," I whispered. How could I possibly decide to end that life? It all felt so wrong and crazy.

But I loved myself too. I thought of what my dad had said. "I know you can do this." Maybe I could, but not with a baby. I was the one who had to take care of myself now. It didn't matter what anyone thought. I was not going to let my life fall apart. It had already been threatening to do so—Jean-Luc, lesbians, Geneviève, and now pregnancy. It had felt like too much and now it was about to spill over the top. But I wouldn't let it. I still had to hold all the pieces of myself together and get through this.

"Bridge over Troubled Water" came on. It was the kind of song that could make you cry. I played it over and over, under the covers. The irony of the last line only made my tears flow faster, the part saying it was my time to shine and that my dreams were on their way.

Chapter Seventeen

Angels

The kind of person I wanted to confide in and possibly borrow money from was standing in the Vert Bois lunch line Saturday. She was tall with long brown hair pulled back in a ponytail. I thought she looked American, and she had a kind face. Maybe she would feel sorry for me if I explained my situation. It was worth a try. I walked over and said hello, cutting into line with her. She was Denise from Pittsburgh, a French major like me.

When we sat down to eat, I told her my story. I made myself tell her about the rape because I wanted this young woman to understand what I was up against. I explained about how the mail strike had left me broke. I started to tear up in the middle of my story but made myself stop because I didn't want to impose too much on her sympathy, especially since we'd just met. I dropped the bombshell. I was pregnant. The strange trust that sometimes springs up between people came to my aid, and Denise agreed to lend me enough money to get me across the Channel with a bit left over for food and necessities.

We walked out to her place on Route de Nîmes after lunch to get the money, stopping by my room on the way so she would know where to find me. I wanted her to feel confident that I would pay her back and not just disappear into thin air. We walked to where the houses gave way to farmers' fields. It was getting to be the hot time of day; the dry wind carried the scent of lavender and the sweetness of ripe grapes. A now-familiar fatigue was stealing over me. We slowed our steps.

"Do you like being an au pair?" I asked, stifling a yawn.

"I don't know yet. It's only been a week. The kids are pretty good. I don't have much time to myself, though. It's lucky you and I met because I'll be eating meals with the family most days. I've been wanting to meet people at the fac. My only free time is on Friday nights and Saturdays." She looked longingly at me. "I'd have liked to have been on my own like you if I could have afforded it. Must be nice to be free."

"Ha, I feel anything but free at the moment. But when I get back—I have to admit I am pretty excited about having my own room and being able to come and go as I please. It's the first time I've been away from home, you know? Is this where you live? It's really pretty." The two-story stone house had a garden with a kaleidoscope of flowers crowding the stone walkway and hanging in vines from a trellis. If you had to be an au pair, this was the place to be. I looked forward to visiting her here in the future, assuming Denise and I became friends, which I already hoped we would be.

"Sit here." She pointed to a stone bench. "I'll be right back with the money." Across the road was a vineyard, its vines loaded with purple grapes. I remembered from my summer on my cousins' farm; it was harvest time. Soon they would be picking those grapes. I closed my eyes, drowsing in the heat.

"Thank you," I said when she returned with an

envelope full of cash and a glass of cool grape juice. I took the money with a touch of embarrassment. "I'll come over as soon as I get back to pay you, I promise."

"Don't worry about it. I know you will. You have an honest face. When are you leaving?"

"Tonight. On the ten o'clock train." I felt a pang when I thought of Jade and me a few weeks ago, excitedly waiting for that same night train to Paris. How carefree we had been then! I looked at Denise's open face, her sparkling hazel eyes and chestnut hair. "Thank you so much, Denise!" I cried, hugging her. "You've saved my life. I'll see you when I get back, okay? Good-bye."

I smiled at her and waved as I moved off down the road. Now I had someone to come back to, someone who understood, a possible friend. When I turned around from the road she was still standing there watching me.

⁂

That evening I was eating in the kitchen with my housemates when I announced that I would be leaving on a trip. "I'm going to see someone in Paris," I said mysteriously. I was in emergency mode and my plans were unfolding almost by themselves. It was weird. I felt like I had a different, more efficient person inside me who knew what to do and was doing it, while my real self was just numbly going along with this person who seemed to think of everything.

"Oh?" said the smiling Charles. "Do you have a boyfriend there?" I didn't answer, but the sudden glow on my face was enough for them apparently, and everyone assumed that I did.

As my housemates talked about school, I went over my plans in my head. I needed to make it to Kenilworth by the next night. I didn't have enough money to stay the night in London or to take the train. My Eurail pass didn't work in England. That would mean arriving in London tomorrow afternoon and hitching north before dark.

I had rejected the other possibility: stopping in Paris to see Geneviève first. I longed to tell her, to rest in the solid safety of her arms. She would lend me money, would listen with sympathy, would help me. But I hesitated. Our feelings for each other were so new and fragile. I couldn't risk contaminating them with this mess. I hadn't told her a thing about what happened in Montpellier. I had told her so many other things about myself but not that. Because I wanted her to continue to see me as "radiant," as she'd called me. Not tarnished and contaminated by some French hippie. And I didn't want her to know how naïve and stupid I'd been. Maybe if she knew, she would no longer be interested in me. I wouldn't blame her if she wasn't. Anyway, it wasn't something you talked about on a first date.

I had another reason for not involving Geneviève at this point—I didn't know whether she would try to talk me out of it. This had to be my decision and no one else's. What if she disapproved of abortion? I knew nothing about her views; I couldn't take the chance. On the way back, I would stop and see her and tell her then.

Standing tensely on the station platform in the stiff night breeze, I thought, *This is it. In a moment, I will step on that train and it will be too late to change my mind.* I experienced an agonizing moment of fear and doubt. *God, am I'm doing the right thing? How is this crazy plan going to work? Maybe I should wait and call my parents.*

I stepped aboard the train. Now that it was too

late, I felt better, sinking back into the routine of travel. I found an empty compartment and almost immediately, a young man in a soldier's uniform joined me. I sat still for a few moments, my eyes squeezed together as the train picked up speed, and opened them to the sight of his friendly face. We talked for a while about his going home on leave. He good-naturedly tried to pick me up, but I shook my head. Not every French man was like Jean-Luc. We lay on benches opposite each other and I managed to sleep for a few hours during the night with my knees drawn up, my raincoat tucked over me.

❧❧❦❦

In Paris, I almost broke down and took the metro to see Geneviève. It was still very early; she would be home now, probably asleep. I don't know what I would have done had the metro been running normally. I waited a long time at Saint-Lazare but no trains came, so I abandoned my rash idea of seeing her and took a taxi to Gare du Nord instead.

What was with this strike business? Maybe there was something I hadn't understood. Was *everyone* on strike? Of all times for this to happen, when I needed to get to England fast. I waited another hour and a half for my train to Calais. I was frustrated by the delay, but it gave me a chance to have some breakfast and read about the strike in the paper. They called it a *grève générale*, a general strike. That explained why nothing was running, except a few trains.

On the train north, I met a Dutch boy, Hans Joachim, and it was great to have someone to talk to in English. He was nice and I relaxed a bit with him. I ended up alluding to my reason for traveling to England.

I didn't go into details, but I mentioned my financial straits.

"These strikes can really mess up your life," he said. I told him I'd be okay, that I had a friend in England who would help me. He stuck close by me. I had this knack for meeting nice people—I was lucky that way. Even the soldier last night on the train had kept me from feeling so horribly alone. And I was getting better at knowing who I could trust.

By the time we arrived at Calais it was midafternoon. I calculated that if I caught a hovercraft right away, I could still make it to Natalie's by nightfall. But the day continued to be one of endless delays. A huddle of disgruntled passengers waited in the terminal at the port asking about ferries and hovercraft. It would be another hour at least for either one, we were told. I was boiling over with impatience and my stomach was tied in a huge knot. Walking always helped me feel better, so I told Hans I'd like to go for a walk alone and left my backpack with him.

The day was warm. I made my way along a service road toward water that turned out to be farther away than it looked. I felt like I was walking through molasses and still the water remained in the distance. At last, I understood. The weird fatigue I had been experiencing lately was due to my pregnancy. *Of course! Duh.* Stubbornly, I forced myself to continue until the road finally veered off and I was surrounded by smelly mud and a salt breeze, with gulls swooping and shrieking in the sunlight. I stood there looking out at the green waves smacking the shore. All the strength drained from my body. *Great. Now I don't know if I even have the energy to get back to the terminal. What if the boat leaves without me?* I spun dizzily on my heel and nearly

fell over. When the stars cleared from my head, I began
to labor my slow way back.

"You'd better eat something," said Hans, when he
saw my face. "Have you had anything today?"

"I had some coffee and rolls this morning," I said.
"I haven't been hungry. Too nervous."

"Wait here." He came back with a cup of hot
sweet tea and a ham sandwich. It tasted so good. I felt
better after that. Hans was heading to The Hague; his
ferry wasn't due for another hour, so he walked to the
hoverport with me. I kissed him on the cheek when it
was finally time for me to board.

"Write to me," he said, thrusting a piece of paper
into my hand. "Let me know what happens." I nodded
and was alone again.

It was past 5:00 p.m. I felt the tension inside me
tighten like a string being pulled to the breaking point.
We sat in the hovercraft for another twenty minutes
before the motors started humming. At last, we were
moving, skimming across the water. I let out a long
sigh of defeat as I saw the sun reflected deep gold on
the water. It would be dark in a couple of hours. Until
that moment, I had still hoped to get to Natalie's that
day. *There is no way that's going to happen. I'll have to
start in the morning, but where will I stay for the night?
I don't have enough extra money even for a hostel.*

I felt my face go stiff with held-back tears, panic
churning in my stomach. Maybe I really should have
waited a few days and called home instead of rushing
off like I did. But the urge to do something had been so
strong, I couldn't resist it. Anyway, it was much too late
now to turn back. I was caught in a sequence of events
and had no choice but to keep moving.

I started to look around the boat. A group of

cheerful-looking Irish boys with backpacks were laughing and joking nearby. Well, it had worked with Denise. There was a space on the bench next to them and I grabbed it. Turning to the slender boy next to me, I said, "Hi."

He grinned at me out of a mischievous, intelligent face. "Hiya." I thought he looked like a leprechaun with his curly black hair, pug nose, and sparkling green eyes.

"I'm Sean," he said, "and this is Trevor and Angus."

"I'm Sophie," I said, offering him my hand. Meeting people was so easy when you were traveling. I asked him where he was staying that night.

"We've got friends in London if we can just find their place. We know the street, but not the number, I'm afraid."

"Yah," said the boy sitting beside him, "this eejit here lost the address."

"Oh, we'll find them all right. I was there once before, but it's been two years, and I'm afraid all the houses look alike on that street."

"Likely we'll find them in the pub anyway," said his friend.

"How are you getting to London?" I asked. "By train?"

"No, there's a bus. Are you going to London?"

"Yes," I said. "Can I take the bus with you? How much is it?" I had a five-pound note left over from before, plus the rest of the money from Denise, although I didn't want to spend that until I'd sorted things out with Natalie.

"Two-fifty, I think," he said. "Where are you going in London?"

"I don't know. Do you think…would your friends

mind? I'm short of money." I explained about the mail strike. "I was planning to hitch to my friend's this afternoon, but it's too late now."

"Yeah, the strikes are a bit of a muck-up. Don't worry, you're going to stick with us," he said, putting his arm around me in a comforting way. I sat there blinking with relief, trying not to cry.

Sitting at the front of the bus with Sean and his friends behind me, I watched the London skyline get bigger as I relaxed into a tired, dreamlike state. It sounded crazy, but I was going with strangers to some unknown apartment to stay the night.

Chapter Eighteen

Gaelic Poetry

"Where are we going?" I asked Sean when the bus had entered the lighted streets of London.

"Hendon," he said. "Northwest London."

After a longish ride, the bus stopped, and I scrambled off after the three boys. We crossed the busy street into a quiet residential lane of brick houses with identical front stoops. "Now, troops," said Sean, "I want you to split up and look at nameplates on each door. You boys take the other side, Sophie and I will do this side." As Trevor and Angus left us, Sean told me the names to look for. "O'Connell, McGee, maybe Donnelly. I don't know if Carroll still lives there. Oh, fuck it, just look for Irish names, will you?"

I went purposefully up the first set of steps, shining my little flashlight on the nameplate. Sean took the next house. I found I couldn't remember a single name. I was so tired it was all I could do to get up each set of steps and back down. Some of the doors had no plates. At the end of the row, I sat dejectedly down at the bottom of the doorstep as Sean approached. The pressure in my bladder was becoming insistent.

"No luck," I said, "What about you?"

"No, it's bloody impossible! Maybe our lot didn't put their names out. Are you all right? You look really knackered. What are you doing traveling alone, anyway? How old are you?"

"I'm twenty," I said defensively.

"Oh, well, you look younger. That's all right then." He kept his bright eyes on me, waiting to see if I would say more.

"I really have to pee," I said.

"Christ, come here." He led me behind the open garden gate. When I was done I sat down beside him again, my chin on my fists.

"I'm pregnant," I said in a weak voice.

"Oh, Christ! And here I've been working you to death. You should've told me." He gave my shoulders a squeeze. "Tell me about it later. Just stay put. I'll go round up the boys."

We trudged to the local pub. I was beginning to think I wouldn't have a bed that night after all when Trevor gave a shriek. "Over here," he called. There was a lot of hugging and backslapping.

Sean introduced his friends. And, looking at me, he said, "This is a little stray we picked up on the boat. Her name's Sophie."

"Pleased to meet you," I said. We all made our way back, and soon, I was inside being greeted by a pretty redheaded girl, the partner of one of the boys in the pub.

"I thought you'd never get here!" she cried. "I've got supper for you in the oven. It'll be hard as a rock by now."

"Sorry, it was slow going in France today," said Sean. "General strike."

"Oh, damn those Frogs and their strikes," she said without rancor. As I ate her stew with homemade bread I thought, *Wow, they just accept me.* Being different is what usually causes separation between people, so maybe I'd found people similar to myself. I thought I must have dropped into Irish heaven; these people seemed like angels to me.

I'd been having that kind of luck for the past two days. Denise and Hans Joachim had been kind. Come to think of it, Jade and I had met a lot of nice people through our whole trip. Jean-Luc was the only rotten one, well, except Jill from Strasbourg who had looked at me funny when I was hugging Geneviève in Paris and never turned up again.

It turned out the boys were from Dublin, returning to school from a backpacking holiday in France. Sean was in law school. "I'm a student, too," I told them and suddenly yawned. The subject of where to sleep came up and I was shown a narrow mattress on the floor in the living room. The one next to it was for Sean. It seemed to be understood that I belonged with Sean. I was his waif. The other two boys were given the floor in one of the bedrooms.

"So tell me your story," Sean urged me as Gladys threw us each a pillow and some blankets. I burrowed into my sleeping bag and in a low voice began to tell him everything.

"You were raped?" he said. "This is getting worse and worse."

"Well, yeah," I said awkwardly, "except if I'd fought harder, he probably would have stopped."

"It wasn't your fault, Sophie."

A flash of rage went through me. "I could kill him!"

Sean said tersely, "I'd help you kill him, darling, but I suppose he's nowhere to be found right now."

"That's right."

"So what are you going to do? No, don't tell me."

He spoke in a high, mincing voice, "You're going to be the pregnant freak at your college and then nobly raise the child alone while you finish university and get a job."

"Not exactly. I'm going to get an abortion."

"Don't know how I knew that. Well, good for you. I always did think women had the worst end of it with getting pregnant and all. Don't know how any man has the balls to voice an opinion about it. Of course, in Ireland, you're supposed to believe that life is sacred. But a woman's life is sacred too. Look at my mam with her five brats. She's never had much of a life the way I see it, though she says she likes it. You deserve your life—don't let anyone tell you different," he said emphatically. "You have someone to stay with in Coventry, then?"

"Kenilworth, yes. My old school friend is there. She'll let me stay with her. She'll have to, I guess."

"She'd better be good to you. I know what old friends can be. My ex-girlfriend is a scold, especially when I'm down. She knows me too well. It's nice to be free. Kind of lonely, though. Do you have a boyfriend? You don't mind my asking?"

"No, we broke up just before I left. But I met someone in Paris…a woman."

"A woman? Aren't you one! Is she beautiful?"

"Yes! I might be falling in love," I said.

"That's great."

We relaxed into the darkness and talked freely about whatever came into our heads: mostly about what it was like to be young and putting all the puzzle pieces of ourselves together. We talked about religion and about chaos. About other things too, crazy Irish things you have to be half-drunk or half-asleep to talk about. Sean quoted snatches of Gaelic poetry—lines from an ancient poem about a woman who had "breasts like the bellies of two foals." It gave me shivers. Were the Irish all poets? I couldn't repeat much of what we talked about now, but I remember the feeling I had with him as though we understood each other perfectly. I was sort of half in love with him, I guess. In a platonic way. We both revered William Butler Yeats, and he told me how Yeats had traveled around Ireland, collecting ballads and legends.

Finally, his words were becoming unintelligible. I kept saying, "What?" and he said, "Never mind. Is it all right if I just hold you for a bit? I won't try anything."

"Sure," I said, and he put his arms around me through my sleeping bag. It felt good. For a second I remembered, by contrast, the way Jean-Luc had touched me through my sleeping bag. But with Sean, there was nothing like that. He was gentle with me. I knew I would never forget his kindness. After a while, we dropped away to our separate mattresses and for the first time in days, I slept deeply.

In the morning, I heard sounds of the toilet flushing, footsteps, and water running. I desperately had to get up and find the bathroom. Last night I was so tired I hadn't even gone near it. When it was my turn I found damp towels hanging on racks all the way up the wall, and clothes draped everywhere. I took a shower and rubbed myself with the last dry towel in the cupboard.

At the breakfast table, dressed in clean clothes, I sipped strong coffee while the redheaded Gladys worked on pancakes. Trevor opened the front door and picked up the *London Times*, tossing it on the table. Looking around the table at their sleepy faces, I knew I was never going to see any of them again. And yet they were my friends. Sean shot me a smile. I sighed with a sense of well-being that I hadn't experienced for a while. I told myself everything was going to work out.

"There's something about the strike in France," one of them said with the paper in his lap. "Sounds like they're negotiating with the government. I bet it will be over in a couple of days."

"Yeah, until the next time," said another one.

"If it weren't for the strike," I said, "I wouldn't have met any of you."

"Hey, it was worth it then," said Sean.

"You have to hand it to the Frogs, though," said Angus. "Bloody intrepid bunch. They get what they want."

"So do we, though, don't we?" said Gladys. "Only we use different methods. We vote. We've got the National Health, don't we? And nobody starves in the UK, do they?"

"Listen to her. 'We' is it?" said Sean.

"Well, I do live here," she said, "and it's not so bad in Ireland, either."

"Yeah, these days. But Ireland's still the poor relation since the English started coming over and stealing everything we had, including the land under our feet," said Trevor.

"Damn Brits, they're still making our lives hell in Northern Ireland, aren't they?" said Sean.

No answer to that. "Have some pancakes," was all she said.

After breakfast, I said, "I have to get going."

"Stay a bit longer," said Sean. "You have all day to get to Kenilworth."

"No, really, I have to go. I'm nervous about seeing Natalie. She doesn't even know I'm coming."

"Well, the M1 is nearby," said one of the Irish

boys. "We'll drive you there. You'll have no trouble getting a ride."

"There'll be lorry drivers on their way to Birmingham, even though it's Sunday. Second largest city in England you know, very industrial."

"Coventry is right on the way. If they don't drop you at Kenilworth, you can get a bus from there or another ride."

"Maybe I should have taken the train," I said.

"Nah, this is much quicker than taking you down to Euston. You'll be fine. It's quite safe to hitchhike here. Besides, we know you can take care of yourself," said Sean. "You're a big girl, right?"

"Yes," I agreed, "and soon to get bigger if I don't watch out." The others exchanged glances. I hadn't told anyone but Sean about my problem, but I knew he'd tell them, and it didn't matter to me if he did.

Sean smiled and looked at me with liquid green eyes. "You've got my address in Dublin. Let's keep in touch. Here's their phone number. You're going to ring up tonight, right? Let us know how you are. Promise?"

"Promise," I said.

Sean's friend stopped the car near the entrance to the busy motorway. I hugged Sean. "Thank you," I said tearfully.

"I won't forget you, ever," he said. "Be sure and call. And write."

"Best of luck to you," said his friend, giving me a quick hug.

I took a step then turned around. Sean saluted from the window of the car.

Then I was on my own again, breathing gasoline-laden air, waving my thumb as lorries lumbered onto the entrance ramp. They were right about the hitching.

I probably waited only about fifteen minutes before one of the drivers stopped for me.

"Where ya going, luv? I'm off to Birmingham." A large, affable-looking man beamed across the seat at me.

"Perfect. I'm going to Kenilworth. Could you drop me there?"

"No problem. Almost right on my way." So I sat beside him, my luggage at my feet, and listened to him chat about his wife and kids in Watford. He kept talking the whole hour and a half, which was good because I didn't have a chance to get nervous or worry what I was going to say to Natalie. When he dropped me off, the driver startled me by giving me a quick kiss on the lips. He winked and waved.

Chapter Nineteen

What Will Everyone Think?

I strode nervously up the brick-lined path to Natalie's door and rang the doorbell. A girl in pigtails and jeans opened the door.

"Is Natalie home?"

"Just a minute," she said and walked over to the staircase. "Natalie! You have a visitor!" she shouted then stood aside watching.

Natalie came down and stared at me. I could see in her sharp eyes that she understood in a moment why I was there, though she pretended not to. Natalie doesn't miss a trick; her brain is so fast. She didn't look pleased.

"Hi," I said.

"Wolnak." She came forward and put her mouth close to my ear, her long blond hair brushing my cheek. "What the fuck are you doing here?" She straightened up and addressed the pigtailed girl. "This is my friend from home, Sophie."

The girl said, "Hi."

Natalie smiled nervously. "Come on up to my room."

I followed her up the staircase. "I have a roommate," said Natalie. "She's not here right now." We sat down on Natalie's bed, covered in the bright red-and-yellow quilt I remembered from her room at home.

"You could at least pretend to be happy to see

me," I said tersely.

"I'm surprised, that's all. What's going on? What are you doing here?"

I sighed. "Well, you remember the incident on the beach at Montpellier?"

"You're pregnant."

"Yeah, and I didn't know where else to go."

"Jesus, Wolnak. I'm just getting settled in! It's not that I wouldn't be glad to see you normally." She stared at me with large frightened eyes. She was twisting a lock of hair between her fingers. During our travels in Scotland we had stopped using last names, but now Natalie had started it again. "What the hell is everyone going to think?"

I let out my breath. "They'll think you have a friend staying for a few days, Cummings," I said, emphasizing the name. "Is that against the rules?"

"Yes, actually. But people do have friends over. They just don't tell the matron. There's a girl who's away for a week. She had to go to a funeral in Scotland. You can have her room. So what are you going to do?"

"I'm going to have an abortion."

"I don't believe in abortion."

"You don't? But you're into women's lib."

"So? I just think it's wrong."

"Well, it's right for me. I couldn't handle a pregnancy, not like this, not now. I was going to ask you to lend me the money."

"I can't help you. I can't do it," she said firmly.

"It's just that there's been a strike in France and I didn't get my first check in the mail. You remember Mom and Dad are sending me my money every month?"

"Yeah. So, why didn't you call them?"

I was silent for a moment. "I don't want them to

know."

Natalie smiled for the first time. "They'll freak out, right?"

"Right." I smiled, too. It was funny in an awful way.

"You have to tell them, Sophie. They're your parents."

"But I'm an adult."

"Are you? Well, I'm not lending you the money, so you have to call them. You should have done it right away. They can wire you the money. If you'd called from France, you could have just said you didn't get the check. Now they're going to wonder why you're calling from England. Now you'll have to tell them."

"I know. But I didn't want to wait in Montpellier until the banks opened tomorrow. I couldn't just sit there waiting. I wanted to already be here. I'll call them and have them wire the money, like you said. I'm sorry, Natalie. I'm sorry to get you involved in this, but you're my friend. Remember what you said that first night in London?"

"We're all we've got?" She smiled wanly at the memory.

"Right. You're my friend and you're all I've got."

"Yes, but Sophie, you could have the baby and give it up. You have to accept the consequences of your actions," she said.

"Fuck that!" I cried, tired of her criticism. "I was raped!"

"Look, I know. Sorry. I just can't help but think about you and Jade, traveling alone like that. Didn't you think something might happen?"

"No," I gritted my teeth.

"Look, Sophie, I said you can stay here. But I don't

want to hear about the abortion. You just do what you have to do and leave me out of it."

"Fine," I said. "Thanks," I added. At least we were back to first names.

"So," Natalie said, her mouth curving up, "how'd it go with your French girlfriend?"

"Oh," I brightened a bit. "Great. It was weird the first night, though. She wasn't even there. She had to travel for her job. But her friend let me in and I stayed there by myself. We'd only met twice before that, you know. I could have robbed the place."

"You have an innocent face. So did you get it on?"

I laughed, a little shocked. "No! I went to my cousins' farm the next day. And Geneviève called there and my cousins figured it out. They gave me a hard time but they were okay about it."

"Yeah, and...?"

"Oh, Natalie, we had the most romantic date ever. We had dinner and talked for hours in this little café. And she's an artist! She went to the Beaux-Arts school. She was in the student riots and all. We held hands and walked all over Paris. I don't know where this is going exactly, but she is so...different and..."

"It was like that the first time I went out with Max," Natalie said with a sigh. "Hey, he wrote me! I've had two letters from him already. One was here when I got back and one came yesterday. But don't try to evade the question, Sophie. Did anything happen?"

I laughed. "We kissed, okay?"

"Wow! Your first kiss. I guess I just wanted to know if this was for real. It was so hard to believe when you first told me. So you really like her?"

"Yes."

"And how was your trip up?"

"Oh, Natalie so much has been happening. I stayed with these crazy Irish people last night in London. I love them. I have to call them so they know I'm okay."

For a moment, I thought Natalie looked wistful. Her careful planning did not allow much for mad adventures. She stood up from the bed. "I want to hear all about everything," she said. "This is such a shock. I'm sorry, Sophie. I'm doing my best. I can't say I'm exactly happy you're here. I was just getting settled in."

"I'll try not to hold it against you," I said grimly.

"At least I'm honest. I'll be fine once I get used to it." Outside the bright sun was shining through red oak leaves. "Come on, I'll show you your room. And then we can go for a walk around Kenilworth."

We stood up shakily, and Natalie looked at me, her blue eyes softening, and gave me the hug she hadn't yet offered. Then she led me down a carpeted hallway past the landing to a row of rooms on the opposite side of the house facing the front. "Here's your room. It's all yours. Just put your sleeping bag on top of her bed, will you? Don't use her sheets. Don't mess anything up." She grimaced with her usual ironic humor.

"No, I'll make sure it stays pristine." I opened the window a crack and could smell the roses from the front walk. As I waited for her, lying on top of my sleeping bag, I thought about Natalie's reaction. If I hadn't met Sean, I'd have dozed on a bench at Victoria Station or something, sustained by the belief that I had a friend to fall back on once I got to Kenilworth, someone who would take me in and help me without asking. It was worse to have her against me than spending a night alone in London would have been. I thought of how Sean had taken me in without asking any questions, compared to the grilling I'd received from Natalie. *If a*

*friend came to my door, I would want to help, period. My
Irish friends are like that too and Geneviève is I think,
and Jade and my family. We're that kind of people.
Natalie just cares about herself. If our positions were
reversed, I'm sure I wouldn't have given a thought to
anything but her plight. Because we're friends and that's
what friends do. Ha! I should have known better. She's so
worried about what people will think and actually told
me that she didn't really want me here.*

*But she doesn't believe in abortion. She has every
right to her beliefs. And after the first shock, she's trying,
You have to give her that. And she's letting me stay.*

I heard Natalie's knock on the door, and I stood
up, determined not to blame her anymore. Propelled
by an unspoken truce, the two of us had a long ramble
around town, crunching leaves as we walked. It was a
beautiful day, almost like Indian summer back home.
Natalie showed me the red Kenilworth castle and we
explored some of the little lanes. A cozy little English
town, it was perfect for Natalie. We stopped at a tea shop
and had sandwiches and scones. It was almost like old
times traveling, except Jade wasn't there.

On the way back, Natalie pointed out the red
phone box up the road from her house and asked,
"When are you going to call them?"

"My Irish friends?" I said, reaching in my bag.

"No, your parents."

"I will!" I bristled. "But I want to find out how
much money I'll need first. I'll call them tomorrow."

"Okay." As Natalie left, I thought about what was
different now from when we were traveling. Even though
Natalie and I had bickered in Scotland, we'd been on
equal footing then. Now I felt at a disadvantage—I was
on her turf.

Chapter Twenty

Everything's Fine

I sat slumped in my chair at the kitchen table staring at the notebook where I had written down what the woman from the clinic had said. Tonight: Go for test. 5:30 p.m. Coundon Health Center, Barker Britts Lane, Coventry. Get bus number 5 at Pool Meadow. Get off at rugby grounds. Clinic up the road by phone box. Bring ten pounds. Tuesday: Bring early morning urine specimen. At 11:00 a.m. see doctor and social worker. Fifty-one pounds, balance to be paid by 5:00 p.m. Tuesday. Thursday: Leamington clinic 7:30 a.m. Overnight. At the bottom I had added, Call parents. I had already talked to the people at the bank early that morning about transferring money, so that was done.

How would I ever have the energy to complete my to-do list? I heard someone come in the front door and straightened up. A cheerful person in a floral housedress under an old green sweater entered the kitchen. "Hi, I'm Mary. I'm the housekeeper. Who might you be?" She had an Irish accent. I looked up into her comfortable brown eyes.

"Sophie, Natalie's friend." I knew I looked and sounded a mess.

"You staying here?"

"Yes." She didn't seem like someone who would bust me, but I wasn't sure.

She sat down at the table. "Don't worry, love. I won't tell Miss Bates. If you're in some kind of trouble, you can tell me. What is it, dear?"

Oh, no, I can't hold out against the Irish treatment. I started to sniffle. Mary looked at the paper I'd been writing on. "Oh, I see. You *are* in trouble. Do you want to talk about it?"

"Well…" as reluctant as I was to tell yet another stranger about my problems, I knew I needed all the help I could get, Irish or otherwise. Especially since Natalie was not being very sympathetic. So I told the housekeeper briefly what had happened… "And my money didn't come because of the strike," I moaned. "I'm supposed to be in France. I wasn't going to tell my parents, but I have to now because of the money, and they're going to be so upset." I paused and tried to slow my breathing, trying to regain control. "I have to pay ten pounds to the clinic tonight," I said slowly. "That means I'll have only five pounds left and I need it for bus fare. I'm going to have to give up food for a while. I'm meeting Natalie for lunch at school. Maybe she'll lend me some money for lunch. She doesn't believe in abortion, you know."

"Has Natalie been mean to you?"

"She's been all right, I guess."

"If you can't turn to your friends when you need them…" Mary frowned.

"That's what I think," I said. "Friendship should come first."

"Here, let me pour you a cup of tea." She pulled out a thermos from her bag and poured the hot liquid into two mugs. Mary held up her cup and said, "Here's to you, Sophie." She dug in her huge purse and pulled out two crumpled bills. "Here's two quid. Take yourself to lunch."

"Oh, Mary, thank you! I wasn't trying to hit you up when I told you all that."

"That's all right, dear. I know you don't want to ask your friend for money. I hope if I was in your shoes someone would do the same for me."

"I would," I said, standing up. "I'd better go call my parents now before I lose my nerve. Bye, Mary. Thank you." Funny how Irish people kept coming to my rescue on this trip. Maybe kindness was a trait they developed as a people over centuries of hardship. It made sense. You learned the value of generosity when you were in need of it yourself.

I walked up the road and felt like I was climbing Calvary Hill. Natalie had given me a piece of paper with the country codes. In the phone box, I poured out the coins I'd gotten that morning at the post office into my hand. It was six hours ahead there. *Mom, please be home.*

At first, there was a long silence, and then my mother's voice, covered in static. "Mom?" My heart was beating a fast staccato.

"Sophie?…okay?" I couldn't hear much. We had a bad connection.

"Mom, I'm okay. I'm in England at Natalie's. I need you to wire me money."

"Can't hear."

"Money, Mom. Wire money. Telegraph. I didn't get the check. There's a mail strike in France."

"You calling from England?"

"Yes." Maybe I didn't have to tell her. Maybe I could just make something up. But, no—Natalie was right. They were my parents and deserved to know the truth. I forced myself to say it. "I'm pregnant, Mom. I have to get an abortion." I flushed hotly with shame and embarrassment.

"Did you say you're pregnant?"

"Yes. I was raped, Mom," I added.

"What?" Mom said.

Oh God. I wished there was some way I could soften the blow. But I had to say it. Telling them was the worst part of all of this. I repeated the word.

"You were raped?" I heard the distress in her voice over the thousands of miles. The connection was better now. I tried to explain, make it sound okay, although it never would be.

"It's not as bad as it sounds, Mom. Really. It was someone I met while traveling. Please don't worry, I'm fine. But I have to pay for an abortion." Then I said, "My money didn't come yet. There's a mail strike."

"How much do you need?"

"Eighty pounds." I'd figured that amount would give me enough extra to live on and get back to Montpellier. "You have to wire it to Lloyd's Bank in Birmingham. As soon as possible." I had to repeat all this again to be sure she got it. "I'll write and explain. Good-bye."

I wobbled out of the phone box, feeling truly terrible now. Rape, Abortion. The words were horrible. I never wanted to cause my parents any pain. But I had no choice. I couldn't shield them. I was their daughter. Just by existing, I caused them pain. Joy too, I reminded myself. Maybe one day I would find out. Maybe one day I would have a daughter too. For the moment, I had an inkling of what it might be like.

I walked firmly down the road. *Still, when you think of it, I am perfectly healthy. I really am fine. I don't have cancer or anything.* I hoped Mom would see it that way too. She and my dad would get over the shock in time.

I walked around Kenilworth at a fast clip as though I could outpace my less-than-happy thoughts. Then I remembered I had to call Geneviève. I stopped at another red phone box, dialing Sylvie's number. Fortunately, she answered.

"Sylvie," I said, "it's Sophie. I expect to be in Paris Friday night. Please tell Geneviève, will you?"

"Of course, Sophie. Where are you?"

"I'm in England," I said. Somehow I was glad it was Sylvie I was talking to and not Geneviève.

"England? But I thought…"

"I had to go back to England for a few days. Tell Geneviève."

"Yes, I will. Good-bye."

Then it was time to go meet Natalie for lunch on campus. Thanks to her careful instructions, I found the cafeteria easily.

"I called them, Natalie," was all I said when I saw her, and she nodded. It was awkward at first sitting there not talking about the whole reason I was there in England. She told me about her theater program, having just come from an acting class. For a moment, I forgot about my problems as I questioned her about it. I could see Natalie becoming an actress; I believed she would succeed at anything she wanted to do.

If only I was as confident as Natalie. I wasn't sure what I wanted to do with my life. I knew I wanted it to be something creative. Plus, maybe I would teach French. What I cared the most about then was learning French really well. I was looking forward to getting back to Montpellier and leaving this mess behind.

That afternoon I lay on my bed writing a long letter to my parents, explaining everything, while trying not to make it sound too bad. I wrote about Jean-Luc and Bernard. I wrote about how I loved Paris, wishing I could tell them about Geneviève, but thought I'd better save that shock for another letter. I told about my visit to the cousins. I said I liked my housemates in Montpellier and was already making friends at the U. I was sure, now that the strike was over, that the letter with the check would be waiting for me. I sent my love to my three siblings. I ended again with, "Don't worry, everything's fine."

After handing my letter over the counter at the post office, I felt lighter. I strolled around in the warm late-afternoon sun, making sure I knew where to catch the bus for my appointment that evening. I was glad my appointments were in the evening because that meant I wouldn't have to spend much time in the house when everyone was home, including the matron and Natalie.

At the clinic, I went through the same procedure as in the French one: produce a specimen, hand it over, and wait. This time, of course, there was no suspense as to the outcome. Over the top of a magazine, I eyed the other patients, wondering which ones were there for abortions and which ones planned to stay pregnant. A couple of them were pretty obvious. I wondered whether I would ever be an expectant mother carrying the heavy mound of her child everywhere she went. I had already numbed myself to that sort of thing after the first emotional night in Montpellier. I couldn't afford to have those feelings anymore. In my mind, the whole problem had turned into a medical procedure. Maybe when it was over, I'd let myself grieve but not now.

When my name was called, I followed the young woman into an exam room. I looked down at my clothes, the same ones I'd worn yesterday, and peered at my ragged fingernails, curling them under. At least I had on clean underwear. I hadn't showered since London, but that was just yesterday morning. I'd combed my hair, but it had grown out and looked shaggy around the ends. A haircut would improve my looks, but I had no money to pay for one.

The nurse came in and asked me a list of questions. When was my last period? She ticked down a list of symptoms. No nausea. Dizziness? Not really, except for that time walking near the harbor in Calais. Breast tenderness? Maybe. Fatigue? Yes. *Confusion, guilt, regret?* She didn't ask about those. She took my temperature and blood pressure then told me to undress from the waist down and gave me a gown. The doctor would be in shortly. *Great, just what I want to do: be examined from the waist down by some male doctor. Maybe it will be a woman.*

It wasn't a woman. The doctor came in and looked at me rather coldly, I thought, though his mouth stretched into a short smile. How did I look to him? I was not one of the revered mothers in the waiting room. He knew what my plans were for this pregnancy and that I had no wedding ring on my finger. I felt like a slut. I had told myself I didn't care what anyone thought. I wasn't going to tell him about the rape.

I submitted to his plastic-gloved probing. I tried to keep everything still, inside myself. He could listen to my heart through his stethoscope, but he would never know what I was feeling.

At last, I was back in the waiting room and was given a paper bag with a container for my next specimen. Then out the door and I was free again, walking quickly through the cool, windy evening, hunching into the collar of my glossy raincoat. I felt like I needed to crunch everything inside where no one could get at it. The only one I had been able to talk with freely about the abortion in the last couple of days had been the housekeeper, Mary.

The bus came and I stepped gratefully into the warm, bright interior. At least no one on the bus knew. A girl in a bright, visored cap with blond tendrils falling over her cheeks smiled at me. I smiled back.

I stopped at the market near Natalie's house to see what I could afford, choosing a packet of crackers and a can of soup.

In the warm kitchen, I waited for my turn at the stove and heated my soup. Natalie wasn't there, but the other girls seemed to know who I was and were friendly enough without engaging me in conversation. I ate all the soup and the whole box of crackers, smiling to myself at the absurd thought that I was eating for two.

The truth is I have no way of knowing whether this child would have been born anyway. Many early pregnancies terminated naturally in the first couple of months. It said so in the magazine. I couldn't remember what the percentage was. A third? Anyway, that might have happened to me naturally. Knowing this helped a little bit. This was just a maybe baby—nothing for sure. *I'm not going to feel guilty. I am taking care of myself and that's my main job now since no one else is going to do it. Still. Damn. Why couldn't things have gone the way I planned? I'd still be in Montpellier with my housemates. I wouldn't have had to worry my parents. None of this would be happening.* But I had a funny feeling that life didn't go the way you planned it, especially not once you were out in the world.

Stopping at Natalie's door, I rapped and stood in the doorway. She was with a petite girl wearing a bathrobe.

"This is Mandy," said Natalie. "My roommate."

"Hi, Sophie," said Mandy. The way she looked at me, I knew she knew about my situation. *I thought Natalie wasn't going to tell anyone!* After all the barbed criticism yesterday, this felt like another invasion.

But the last thing I wanted was any more unpleasantness. I forced myself to speak normally. "Natalie, I'm so tired. I think I'll just read and go to sleep. Do you think it would be okay if I took a quick shower tomorrow morning after everyone's left?"

"Better not," she replied. "There's no hot water after nine and it'll be busy in the morning before that. Now is a better time, since it's still early."

"Okay, thanks," I said and closed the door.

In the shower, I tried to wash away the look the doctor gave me along with Mandy's knowing eyes. I tried to wash away my mother's startled voice on the phone and my own guilt. *Innocent. I am innocent and pure. All the dirt is washing away down the drain.*

Chapter Twenty-One

Drifting Away

In my dream, I was sitting face-to-face with Natalie on the shore of a big lake in Scotland. I had my back to the water and we were arguing, when suddenly I looked down and saw that the piece of shore I was sitting on had broken off. I was drifting out into the middle of the lake! Rather than jump off and swim back, I sat there helplessly. Natalie stood and watched, not attempting to help me at all. She didn't seem to care. Then Natalie turned into Geneviève, her eyebrows furrowed as she stared at me. I felt angry and abandoned, not only by Natalie but now by Geneviève, too.

The bedside clock showed a little after 5:00 a.m. My stomach burned from hunger, and I had to pee. I put on my robe and padded out into the silent hallway in my socks.

I tiptoed downstairs to the kitchen. In the large pantry, each shelf containing food was labeled with a resident's name. I avoided Natalie's and carefully took a piece of bread from one, another piece from someone else, a biscuit from a third person, a tea bag and apple from a fourth. Then I made a strong cup of tea, sweetened with stolen sugar cubes. I enjoyed a solitary breakfast as reddish light began to fill the window.

◈◈◈◈

At the clinic that morning, I dutifully handed in my paper bag with the bottle inside. There hadn't been time to read much more about pregnancy in the mommy magazine before my name was called. This time, I saw another doctor who was much nicer than the first and seemed very calm and matter-of-fact. I didn't even have to undress this time. He explained to me about the D and C and that I might feel cramps afterward. There would be bleeding, like a period. I might feel weak and should rest in bed for a few days. I most certainly shouldn't travel until I felt stronger and the bleeding stopped.

I didn't say that I intended to travel as soon as I got out the next morning. They'd told me that I was going to stay overnight after having the abortion. This seemed an unusual luxury, but it must be because the clinic was private and not part of the National Health. I pictured nurses bringing me cups of tea. I wouldn't mind that at all. It would be nice. And I wouldn't have to face Natalie again. I was sure that a day and a night of rest in the clinic or whatever it was, would be enough. Then I was going to hightail it out of England to see Geneviève. Whenever I thought about that, my pulse gave a leap, and it did so now despite my bad dream about her and Natalie.

The social worker I saw next asked me for background on my pregnancy and I gave it to her. I explained that I felt the rape had been partly my own fault. The woman clicked her tongue. "It's never the woman's fault in a case of rape, dear," she said. "You must believe that."

"It's just that I keep thinking of what I could have

done to prevent it."

She shook her head and made brief notes. "Would you believe me if I tell you that they all say that? You must try to be kinder to yourself. You did what you could at the time. Yes, you'd surely do it differently now, but I hope you never get the chance to find out." She smiled and shook my hand. "Good, luck, Miss Wolnak. You're going to be fine. Just be patient. It will get better." I nodded. "Now we'll want the balance of the fee by five o'clock today. Otherwise, you'll lose your place. Will that be any problem?"

"I'm waiting for the money to come by wire from the US. I don't know how fast that works, but I think it will come this afternoon."

"It should be all right," she said reassuringly. "You'll soon be back at school, and I'm sure you'll be very careful after this. The clinic will give you a prescription for some antibiotics and birth control pills."

"Yes, the doctor told me."

"Be sure to take them, all the pills, will you?"

"Yes, of course. Thank you," I said.

Walking out of the clinic into an overcast, windy day, I knew I wouldn't fill the prescription for the birth control pills. Instead, my mind went back to the problem about the money. When I'd called the bank in Coventry this morning, they'd said I'd have to go to a Birmingham branch. I'd asked for directions, and they'd even told me what bus to take from Coventry. I decided to go straight there as I turned up the collar of my raincoat and waited shivering for the bus on the high street. Underneath my coat I wore my wool sweater and even had on a knitted cap I'd borrowed from Natalie, but nevertheless, the cold wind went right through me.

I looked longingly at the tea shop across the street. I hadn't been having any problem with morning sickness; maybe it was too soon for that. All I knew was I was hungry all the time. I imagined everything I would eat when my money came. Bangers and mash, fish and chips, mushy peas—I didn't care about how weird the names were. It all sounded good.

Birmingham seemed as enormous as London. I walked for about half a mile through throngs of people, passing The Bull Ring shopping center and a Woolworth's. Then I spotted Lloyds Bank. It was almost 3:00 p.m., and I thought there was a good chance the money would have come. "I'm expecting some money from the US," I said breathlessly to the clerk at the reception desk. I gave my name and he went and conferred with a teller, who returned shaking his head. My spirits sank. "I'll be back in an hour," I said and left the bank.

Well, it had to come soon. But what was I going to do while I waited? I was hungry but couldn't eat. I walked past restaurants, boutiques, and office buildings. It was warmer here than in Coventry; the tall buildings probably shielded the streets from the wind. I flowed along with well-dressed people who were laughing and talking. I made sure I remembered the way back to the bank. Then I spent half an hour restlessly reading in a public library as my stomach rumbled and I kept losing my place. This was no good. I put down my book and just sat and gazed out the window trying not to think about food.

After forty-five minutes, I returned to the bank. Still nothing! In another hour it would be 5:00 p.m. and the clinic was only holding my spot until then!

"What time do you close?" I asked the teller.

"Six o'clock, miss." The vise was tightening.

Back on the sidewalk, my pace became slower than the flow around me until I was just crawling along.

I remembered screaming in the shower with Jade. I wished there was somewhere I could go and do that right now. I had slowed to a halt so all the people had to part around me. I felt like I did in the muck on the ferry road in Calais. I couldn't seem to move. Where was my emergency self? As though in response to my call, I felt her moving my feet again toward the bank. I settled into a chair in the bank lobby where the clerk could see me. At five minutes to 5:00 p.m. I approached him. He looked at me sympathetically. "Still nothing?" I asked. He shook his head.

I went out to telephone the clinic. "Hello," I said, giving my name. "I'm the person waiting for the money from the US. It hasn't come yet. Please, could you wait until the bank closes at six?"

"I don't know. Just a minute please." I had stopped feeling hungry; instead, my stomach was twisted and tight as I waited in the phone box, pressing the receiver to my ear. Finally, the voice returned to the line. "Yes, we'll wait until six."

"Thank you," I gasped, and hung up the phone. *6:00 p.m.! That's in an hour. What if it doesn't come by then? I'll lose my place. I'll have to wait until they have another spot open and who knows how long that would be. I have to get this done and go back to France! School will be starting and anyway, I can't stay with Natalie any longer. Kathy will be back and the matron might find me out at any time and then I'll be out on the street. If only I can get the clinic to wait until sometime tomorrow, but they seem so strict about it.*

Back in the bank, I sank into a chair and closed my

eyes. *Please, God, make it come soon.* How long did it take for money to cross the Atlantic cables? If only I had taken it all with me in the beginning. To be fair, letting my mom send checks piecemeal had seemed sensible at the time. But how humiliating to have to rely on my parents to send me my own money. It's not like I was asking them to pay for anything.

I closed the book and put my head in my hands. I really couldn't take this anymore, not after everything I'd been through the past few days, not after the strikes and the delays and no money and hunger and Natalie being difficult. Not after talking to my mother.

I'd stopped paying attention to the time when I was startled to feel a hand on my shoulder. The clerk was standing there smiling warmly at me! "It's just arrived," he said, as I broke into a huge grin. "Please step over to the window." I glanced at the clock behind him. It was a 5:45 p.m. *Unbelievable! It got here just in time.* Stretching out my hand, I watched dazedly as twenty-pound notes were piled onto it. I shoved them in my purse and sailed to the door, turning and waving to the clerk as I passed. Then I went back to the phone box.

"Hello, it's Sophie Wolnak again. I've got the money!" I squealed.

"That's all right then. We'll hold your place. Take your time. We're open until nine."

"Thank you so much," I said effusively and went floating down the street in search of a restaurant. Suddenly my appetite had returned and I entered the first decent-looking place I saw.

I gazed around at the other people there, trying to slow my breathing. It was hard to relax after being wound up for so long. The chicken, mashed potatoes and peas I ordered were delicious. For the first time since coming to Natalie's, I felt that everything was going to work out.

On the way back to the bus stop, I popped into a sweet shop and bought Natalie a box of Scottish shortbread. It was so much fun to have money to spend. Then I took the bus back to the clinic in Coventry, paid my bill, and stopped for a few groceries at the market nearby.

Across the street was a hair salon called Slick Chick. Terrible name, but on a whim, I went over. They weren't busy and took me right away. In the chair, I closed my eyes. "Do what you want," I said. "Something trendy," I added. Then I relaxed as the young woman clipped my hair. Anything would be better than the mop I'd walked in with. It was nice to just let go and let someone else take over. When she was done, I looked in the mirror and saw a pale young face with large, sparkling blue eyes underneath a gleaming short cut with blond bangs. I turned my head from side to side and the face in the mirror smiled.

"Definitely cute," said the hairdresser. "You need some hoop earrings in a bright color to go with it. The shop right next door has them."

"Thanks," I said as I paid, and with a springy step, I visited the shop. I came out wearing some yellow-green earrings to go with my coat.

By the time I opened Natalie's front door, I was feeling truly invincible. I was the girl with the sexy haircut and trendy new earrings. The pigtailed student who'd let me in the first day was sitting near the door. She had a pinched expression on her face. "Oh, Sophie," she called out, "the matron wants to see you."

My buoyant mood deflated like a punctured balloon. "Oh, great. I can't face the matron now," I said. "Not after the kind of day I've had."

"Well, you've got to. She said to send you in as soon as you got back. Anyway, Miss Bates isn't so bad. She's nice, really."

"Okay, where is she?"

"Straight back down that corridor, all the way," said the girl.

I knocked, feeling small. It was so like being a schoolgirl having to go to the principal's office. Would she make me leave?

"Come in," came a stern voice, and a middle-aged woman wearing a skirt and blouse turned to look at me, her dark graying hair in a braid. She was seated on the sofa in a small sitting room with the television on. She stood to turn it off and motioned for me to sit down.

"I'm Miss Bates," she said, "I'm sorry to be in the position of having to enforce the rules of this house, but that's my job. I found out this morning that we had someone staying here. Of course, it happens." She looked at me questioningly, but with tolerance. "I was told you were in trouble."

"That's right," I said, and again found myself having to explain my story to someone in authority.

She sighed. "Nothing shocks me anymore. But I have to say, that was foolish of you to have trusted those boys. I'm sorry you have to bear the consequences." She spoke with dignity but not without kindness. "I feel one must keep one's reserve, you know? Trust no one."

"No one? But don't you think you have to trust someone?"

"Well, yes. But you know what I mean." She waited for me to respond.

"You mean until you're sure, I suppose. But sometimes you can know enough about a person in a minute. You're right though. With those boys, I didn't really trust the one who hurt me. I was stupid."

"Well, I'm glad you learned something. How much longer do you plan to stay in Kathy's room? It's lucky she's away."

"One more day, that's all. Thursday, I'll be gone," I promised her.

"All right. I'll take your word." She smiled warmly, seeming reluctant to let me go. "What are you studying, Sophie?"

"French lit, art history."

"What do you plan to do when you're out of school?"

"I don't know exactly. Teach. Maybe be a writer."

She looked gravely at me and said, "Yes, I believe you may," and ended the interview. Her solemn pronouncement, however unfounded, touched me deeply. I thanked her sincerely and went back to the front hall. Natalie was sitting in the living room.

"Sophie!" she said, coming over. "I like your haircut. Really!"

"Thanks," I said.

"I heard you saw Miss Bates."

"Yep, news travels fast around here."

Natalie nodded worriedly. "I wonder who told?"

I shrugged. "It doesn't matter. She's letting me stay. In another day, I'll be gone. Here," I said, fishing the shortbread out of my bag and extending it to Natalie like a peace offering. "I got you a present."

Chapter Twenty-Two

Little Maybe Baby

L eaves were blowing everywhere when I opened the door of the large Victorian house that served as an abortion clinic on the outskirts of Leamington. I sank into a chair in the little waiting room knowing I had nothing more to do or take care of.

I still felt prickles of guilt, but the social worker had said it was okay. Everyone felt that way. One other young woman was there, also alone, dressed in a tartan skirt and cardigan. I sensed that she too was relieved that the time had finally come. Soon we could leave all this behind. Day would pile up after day. I would get into a routine. I would go to class and study, and in the evenings and weekends see my new friends, maybe go to parties. I'd forgotten what it felt like to live a normal life.

Lying on the operating table as the sedative started to take effect, I said to myself, *Good-bye, little maybe baby.* The nurse told me I might have a funny dream or say something weird. In fact, I did have a sort of dream; I saw Geneviève holding my baby as though she had rescued it. I thanked her and then I was waking up already. I felt like a weight was pulling on the lower part of my body. "Did I say anything?" I asked the nurse as she helped me off the table into a wheelchair.

"You said you had to go to the bathroom, love, that's all," she said. "Do you want to?" I said yes, and she wheeled me to one nearby. Someone had stuck a pad to my underwear and it was covered in blood. That was what I'd been hoping to see for so long, but it didn't matter now. The nurse wheeled me down the corridor to a large room with lots of other beds where women were sleeping, reading, or sitting on the edge of the beds chatting to each other. It was sunny in there; the gauze curtains let in light.

I got in under the covers and closed my eyes. At last, I could be still. I had been thrashing around like a fish on a hook, but now it was all over. I could rest. I felt numb all over except for an ache in my abdomen. It might have been a bad period. I just lay there thinking about how much I needed this time to lay low. My nerves had been taut, my insides clenched for days and days, even since back in London with Dad. The only break I'd had from feeling that way was the night I'd spent in Paris with Geneviève and the night with the Irish people.

I lay there watching the patterns of the tree branches moving against the gauzy curtains and I slept until someone came around with a trolley calling, "Tea, who'd like a cup of tea?" I sat up. I did want one, and it was just the way I imagined it, being brought tea and biscuits by kind nurses. Except they were probably aides, really. I sipped the hot liquid and gazed around the ward. It was quite a cheerful place. Some of the women were walking around, visiting at each other's beds, or sitting in front of the television. The one in the next bed looked to be in her forties; she was knitting. It was comforting to be in a room with women all in the same situation as myself. I was young—my circumstances were different from the woman next to me. Maybe she was married. But it didn't matter. I didn't have to explain myself to anyone here, didn't even have to talk at all if I didn't want to.

They served us a nice lunch too. I spent the whole day that way, in bed except for getting up to go to the bathroom. Every time I woke up, the light was a little different through the gauze curtains, until finally dusk set in. I kept seeing an image of Geneviève with my baby, which made me vaguely happy in a weird way.

When I left the next morning, I walked slowly down the lane toward the road, beneath trees with yellow leaves, my backpack on my back. I watched the birds soaring in the sky, the wind ruffling the wheat in the fields. But these things did not evoke any pleasure in me as they usually would. I was tired. I hadn't expected to feel like this, although the doctor in Coventry had warned me I'd need to rest for a few days.

I stopped at a Boots pharmacy on the high street to fill my antibiotic prescription and buy more pads and pain pills. Then I took a bus to the train station and began my journey to London and Paris. When the train stopped in London, I stayed in my seat.

I couldn't seem to feel anything. I thought about Geneviève and couldn't muster any enthusiasm. I didn't get depressed very often and when I did it hit me hard. I felt like a stranger to myself. I thought, if I just wait, the person I used to be will come back—I have to believe that.

The day continued in this strange vein. Nothing seemed real. On the boat, all I wanted to do was sleep. My abdomen ached. I wasn't hungry. I lay down on a bench and dozed to the rocking of the waves, which helped. Then we landed in Calais and I boarded a train to Paris. On the train, I bought a bottle of water and a sandwich and took another pain pill. I wondered whether Geneviève had received my message from Sylvie; probably she had. I wondered whether she would be there at her apartment or traveling like last time.

I probably should have told Geneviève about the rape. I talked to her about so many other things but kept back that important bit of news. What was she going to think now when I told her? I had a bad feeling. Maybe if those stupid trains had been running in Paris when I was on my way up, I might have told her then. But that didn't happen.

I closed my eyes and saw Geneviève's face in the dream about her saving my baby. Only this time she was looking at me with reproach in her gray eyes and holding the newborn infant tight to her chest.

It was early evening when I got to Gare du Nord. Being in France after England was like jumping into a swimming pool. It was like being in a completely different medium: not only the language but the whole feeling was different. This was starting to be the Paris of the real world to me, not the fantasy place Jade talked about. My depression lifted for a moment. I felt some warmth seep into me as I walked by the café where I'd stopped for breakfast on the way up and saw the same waiter. He caught my eye as he was carefully transferring tiny espresso cups from a tray to someone's table.

Entering the metro station, I trudged down the long corridor where an accordion player was dredging out a melancholy tune. I stopped and fumbled for a franc to put in his hat. "Play something happy," I pleaded after he'd finished his song. With a nod of the head, he squashed the halves of his instrument together, running his fingers over the keys. Out came "La Vie en Rose." With a little thrill at the familiar tune, I quickened my steps down the tunnel, the lilting music reminding me of how happy I'd felt the last time I was with Geneviève.

But a little later, when I slowly climbed the steps to her dimly lit street, my anxiety and depression returned. I knocked on her door and at first, I could hear nothing inside, then footsteps and the floor creaking by the door. "Sophie?" she said, opening the door. She took my hand, pulling me into the kitchen, kissed me, then closed and locked the door.

"You cut your hair." She led me to the sofa. "I like it." A lamp produced a patch of light over the table with the clay sculptures. "What's wrong?" she asked, glancing at my rigid posture. "Sylvie said you were in England again."

I nodded, wondering where to begin. Geneviève waited. Finally, I let out my breath and said, "Remember those two men who were sitting with Jade and me at that table in Montpellier?"

"Yes. I thought they were your friends but you said not."

"No, we'd just met them. I was supposed to be finding a place to live, but instead we spent the day with them and ended up on the beach at Palavas."

She looked at me somberly. "And so?"

"Well, we camped with them on the beach that night."

"But they would think you wanted sex with them if you camped."

"Apparently. I smoked too much hashish, too."

"What are you telling me? Did one of them have sex with you?"

I nodded. "I didn't want to."

She stared at me. "You told me nothing of this." Her voice rose. "Why? I could have helped you! Such a bad thing and you told me nothing!" I had never seen her angry before. She looked at me with steely gray eyes. "It's not the kind of thing you talk about on a first date," I said. "Or even on a second date."

"You should have trusted me."

"I hardly knew you!" I retorted sharply. I saw the hurt expression on her face; I didn't want the conversation to go this way. "I'm sorry, Geneviève," I said more softly. "I'm sorry I didn't tell you. I didn't want you to think of me as a stupid American. Even though that's what I was."

She took a deep breath as though trying to calm herself. "No, no." She bit her lip and shook her head before speaking more gently. "I am sorry too, Sophie. I should not be angry with you. I should be giving you sympathy instead." She rose from her chair and stood by me. "I would never think you were stupid."

"But I was! Other girls I know would have managed to stop him. I just sort of gave up. In the culture I grew up in, girls are supposed to be nice. We are pleasers," I said bitterly. "Maybe there is something wrong with me."

Geneviève put her arms around me as I shook but did not cry. "*Ça y est,* Sophie. It's okay. There's nothing wrong with you. The man was a rapist. Normal French men would have stopped if you said no." I looked up at her, half-convinced. "Rape happens because there is a rapist," she went on emphatically. "No other reason." She looked at me intently. "Okay? Do you believe me?"

I nodded. She was right. I knew all along that Jean-Luc was different from other French men, but I think I needed to hear it from a French person to really believe it. I flexed my shoulders as if a real weight had just been lifted from them.

She smiled. "You know, I don't see you as the

pleaser type, really. You seem very original to me. You seem to do what you want."

"Really?" I brightened, liking the sound of that. "I hope you're right."

Geneviève sat back down on her chair and looked at me, seeming to know there was more to the story. "So then what? Why were you in England?"

I sighed, wanting to get through it quickly. "Well, when I got to Montpellier I found out I was pregnant." There, I had said it. Geneviève sat with her arms crossed, listening closely. "I guess it was the wrong time of month," I said, unnerved again by the frown on her face.

"So, when I met you, you were already pregnant?"

"Well, I was, but I didn't know it yet. Then in London I was tired, and I realized my period was late. I didn't want to believe it."

"I wish you had told me," she said, but this time in a more resigned way.

"I know."

"So then what happened?"

"I got a test in Montpellier. It was positive, and I went to England to get an abortion." Geneviève nodded slowly, staring at me. She lifted her arms, which had been crossed in front of her, extending her hands as if she were going to catch a ball. They were shaking. It was like she was looking at things inside her mind, not at me. She continued to stand there as tears emerged from her eyes and trickled down her face. I just watched her, incredulous, helpless. "Geneviève..."

"Excuse me, just a minute." She lurched from the room into her bedroom. I could hear her through the closed door. She was crying noisily, like a small child, without trying to muffle her voice. Well, she's Latin, I thought. They express their emotions. I listened, confused, sinking deeper into the couch. I couldn't cry along with her, so I just sat there miserably waiting for her to return.

At last she did. Her eyes were swollen and red. Her whole face looked puffy, but she had dried her eyes. Sitting heavily beside me, she took my hand, saying, "No, don't look at me. I look terrible. Excuse me for leaving you here alone. But I had to."

"Why?" I asked. "I'm the one who should cry."

"I have always wanted to be a mother. When I realized that you could have...as soon as you said you were pregnant, it was as though it was me, and I saw myself with a baby. Except I knew what you were going to say. I knew that it was gone." She shuddered.

I leaned over and said into her shoulder, "I had a dream that you saved the baby. I knew you would have been a great mother."

She nodded stiffly. "Perhaps one day." We sat there for a long time, huddled together, her soft, warm bulk against me.

Finally, she said, "I dreamed about you too."

"Was it a good dream?"

"*Oh, mon dieu, oui.*" She stroked my cheek and kissed me. It was our second kiss. As with the first, I was drawn quickly into it by her sensual mouth and tongue, my arms gripping hers with instant passion. And like the first time, I was disappointed when she pulled back. I wanted more. Although her pupils looked dilated, and I was sure she wanted to go on as much as I did, she began speaking again about practical matters. "Have you eaten anything?" she asked.

"Not since a sandwich on the train," I said. She went to the kitchen while I sat on the sofa wanting her. I heard the sizzle in the pan as she cooked us an omelet.

The smells from the kitchen were as tantalizing as Geneviève herself. But she was right, I needed to eat, and even more, to sleep. I was exhausted with travel, with emotions, with everything. I sat and ate with her and went into the bathroom and took off the clothes I'd put on that morning at the clinic in England. I sank into the hot water, feeling grateful that the hard part was over, replaying our kiss at the end. I almost fell asleep in the old claw-foot tub. Geneviève roused me by rapping on the door. "Everything okay?"

"Yes! Coming!"

"I am going to work on some sculpture," she said through the door. "You can sleep in my bed. I will be there later."

"Okay." I got out before I fell asleep again, dried off with one of her towels, and put on my pajamas. I brushed my teeth and took another pain pill before I staggered into her bedroom, which felt familiar from that first time. Incredibly, only about two weeks had passed since then. I wondered for a second which side of the bed to sleep on and flopped onto the side near the door and drifted into a deep sleep.

Chapter Twenty-Three

Place des Innocents

I eased myself out of bed carefully the next morning so as not to wake Geneviève. She opened one unfocused eye then closed it again. In the bathroom, I changed my pad. The oval of blood was a little smaller than yesterday. After washing my face, I ventured back into the bedroom. Geneviève was sitting up in bed in her red pajamas. "How are you, Sophie?" she asked, her voice hoarse from sleep.

"Better. Did you go to bed late?"

"A little after midnight. I started a new sculpture."

"Oh? What about?"

"Not sure yet. I just needed to get my hands into clay last night. It felt good." Geneviève rose and raised the blinds, letting in a little light from the courtyard. I followed her into the kitchen and watched as she began to make coffee.

I glanced through the door out the bedroom window. "It's kind of dark here off the courtyard, isn't it?" I said.

She nodded. "It brightens up in the afternoon."

"I like it like this. It's quiet. I like the trees."

"It's quiet now. Just wait until school lets out."

"Oh, that's right. Children in France go to school on Saturday mornings."

"Yes, it can be noisy in the courtyard when they

get home. Right now, you can hear the birds."

"Does someone feed them?"

"Oh, yes. There are old ladies here who live for the birds. Others keep cats. The two groups are always at war." She had her back to me as she measured coffee.

I thought about her reaction last night when I told her about my abortion. Geneviève was such a good-natured kind of person that it was all the more disturbing when she did get angry. As though following my thoughts, Geneviève said, "Sophie, you must have passed through Paris on your way north. Why didn't you stop and see me?"

"I thought of it, but there was no metro. The strike, remember? And anyway..."

"What?"

"I was afraid you might try to change my mind."

"But to think you could have had a baby, half French and half American!" The noise of the coffee grinder intervened. "You could have had the baby," she continued, "and who knows, maybe we would have been together then and raised it together, or if not and you didn't want to keep it, I could have adopted the baby."

I stared at her broad back as she moved around the kitchen. She was talking about a possible future together that I hadn't even begun to contemplate. Things were moving too fast for me to keep up with. "Sure. That could have happened," I said cautiously.

Geneviève set a steaming bowl of café au lait on the table and brought one for herself. Then she shook her head. "Sorry. I'm getting ahead of things, *n'est çe pas?*"

"No, no problem." The way her warm gray eyes caressed mine made me relax and feel that everything was going to be okay. We sipped our café and spread slices of French bread with butter and jam. French butter was different and so was the jam. My cousin used to make jam like this from her own strawberry patch. It tasted like mornings past in the farm kitchen listening to the drone of the milking machine.

She touched my hand across the table. "You said last night you were depressed, Sophie. Are you still?"

"Yes."

"Do you want to talk about it?" she asked.

I shrugged. "It's just that…I was supposed to go backpacking with Jade and Natalie, then start school, right? I mean, those things did happen, but the rest…" I shook my head, tracing the worn grain of the tabletop with my finger. "I got pregnant and had an abortion— not exactly on the agenda. I had to tell my parents that I was raped! I still can barely say that word. Imagine saying it to my poor mother! Well, and I met you," I added.

"That wasn't on your agenda either." She smiled.

"No. But I *was* looking for something…or someone."

She smiled. "Did you tell your parents about us?"

"Hey, it's a little soon for that."

"I know, I know. Sorry. Tell me more about what happened. Was it awful?"

I gave her an abbreviated version of the story, starting with describing my "emergency self" who took over.

"*Tu es très courageuse.*" She gazed at me sympathetically.

"*Merci,*" I said, cheering up a bit. I had not thought of myself as brave. I knew it would be impossible to stay down for long around Geneviève's compliments. But then I remembered how angry she had been last night at first. "I had a dream about you," I said. "Another one. It was when I was at Natalie's."

"What was it?"

"Well, I was sitting and talking to Natalie by a lake, and then the piece of the ground I was sitting on broke off and I started floating away. I was so scared. Natalie just watched me, and you were there too, but neither of you tried to help me—you just let me drift away."

"What was that about?" she asked.

"Fear of abandonment?"

"I think you were losing the solid ground under your feet. Natalie didn't support what you were doing, and you were afraid I wouldn't either."

"Well, it sounds like you wouldn't have."

"That's not true." She kept her clear gray eyes on my face as she lifted her coffee bowl and took a sip. "I would have discussed options with you, sure. But I would have supported your decision, Sophie."

"So you're not angry about...what I did?" I asked.

"No. I told you that you are the artist of your life, remember?"

"Of course. I think that's when I really started to fall for you, when you said that."

She smiled. "So I said the right thing."

I nodded. "Speaking of artists, can I see the sculpture you were working on last night?"

"It's not finished, but yes." At her worktable, I lifted the sheet of plastic and the wet cloth underneath. There was a mound in the middle. Around it was what looked like bones, at least the three that were finished did. There was the beginning of a little squared-off structure, like a house, on the edge.

"I like it so far," I said, sitting on the sofa. She sat

beside me. "So what's the sculpture about?"

"Well, last night the words, 'Cemètiere des Innocents' came into my head."

"What's that?"

"An old cemetery in Paris. The name refers to the slaughter of the innocents by Herod." I nodded, intrigued. "Anyway, I've seen pictures of the place. It used to be the main cemetery of Paris until the eighteenth century. There were just bones in it, actually. You know, they used to cover the bodies with lime in pits outside the city until the bones were bare. It sounds barbaric to us now. But it made sense to them. Then they brought them to the cemetery. Nobody really minded having the bones around. They were in a little vaulted building that ran around the square. There were houses there too. It's just a square with a fountain now."

I smiled grimly. "Do you really think talking about cemeteries and bones is going to help me get over my depression?"

She laughed, then sobered up. "To heal I think you have to go where the pain is."

"Oh. Right." You couldn't just ignore it. I wondered whether I had done that. Had I stuffed my feelings and tried to distract myself by traveling? It was true: being in Paris, meeting Geneviève, and later discovering my pregnancy had all distracted me from the pain of being raped. But I had felt it intensely in the beginning. I had talked to Jade, Natalie, and others. And sometime in Scotland, I had truly started to recover.

"I always try to think of places that can sympathize with how I'm feeling," said Geneviève.

I closed my eyes, trying to see what she meant. "Your sculptures are all about places, right?"

"*Oui.*"

"Places and their history and how you feel about them. So if you go to a place that is somehow like how you're feeling, even if it isn't that way anymore..."

"When I'm in a place, I can feel what it was like before," she said.

The killing of the innocents. She was right. What was actually hurting me deep down was the killing of my child or of what could have been my child. Apparently, Geneviève's own emotions took her to the same place. "Why don't we go see this square, then," I said, standing up. "The doctor said I'm supposed to rest. The hell with that. I'll just sit down when I'm tired."

"It's not far. It's next to where Les Halles market used to be, in the same direction we went last time."

I entered her bedroom, where my backpack leaned against the wooden wardrobe, and removed a long-sleeved shirt and jeans, pulling my warm sweater on over them. When I emerged from the bedroom, Geneviève stood waiting, wearing a brown leather jacket.

"You look pretty hot in that jacket," I said teasingly.

"You should see the leather pants that go with it." She grinned back.

"Really?"

She looked down at her solid, big-boned body. "Just kidding. I guess they save those for skinny people like you."

I laughed and took her arm as we set off down the stairway and into rue Vivienne. The air was crisp but the sun was shining. The tourist in me revived.

"By the way," she said as we strolled down her block past the closed-up wine bar, "tonight some friends of mine are getting together at a café on the Left Bank. Would you like to meet them?"

"Sure."

"They're old friends from school. We meet once a month or so. They don't know about you. It would be a surprise."

I had a dark feeling that I might also meet one or more of her old lovers that way or even current ones. I brushed those thoughts away.

"But it depends on how you feel tonight," she said.

I was fine until we passed the imposing National Library, when I began leaning more heavily on Geneviève. A melting feeling went through me at the touch of her encircling arm. We crossed the street near Club 18. We had only been walking about six blocks when we entered the ancient, arcaded courtyard of the Palais Royale, which Geneviève had pointed out to me that first night. My eyes were dazzled by the sun for a moment before I could see the huge rectangle of grass with a fountain and geometric trees in the middle like the ones in the Tuileries. Since fall was now here, the trees were half golden. A pair of female joggers passed us on their way out of the courtyard.

"It's so quiet," I said. She sat on a bench. How strange to be in the middle of Paris in this secluded place. Nearby, a bird twittered. Instead of sitting, I lay down on the cool grass and looked up at Geneviève's back and the sky above. "Did you say this was where the Revolution started?" I asked.

"Oh, yes. It was a very different place then, with shops and cafés set in the arches."

There were still a few shops. We'd passed one that sold toys on the way in. "Do you think the revolutionaries still meet here? Do you believe in ghosts?" I asked, smiling.

"But of course," she replied seriously. "I can sense

when someone like that is near me."

"Really?"

"Yes, I think a lot of people can, or else why would we even talk about ghosts? At home in Reims, I used to wake up sometimes at night, feeling someone in my room with me. It scared me half to death the first time."

"*C'est horrifique, ça.*" I laughed. "Is anybody here now? Are the ghosts listening to us talk about them?"

"You think I'm crazy, right?" She raised a brow.

"Well..." I grinned. "No, I don't think you're crazy. My mother taught me about angels when I was little."

"You were raised Catholic?"

I nodded. "You too?"

"*Oui.* I am no longer *croyante.* But I believe in Saint Geneviève on her hill. I swear I can feel her up there. But, you were saying about angels...?"

"Well, like my Irish friends and the boy on the train and Natalie's housekeeper and Denise who lent me the money. If they weren't angels themselves, I'm sure it was angels who brought them to me."

"I think they brought you to me too." I felt a flood of warmth at her tender words. "You and I," she continued, "we understand each other, don't we, *chérie?* We are different from each other, yes, but also the same. Despite the cultural barrier?"

"Yes," I said, tears moistening my eyes. She extended her hand to help me stand up. We slowly left the enclosure, our arms linked, continuing that way to rue de Rivoli, where we turned west. She pointed forward. "If you keep walking on this street, it turns into rue Saint-Antoine, where I work."

We passed the Louvre across the river on our right then turned north. Ahead, I could hear the sounds of cranes and trucks working on a vast construction site. "Les Halles," Geneviève said, "huge pavilions where you could find every kind of food. They were here since the twelfth century. This place used to be called 'the belly of Paris.' For nearly a thousand years it supplied all the restaurants and shops of Paris and defined the whole district." We looked at the dust and rubble that remained. In the debris, I could still feel, and almost smell, the centuries of time. Geneviève said, "Back in the thirties, hobos used to come here for handouts, and there were dance halls and brothels. Then, in recent times, it got too difficult to bring transport in, so they moved the market to the suburbs."

"Can you imagine swinging a wrecking ball into something nine hundred years old?" I asked.

She shook her head. "It's one of the places I really used to like when I was a student. I am sad to see it like this. Maybe I'll do a sculpture about it."

"What are they building here?" I asked, pointing at the fenced construction area.

"Some kind of underground shopping center."

We passed some shabby bars and restaurants. "The Smoking Dog! That's a funny name," I said.

We stopped at a little square. "Here it is, la Place des Innocents," she said. The fountain was a domed, vaulted tower with a cross on top. The gleaming water spilled down its height in a series of steps.

"Beautiful," I breathed.

"They moved it here from another site after the cemetery closed," she said. "It dates from the Renaissance."

We sat for a while and watched the water tumble. "So what happened to all the bones?" I said finally.

"They got overcrowded."

"Yeah, they would after a few centuries."

"So they moved them to the Catacombs," she said.

"The Catacombs?"

"Underground tunnels, very old quarries from Roman times. They run under the hills, like Montparnasse, south of where we walked last time. The bones are there. You can see them lined up along the tunnel walls."

"Really? Have you ever been there?"

"No."

"Want to go?" I said.

Geneviève brightened. "I think it's a long walk once you're underground and there may not be a place to sit down."

"Oh, come on. I can rest before and after. Don't you want to see it?"

"Well, of course I do. And I think it's only open on Saturday. That's today! But are you sure you feel up to it?"

"Yes! I'm in the mood for it now after all the talk about ghosts."

"We should have a flashlight," Geneviève said worriedly.

"I've got one in my bag," I said. "It's a little one, from backpacking."

"Okay, we'll go. I know it's down Saint-Michel. We can take a bus. But first, let's eat lunch at the Smoking Dog."

Chapter Twenty-Four

Les Catacombes

"Geneviève?" I said nervously as we joined the queue that snaked along one side of the square.

"*Oui?*"

"Do you think we'll meet any, uh, ghosts down there?"

"I've never heard about any. I've heard it's very peaceful."

"Well...I don't know what to expect. Tell me again why we're doing this?" I asked, feeling a bit giddy.

"We are going to share an experience. You said you wanted to go."

"I do want to go. But this is definitely not my idea of a romantic date." I had a feeling it *was* her idea of one. I took her hand as the line slowly moved forward. When it was our turn, we paid the one-franc fee and were told not to touch anything and not to smoke.

We descended the stairs. As we walked down the spiral stone steps, we could feel the air growing cooler and heavier. Holding hands, we entered the first tunnel, which was quite dark and narrow, lit only by small lamps on the walls. Water droplets glinted on the ceiling. I used my flashlight as our feet crunched on gravel. It was a long march in semidarkness, but no one spoke; they were probably thinking about what was to come.

Next we passed through another arched passage to a wider, better-lit corridor where the bones were. They were higher than my head and maybe ten feet deep, all the thin limbs stacked neatly like logs, then a row of skulls, more bones, and skulls again stacked on top. I had never seen anything like it.

Geneviève and I gazed in fascination and only kept moving because people were coming behind us. Nobody talked much, or they spoke in whispers. Time seemed suspended in the silence.

A plaque on one wall read: *Ossement du cimetière des Innocents, deposé en 1787.* There were similar plaques farther on designating other churchyards and the dates the bones were transferred.

Along the way, we passed junctures of other passages that were gated off. The place went on beyond where anyone was allowed to go, but you could see as you passed that the blocked passages too were filled with orderly stacks of human remains.

It seemed to me there was something sociable about this citadel of the dead that drew lines of living people down here every week. It was a show that everyone was a part of. Geneviève and the other young people talking in whispers around us had the same DNA as those who were resting here. They probably looked much the same as these people did when they were alive, and they would look this way one day when their lives were done.

That tiny thing inside me never had a chance to grow bones and have a life or die when it was old. But if it had, it would have been a part of this spectacle too. I felt a lump rise in my throat. Anyone who'd ever had an abortion must have felt this same haunting loss of what might have been. I'd been unable to feel it until I came down here, however. Tears sprang into my eyes.

Geneviève saw my face. "You're crying, Sophie," she whispered. I nodded. She put her arm around me and we walked on through the tunnels. At one point, when we were alone, I turned off the flashlight. In the darkness, I reached up and my lips found hers. We kissed until I heard the crunch of feet on gravel and I turned the light back on.

"Let's get out of here," I said, my pulse still pounding from the kiss, and she squeezed my hand in assent.

We hurried down the long tunnel toward the exit stairs. Back outside, both of us blinking in the brilliant sunshine, she asked laughing, "Where are we?" We looked around at a strange street.

"Not where we started, anyway!"

We crossed the street, squinting in the sun, our arms around each other. I felt my steps dragging and I leaned on her. "That was incredible," I said.

"Did you like it?"

"I loved it! It wasn't creepy at all." I paused. "Well maybe a little."

"No," she said. "*C'etait très beau.* It was beautiful." She had a thoughtful look on her face.

"Let's go sit down," I said. "I'm really tired now."

We sat at a café and ordered a pot of green tea. "All those French…" Geneviève shook her head.

"I know. A place like this would never exist in the US," I said. "We don't go back that far."

She pulled out a pen and began doodling on a napkin. "Here's the fountain in the middle, and then around the outside…" She drew a circle of double lines around the circumference of the napkin. "I'll put the little skulls and bones around here. It will form a circle, you know, a circle of life and death."

My chest swelled with awe and pride. Here was a person who could pull out a piece of paper and draw lines and figures on it that had to do with life and death. She was an artist with a big heart. I put my hand on top of hers that held the pencil.

"Did it help you to cry a little?" she asked, noticing that my eyes were again wet.

I nodded. "I couldn't do it before. You were right—it needed to be something extreme. Thank you." She shrugged and stuck out her lips in a typically French way, which meant it was nothing. "No," I insisted. "I never would have done this on my own. It was you. Your obsession with history...the way you look at everything." I made an arching gesture with my arm. Often, when I spoke in French, the words tumbled out with a life and meaning of their own, so I wasn't surprised at what next came out of my mouth. "*Je t'aime.*"

Geneviève squeezed my hand and whispered, "*Moi aussi.*" I had just said, "I love you," and she'd said, "Me too." Maybe it was too soon and maybe it wasn't, but because we'd said the words in French, I didn't feel self-conscious about the exchange as I might have if it was in English. Anyway, even though we hadn't known each other long, it was true. She leaned across the table and kissed me gently. When I looked around the café, the other patrons were still in the same positions as before, not looking our way. I remembered Kari or Annik saying that was why they adored Paris—you could kiss in public and nobody cared.

As we left the café, she asked, "How are you? Tired?"

"Yes, very," I said. "I just want to go back and sleep."

While we waited for the bus, Geneviève kissed me again. I felt my body melt into hers, like a seal into soft wax. It was an effort to pull away. I knew that part of me was still going to be sad and it would take time for that part to get better, but for the moment, I was happy.

Back at her apartment, I took off my thick sweater and lay down in bed. "Do you want company?" she asked. I smiled and beckoned to her. "You're not too tired?"

"No," I said.

She smiled, gazing into my eyes. The late-afternoon light filtered in through the bamboo shades as children's voices rang in the courtyard.

We held each other, her full breasts pressing against my smaller ones. I curled up and buried my face in her neck, smelling the clean fabric of her T-shirt mixed with a faint odor of her cologne. "You're so beautiful!" I breathed.

"You, too," she answered, her gray eyes softly meeting mine.

I ran my hands over her smooth back, felt the flesh of her hips through her clothes, her muscular back and rounded stomach; all the while, her hands caressed me. I had no clear idea how to make love to a woman. I didn't even know whether that was what we were doing, but gradually, our bodies became more closely joined, our kisses more intense. As we kissed and pressed against each other, the subtle ache in my groin grew in intensity and the friction between my legs pushed me toward the edge. An orgasm rippled through me. After a long moment, I exhaled slowly and sank into her arms. It must have been an hour before I felt her move.

"Are you going to meet your friends?" I asked.

"Pretty soon," she said, smiling at me.

"I'm so happy," I said. "Don't go yet."

Geneviève wrapped her arms around me and held me for a few more minutes before she kissed me once more and stood.

"Want to come with me?"

"No, I need to rest some more," I said. "Just come back soon. Could you bring them here?"

"That's a good idea. I'm sure they'll be curious enough to come. Are you hungry?"

"Yes, but I'll get myself something."

After she left, I closed my eyes and saw the tunnels full of bones and the fountain we'd seen this morning. I'd forgotten about the fountain. I pictured the way the water at Place des Innocents endlessly cascaded in the sunlight and the image soothed me back to sleep.

It was dark when I awoke again. I looked for her before remembering she had left. Was I still technically a gay virgin? I smiled. I didn't feel like one. I'd taken another step away from total innocence. I got up and washed my face, combed my hair, and put on my new earrings, which lay on the back of the sink.

I had just finished dinner and poured myself a second glass of wine. A brass candlestick stood in the middle of the table. A heavy glass ashtray and matches lay beside it. I lit the candle and gazed at the flame. Voices and laughter rang in the hallway and a key scraped in the lock.

Four women came through the door with Geneviève. They were flushed and disheveled, still laughing, their arms around each other to various degrees. Geneviève bent over the table to give me a kiss as everyone else converged around me. I stood up.

"Sophie, this is Katrine." The woman was short, with large, heavy-lidded brown eyes, short brown hair, and a sardonic smile. She stepped forward to kiss me. "Katrine used to be my roommate here, one of them." Geneviève introduced the others one by one as each woman kissed me on the cheek. French introductions and greetings were so complicated. Apparently, I warranted a kiss because of my relationship to Geneviève, or maybe once you've had some wine, the distinctions blur. "Dany, Colette, and Stephanie," she finished as they trooped by me with their greetings. Dany had her arm around Colette; they seemed to be a couple.

"*Elle est belle, n'est çe pas?*" Geneviève laughed, spreading her arms extravagantly. "She's beautiful, isn't she?" Her friends all grinned and nodded.

"We are *les gouines des Beaux-Arts,*" said Dany, who sported very short hair and had wild blue eyes.

"Except me," Stephanie said, waving a slender hand, her blond wavy hair spilling over her face. "I'm straight. And I went to the Sorbonne."

"Sit down," said Geneviève as she pulled out glasses and a bottle of mineral water along with a bottle of wine. "My friends wanted to meet you, Sophie. That's the only way I got them to walk all the way over here from the Left Bank."

"Oh, it was worth it," said Dany, shrugging out of her leather jacket and pulling a packet of Gauloises from her shirt pocket. "And it's not so far. We wanted to see Geneviève's new girlfriend. It's about time she settled down."

"Hey," said Geneviève, "don't scare her. We're just getting to know each other."

"Sorry," said Dany, bowing her head to light the cigarette with the candle. "It's just that we know the way she usually talks about a new woman, but I've never heard her go on about anyone like this before."

"Stop, please!" said Geneviève, this time clearly embarrassed. "I didn't bring you here to humiliate me!"

"That's right," said the willowy Colette who had long, straight dark hair and almond-shaped eyes. "Let's talk about something else."

"How are you?" asked Katrine. "Geneviève said you weren't feeling well."

"I'm better. I had a good sleep. Merci." They were all looking at me expectantly. Had Geneviève told them everything? I looked at her, and she nodded. "I just had an abortion," I said.

"I told them. Do you mind?" Geneviève asked.

I smiled. "*Non, ça va.* They're your friends, and you were in pain. Of course you would tell them."

"But I should have asked you first," Geneviève continued. "It is common politeness, but I didn't think of it."

"It's okay," I said.

Dany said, "It's very painful for you to be so far from home and to have to make such a decision. We support you, right?"

The others chimed in, "*Oui!*"

"*Merci,*" I said, touched by their solidarity as they all looked at me, each face so different but all with the same expression of kindness. "It's very nice to meet all of you. Did you all know Geneviève when she first came to Paris?"

"*Mais, non,*" said Geneviève. "First I had to go through a time when I believed I was the only lesbian in Paris."

"At least you knew what you were," said Katrine. "It took me years of denial before I could admit it."

"What's to admit?" said Colette. "It's a great thing!"

"*Mais, oui!*" They all gave yells of approval.

I smiled timidly. "I don't know if I qualify as a lesbian. I've been with men before."

"You are liking a woman. That is all that counts," said Katrine.

Maybe you'll become one of us. That was what Geneviève had said when she came to see me the first morning at the hostel. "So, since I am with a woman," I replied, "everyone will see me that way, and maybe I'll also see myself that way," I said tentatively. "I don't know yet. Maybe it's not that important."

"Questions of identity are always important," said Geneviève. "But you don't have to figure it all out right now, *chérie.*"

They were a fun group. I made them talk about how they'd all met, and there was much laughter as bottles of wine disappeared. We talked late into the night until the group finally trooped out with promises to meet me the next time I was in Paris.

Chapter Twenty-Five

Romanticism

The pile of letters spilling over my desk in Montpellier was evidence that the strike was over and that the Nguyens had used their key to my room to deposit my mail. I saw four letters from the US! One was from Jade, two from Mom, and one from my sister. As I fell upon this bounty, I saw a letter from Ireland. Sean! And one with a colorful Dutch stamp. With an hour until I had to be at my first class, I carried all the letters to my bed and curled up on the pillow where my penguin had been holding my place. I caressed the stiff envelopes, smelling them and feeling the different textures.

I opened the older one from my mother first, dated early September. There was a letter in it and a check. Well, better late than never. Then I opened the one from her dated just last week. She must have written it right after my phone call! My cheeks flamed as I read her short note.

Dear Sophie,
After your phone call, I told Dad and we both cried. I hope the money came and everything went all right. We are waiting for your letter so we can understand better what happened. Just remember we love you no matter what.

Mom and Dad.

My eyes were moist as I opened Jade's letter.

Dear Sophie,
How are you? Did your period finally come? Please let me know ASAP as I am very worried about you. I MISS you. I had no idea a trip to Europe could change my world as much as it has. If I could go back there right now, I would. I just can't get into life here as if nothing happened. Minnesota seems like a strange place to me. I feel so alone here. It's the first week of classes. I'm taking French. Do they have a French course there I could take? Seriously, I may come next semester. My dorky friends here have lost their charm. Do you think I am going nuts? Should I go for counseling or something?
Love, Jade.

Jade might come back? Is she serious? I put down the other letters and got ready for class. *Wow, it would be great to have her here. I can't wait to call her.* I tried not to think about my mother's note. Probably by now she'd received the letter where I explained everything. I hoped she didn't take it too hard. I took a deep breath. I had other things to think of now. *I am a student at Paul Valérie University.*

I'd have to buy books and supplies this afternoon. And open a bank account. Tomorrow I needed to go to Denise's place to return her money. I really wanted to call Jade. She said she was worried about me. I'd call her after my classes.

My first class was a large ninety-minute lecture on Romanticism in French literature, which met once a week. I sat near the back and focused hard on the professor's face, past the backs of students' heads, trying to understand everything he was saying. Some of it passed me by, but then it was only my first day. We were going to have to hand in weekly essays in addition to exams at the end of the semester. During the break, I stood up and stretched, letting the buzzing wave of my classmates' French wash over me.

Then I had Russian class, which was small. It met three times a week. My housemate Charles's girlfriend was in that class.

"Sophie! *Ça va?* How was Paris?" she asked.

Here we go, I thought. "*Magnifique!*" I answered truthfully.

"How did you meet your boyfriend? He's French, right?"

"Yes," I said. "We met at a club when I was traveling."

"Ah, *oui?*"

It would be so different if Geneviève were a boy. How I'd boast about her then.

I went to the bookstore. I had to get *Adolphe*, by Benjamin Constant; Chateaubriand's *Atala*; and *Les Miserables*, by Victor Hugo. I was drawn to *Atala* by the picture of the Indian couple tenderly embracing in the forest. I read the jacket: Atala had made a vow on her mother's deathbed to remain a virgin. Why the hell would a mother want her daughter to do that? Bad choice, Atala.

Of course, I couldn't stop thinking of Geneviève. Every little thing led to more thoughts of her. She was so strong and good. She was an artist. I had to get a grip on myself if I wanted to become a serious student of French literature.

I picked up *Adolphe*. This one, I knew from class,

was about a young man who has an illicit affair with an older woman. Older woman! Leafing through it, I could see that it contained detailed passages about states of feelings. I recalled the phrase from class: *les vagues des passions*, waves of passion. I knew about those too.

I went to Vert Bois restaurant where I saw some familiar faces. Evidently, this was where I would be able to make friends, coming here twice a day, except Sundays or when I cooked at home.

I sat with Carly and Rose, students from Antioch College. They were in the Institut des Etrangers, like all the Americans I'd met so far, but were also sitting in on one or two regular classes such as the ones I was taking. It turned out they would be in my art history class.

Carly had flowing strawberry-blond hair; she was talkative and lively. Her friend Rose was quieter, with long dark hair, small bright eyes, and rimless glasses. She wore baggy denim shirts to hide her full figure. Both were intelligent with quick humor. They were potential friends, for sure.

After lunch, I hurried to the post office to telephone. There were phones at the fac, but the post office had private booths and you just paid the clerk when you were done. I hoped Jade would be home. It was evening in Minnesota. The phone rang three times before someone picked up. "Hello?" a voice said clearly.

"Is Jade there?"

"No. Can I take a message?"

"Sure."

"Is this her roommate? This is Sophie."

"Oh my God. She talks about you all the time! Just a minute—let me get a pen."

"Um, tell her I had to get an abortion. Okay? But I'm fine. I like school. And she should come. Got that?

Tell her to come! There's a course of French she could take."

"Okay, I got it."

I hung up the phone feeling low. I had so wanted to talk to her, and I probably would not try again. That call had just eaten up five francs.

I stopped at Café Tout Va Bien before heading back. This was the same café where Jade and I had met Jean-Luc and Bernard and where I'd first glimpsed Geneviève. The outdoor tables were full of students; the sun warmed my skin. I sipped a double espresso very slowly to make it last and opened my book.

Sitting there, my eyes went from the small print on the page to the vast Place de la Comédie where pigeons flapped and old buildings gleamed in the sunlight. I started reading *Adolphe*. After one paragraph, I lost the thread and began listening to the conversations around me. I was lonely sitting by myself. But I couldn't afford to sit around chatting in cafés even if I'd had someone to chat with. I had to work harder than the French students to pass my exams. I was going to get credit by taking equivalency exams at home, but even so, I wanted to do my best.

Having finally blocked out the voices, I got involved in *Adolphe*. His transports of emotion kept reminding me of my feelings for Geneviève. Maybe I shouldn't have taken a course in Romanticism.

On the way back, I used the check from home to open a bank account at the Credit Lyonnais. Vert Bois would soon open for dinner. I went in and sat in the lobby and pulled out my book again, plunging back into the passions of *Adolphe*.

A shadow crossed my book. Someone was standing over me. I looked up. It was Bernard! I could hardly believe my eyes. He was grinning with his crooked teeth, wearing one of Jean-Luc's necklaces and a sweater that was a little ragged around the neck. His dark curly hair stood up around his head.

"Bernard!" I shook his hand. Then in a sudden panic, I glanced around for Jean-Luc.

"He's not here," said Bernard, sitting in a chair next to me and crossing his legs.

"Where is he?"

"He went to Aigues-Mortes to an art fair."

"Don't you usually go with him?"

"No, no, not always," Bernard said, watching my face. "I'm very happy to see you, Sophie. How was your trip to England?"

"Good. I had to make a second trip there. I just got back this morning."

"Oh?" He uncrossed his leg and leaned forward. He could tell something was wrong.

"I got pregnant, Bernard. From Jean-Luc."

"Mon dieu!" He wasn't smiling anymore.

"I went to England to have an abortion."

"How do you feel? Are you okay?"

"Fine. I'm better today. I stayed with my *petite amie,* my girlfriend, in Paris." I told him this because I had for some reason trusted Bernard from the first moment I saw him.

"Ah, *oui?*" Another toothy smile, more gentle this time. "But I didn't know you had someone in Paris, Sophie. *C'est chouette!*"

"I didn't have anyone. It's new."

"I didn't like what happened on the beach," he said, frowning down at his lap. "I didn't feel right about it. You're young. And I didn't think you were interested in Jean-Luc. He and I—we are together too, like with your friend in Paris."

"You are? I wondered about that."

"Yes, and I don't mind normally. It never means anything. And it doesn't happen often." He twisted his hands nervously and attempted another smile. His large eyes told a different story than his words. "I'm sorry, Sophie. It was bad luck, eh?"

"Yes, very. But I'm okay now. I still get sad. But I'm happy mostly."

"Happy because of her?"

"Geneviève? Yes, and happy to be back at school. And to see you." I smiled.

Students were strolling past us in groups, or singly, and standing in line. "Can you sell me a meal ticket?" Bernard asked. Only students could buy tickets, but sometimes people would stand in the lobby and try to buy one from a student.

"Sure. Bernard, will you tell Jean-Luc?"

"I suppose. Unless you don't want me to."

"I don't care. But I don't want to see him. Will he come here?"

"No, he won't come."

I sighed. "Thank you. Come on, let's get in line."

Bernard walked me back to my place after dinner, his steps matching mine. I crossed my bare arms in front of me. I had forgotten how cool it got at night here. "Come in for just a minute," I said, "so you can see my room."

We went through the door into the front hall and M. Nguyen was standing there, smiling as he always did. "Welcome back, Sophie. Did you have a good voyage?" He shot a narrow glance at Bernard.

"*Oui, merci. Bonsoir,* M. Nguyen."

"*Bonsoir,* Sophie." He turned and went upstairs.

At the end of the hall, I said to Bernard, "Here's my room," and opened the door.

"*Chic.* Now, I know where you live. I will come and visit you, all right?"

"Yes, okay. Where are you staying?"

"We're at Aimée's place. Remember where we took a shower? We're staying there until we move to Aix. In the summer we camp a lot, but in the winter we stay with friends or in hotels."

"You make enough money selling jewelry?"

"We do okay."

"Bonsoir, Bernard." I kissed him French-style on both cheeks and watched his thin back retreat down the hallway and out the door, which closed with a thump.

I stood in the shower off the kitchen frowning, the hot water stinging my body. Seeing Bernard had brought back all the bad feelings about Jean-Luc. And yet, at the same time, I had been truly happy to see Bernard again. He was a familiar face, almost like an old friend.

Back in my room, I put on my pajamas and grabbed some paper and a pen, feeling calmer. Gathering up the letters that still lay on my bed, I propped up my pillow and cushion against the wall and got under the covers, my stuffed penguin beside me. Everything felt so strange and new. But at least the first day was behind me and Jade might be coming next semester. I turned on my little lamp and read the letters all over twice. I spent the rest of the evening writing a longish letter to Sean, thanking him and detailing everything that had happened after I left him in London.

＊＊＊＊

Once I turned off the light, I thought only of

Geneviève. We'd spent our last few hours in Paris sitting in the Vieux Sabot wine bar. The afternoon was deepening and rosy sunlight winked in the upper windows of Geneviève's building opposite. We sat at a table near the window, heads bowed together, drinking wine and eating aperitifs.

"Maybe Sylvie will come in," she said.

"I'm thinking about my train and having to leave."

"Don't think of that yet, *chérie*. It's only four o'clock. Your train isn't until nine."

"Okay, I'll try to think only about how beautiful you are."

"Yes, and I'll do the same thing."

"Think about how beautiful you are?"

She laughed. "Yes, and how lovely you are, too. I'll come down and visit you in October, *d'accord*?"

"I was hoping you would. Geneviève...is there anybody else you've been seeing?"

She hesitated. "One or two."

"Will you continue to see them?"

"No. Not if you don't want me to."

I laughed self-consciously. "Well..."

She covered my hand with hers. "Don't worry, *chérie*. You are the only woman I want."

We sat in silence for a while. She kept looking at me like she wanted to ask me something. Finally, I said, "What?"

"Well, have you ever thought of transferring to Paris? You haven't even started classes yet. It would be so easy to do it now."

I looked down uneasily. "I'm not ready for that."

"For what? To see me more often?"

I shook my head. "It's not that."

"Okay," she said. "I know you want to be on your

own. But what about later? I could help you find a place with other students. We wouldn't have to say good-bye so much."

"Maybe when I'm ready. I need some time."

"You've never lived alone before, right?"

"Right."

She smiled sadly. "We're not in the same place in our lives right now, are we?"

"No."

She shrugged. "I can be patient."

I hoped it was true.

Chapter Twenty-Six

Drunken Bees

"They're harvesting the grapes," Denise said. "It's called *le vendange.*" Sitting on a bench in the front garden, we watched rows of workers picking grapes in the vineyard across the road. "M. Ferrell, who I work for, manages the vineyard," she said. We watched the little trucks driving slowly between the rows of leafy vines while workers emptied their baskets into them. "So how did it go in England?" she asked.

"It was tough. But thank you so much for trusting me with your money, Denise. You were a lifesaver." She nodded. "The strike held everything up at first," I said, "but it all worked out. Maybe it was all my mom's prayers—I'll tell you all about it later. And then I had a super romantic weekend in Paris."

"You did?" she said, surprised.

"Yeah, I met someone when I was there the first time. I saw her a couple times and then again last weekend."

"Her?"

"Yeah." My face grew warm. "My first gay relationship." I waited to see Denise's reaction, but she seemed to get over her surprise pretty quickly. "I wanted to find out what it was like to date a woman," I continued. "But I didn't expect to feel the way I do."

"What do you mean?"

I leaned toward her. "Well, even though she's French and I'm American, we really *get* each other, you know? It's not just because she's a woman or anything. Or maybe it is in a way. I don't know." I shrugged, embarrassed.

Denise picked up on my discomfort. "But that sounds great." She looked at me. "It sounds like things are going well with your girlfriend. So, is there a problem?"

"No. It's just…too much." I sucked in my breath. "I mean…" I pressed my lips tightly and shook my head, then let out a long sigh. "I've just been through this whole abortion deal, you know? If I hadn't already met her, I don't even know if I would be looking for anyone right now. I mean, I'm glad I did meet her and everything, but the timing kind of sucks, you know?" Denise nodded. "She'd like me to move to Paris." I shuddered and shook my head. "I can't even think about that right now. She's been on her own for years. I'm fresh from leaving home! Well, maybe not so fresh anymore." I calculated. "Almost two months now? Anyway, I'm actually glad we have a long-distance relationship. That's the only way this will work for me, I think."

The door of the house opened and a little girl of about four with wild black curls dashed out and buried her face in Denise's lap. "*Maman* says you should come and eat dinner," she said in a quiet voice.

"Okay, Christy. I'll come in a minute." Denise put her hand on the girl's head and turned to me, her hazel eyes serious. "So go on, Sophie."

I shrugged. "I never thought I would fall for a woman," I said. "All the plans I made when I was younger…"

"Like what plans?' Denise asked.

"Oh, you know." I sighed. "Getting married, having kids, all that. With some guy."

The image flashed before me of my high school boyfriend Sam as I used to picture him married to me, presiding at the dinner table with a brood of cherubic children sitting around it, myself serving the dinner I'd cooked. Sam would smile at me lovingly. We would have kids who looked like both of us. Of course, if it turned out the person I was picturing wasn't right for me, then it wouldn't matter what my children looked like, would it? Or for that matter, if I found out I was supposed to be with someone of my own sex?

"Are you worried that she might be 'it'?" Denise asked.

"It?" I swallowed, unsure if I believed in such things. "It's too soon to tell," I said feebly.

Denise ignored me. "If it turns out she's the one, then you're in luck, Sophie," she said seriously. "I say go for it. You may not get another chance."

"What?" I burst out. "We're young, Denise. We have hundreds of chances ahead of us!"

"How can you say that?" she countered. "I thought you were in love!"

"I am," I said. "But the fact is I have to go home at the end of the year and finish my degree."

"Well, my mom always taught me to grab opportunities, Sophie. She met my dad the summer before she went to Stanford for graduate school. He was living in Pittsburgh, going to Pitt. She didn't want a long-distance relationship, so she broke it off. She figured she'd meet someone in California. But she never felt like that about anyone else, ever. Meanwhile, he married someone else, then later got divorced. It took my parents ten years to get back together."

"Okay, I get it." I wanted to laugh. What an idea, comparing me to her parents! I just couldn't look at things the way Denise did, try as I might. But her story had somehow lightened my mood.

The little girl who still huddled in Denise's lap tugged on her sleeve. "I'd better go," my new friend said, standing up. Christy rose with her, clinging to a leg, and peeked at me with enormous black eyes. Denise smiled. I liked the way the corners of her eyes crinkled. "Hey, do you want to go to a wine festival in Avignon on Saturday?"

"Sure!"

"Be here by 9:00 a.m."

"Here, write down your phone number." I handed her a notebook and pen from my bag, which she scribbled on.

After waving good-bye, I strode in the opposite direction from home, past leafy vineyards framed by distant blue hills. As I went along, my steps became more buoyant, as though my shoes were filled with helium. I plunged off the road into an orchard that sloped down brushy hillsides full of gnarly shrubs. Trees closed in around me as the fragrance of Mediterranean plants filled my nose. I sighed blissfully and walked deeper into the wooded ravine. I felt just like Atala, exploring the primeval forest.

The cider-sweet smell of apples filled the air, and I started to search for the source. Down another slope I found it: mounds of rotting golden apples that had been dumped there, with bees and flies buzzing madly about the puckering, oozing skins. It took me a moment to figure it out. Maybe the apple harvest had been overabundant this year, and they did this to keep prices down.

Then I laughed. The bees were drunk! That's why they were zigzagging around like that. I recognized the odor of cider alcohol. Dropping my bag, I began to run, careening around the orchard with the bees. Why not? No one could see me. I could do whatever I wanted. I had my energy back, and more! I forgot about the weighty conversation I'd just had with Denise. The memory of my weekend with Geneviève soared through me. I spread out my arms, vibrating them up and down like bees' wings.

On Saturday, the grape festival in Avignon was like a sequel to my silly, joyful dance with the bees. Denise and I stood with her au pair family and watched as a row of women in long dresses with ruffled white bodices and white caps on their heads did a kind of bouncy line dance. We removed our sandals, rolled up our jeans, and climbed a ladder into the wooden grape-crushing vat. Screaming with laughter, Denise and I held hands and stomped together for dear life. The viscous mass on the bottom squelched between our toes and splashed up to our thighs, completely soaking our jeans. The grape aroma was so powerful, I felt like I was drinking it. And of course, I was reminded of Geneviève. These were the same grapes that made the Côtes-du-rhône wine we'd drunk last Sunday.

◈◈◈◈

I got home from school on Monday, to find a letter from Geneviève on the hall table along with one from my mother. I opened Geneviève's envelope while still standing in the hall. Her note was short. She was planning to come down the next weekend to see me! I stuffed the paper in my bag where I could still feel it vibrating. From the kitchen, my German housemate, Gerti called to me, "I saw you got something from Paris. Was that from your boyfriend?"

I didn't know what to say. Should I just tell her the truth? Probably. I wasn't ashamed. I approached the stove to check out Gerti's soup. It smelled like thyme and mushrooms. "Mmmm," I said.

"What's his name?" she persisted

"Geneviève," I said with a grin.

"A woman? No kidding? I never guessed." She smiled. "That's great!"

Thanks, Gerti." I felt relieved that it was okay to talk to her about Geneviève. I'd kept so many secrets about my girl crushes as a teenager that I wasn't sure if I had to keep on doing that.

"Long-distance relationships," she said. "They are kind of..." We were both speaking in a foreign language, French, and I knew the problem about describing emotions.

"They are *difficile,*" I finished.

"Right. But worth it, yes?"

I nodded. "She is coming to visit." Gerti high-fived me.

After my success with Gerti, I couldn't resist pulling out Geneviève's letter at the restau-U, and waving it at Carly and Rose. I blurted, "My girlfriend's coming to visit me next weekend!"

"Girlfriend? You mean from home?" asked Rose.

"No, I mean from Paris. She's my girlfriend, you know, petite amie?" Why wasn't there an unambiguous expression for it in English like there was in French? I watched the surprise on their faces with amusement.

"I didn't know you were gay," Carly said.

"Well, I don't know what I am. It's all new for me. But anyway, she's gonna visit. You'll get to meet her."

"Hey, that's fantastic," said Carly.

"Yeah, good luck," Rose said.

The charming Carly managed to make the acquaintance of a French student, Daniel. He was a smiling, bearded young man, small and wiry, who talked with a slight lisp due to a cleft palette. A faint scar shone white on his upper lip. Daniel also talked with his hands, and indeed, his whole body, to augment his deficient speaking voice. He started sitting with us, and some of his French pals gravitated around us as well.

"Hey, I'm going to take a class in mime at the Cultural Center," he said. "Anyone want to take it with me?" We all ended up signing up for mime. After that, on Friday nights I went with Daniel, Rose, Carly, and Denise, plus a few others to mime class. We pretended to be tortoises, cats, and whales, all without making a sound. Mime was all the rage. In our free time we practiced. It was hard to do it without laughing, though. We tried to keep serious faces like Marcel Marceau.

༄ ༄ ༄ ༄

One evening I saw Bernard in the lobby of Vert Bois as I walked in the door. He looked upset. "Sophie," he said, taking my arm and leading me to a corner bench. "I have to talk to you."

"What's wrong?" I asked fearfully. He was a mess, his eyes swollen and red, his hair matted and standing comically up in a point. I reached to smooth out his curls. He attempted to smile, his crooked eyetooth peeking shyly out from chapped lips.

"I broke up with Jean-Luc."

"What? Why? What happened?"

"You know. Things haven't been going well between us for a while. I told him I wasn't going to Aix with him this winter. I'm staying here." He closed his eyes briefly as suppressed sobs broke in his chest. The words came out in jerks. "I've had enough. It wasn't just what happened with you, Sophie, but that was when I knew I couldn't go on. I kept pretending everything was okay." He gazed at me, his dark eyes glistening. "I want a lover who wants to be with only me, Sophie. I told Jean-Luc that, and he wouldn't promise anything. He said I should be glad he doesn't go with other men. It's true, he doesn't, as far as I know. But he didn't even say he loved me, though he's said it before. He kept asking me to stay, that's all. I packed up my things. I haven't got much. He's a lousy shit. Why should I stay? Do you know what he said to me when I was ready to go?" I shook my head. He said, "You are completely lost, Bernard."

I sucked in my breath. "He's a shit." I slid my arm around Bernard's bony shoulder. "You'll be fine," I murmured in his ear. "You're not lost. How long were you together?"

"I don't know. A year and a half?"

We sat shoulder to shoulder for a few minutes, staring into space. Then I asked, "What are you going to do?"

He shrugged as if it didn't matter. "I'll get a job in a café or restaurant washing dishes. That's what I did before."

"You could go to the university," I said, in sudden inspiration.

"I don't know. I'm not that smart. Besides, I need money."

"I think you are smart. You can work and take classes. You can work at night."

He shook his head. "Maybe. Right now I have other problems. Like where to sleep. Sophie, could I stay with you for a few nights? Until I get a job and find a place?"

"No way, Bernard. That won't work." I remembered the way M. Nguyen had looked at Bernard the night he'd walked me home. I studied him. "You'll never get a job looking like that. First, you need a shower. I'll trim your hair for you, just a little bit." He looked at me hopefully. "I'm a good haircutter. Do you have money?" He nodded. "Okay," I said, taking charge as I would with my younger brother. "Come and eat with me and then go to the public bath, you know where it is?" He nodded. "Then I'll meet you here and I'll have my scissors with me. Do you have a good shirt?" He looked uncertain. "Buy one tomorrow. Just so you look clean, not like a hippie, okay? That doesn't fly too well in this town unless you're selling jewelry."

"Sure," he said. "I know how to find a job. I know all that. I'm just not thinking straight right now." He hung his head. "I guess I need someone to boss me." The ghost of his usual grin appeared on his face.

"Here, I'll give you a meal ticket for free. That's my good luck present."

As we moved toward the meal line, I felt my spirits lift. Not only was I helping Bernard, but I felt like I had scored one over Jean-Luc. He'd cruelly told Bernard that he was lost. Well, we would see about that.

We stood in line behind a boy with long wavy hair, a cowboy hat on his head. When it was our turn to enter, shouts suddenly rang out from around the whole room.

"*Chapeau! Chapeau!*" Pieces of bread started

raining hard upon us as we ducked. I blinked in shock. "Take off your hat!" someone said to the offending boy. Bernard and I started laughing as we balanced our trays carefully while stepping over pieces of bread on the floor. Bernard followed me to a table where Carly and Rose were sitting.

"This is my friend, Bernard," I said. Carly aimed her dimpled smile at him.

"Bonjour, Bernard," said Rose. Some of Daniel's friends came and joined us, glancing at Bernard then at me.

"Are you a student?" one of them asked him.

"Mais, non," Bernard mumbled.

"This is Bernard," I said. "He's thinking about registering here."

"I don't know," Bernard said uncertainly. "I passed my *bac*, but I don't have my scores with me."

"Why don't you write your school and get them?" asked one of the boys.

Bernard smiled confusedly. "I'm not thinking straight. It's just that I never thought I could do that." He caught my eye as I smiled encouragingly. "But maybe I can."

Chapter Twenty-seven

This is Geneviève

On Saturday morning I waited near the sleeper cars for Geneviève to emerge, watching each face anxiously as people stepped off the train. Suddenly something soft and warm bumped into me from behind and my stomach lurched as two arms encircled me.

"Hey! Where did you come from?"

"I came out the other door." Her full, deep voice was close to my ear. I turned and embraced her. My head nestled on her shoulder. I could barely stand up on my own. Raising my head, I looked up at her cupid's bow mouth as she bent her head and kissed my lips gently. Passengers from the train walked around us.

"Mon dieu, I am glad to see you, Sophie," Geneviève breathed, breaking our silence. She took my hand as my stomach did a flip. Neither of us seemed very adept at walking. Geneviève slung her duffle bag over her shoulder with one hand, still holding mine with the other, and we staggered out of the station to the bus stop.

At my house, I opened the front door as morning light leaped across the hall into the kitchen where Charles, Gerti, and her boyfriend Wolfie were sitting and eating breakfast. All eyes turned to us. Wolfie was visiting Gerti for the weekend. Lee, my neighbor across the hall, eyed us over his coffee.

"*Salut*, guys," I said. "This is my friend, Geneviève. She's visiting from Paris." Everyone said hi and seemed at ease. "See you later." And we continued down the hall to my room.

"Nice. You'd never get a room this big to yourself in Paris." Geneviève pointed to the wall. "Your roommate's bed would be right over there." She sat down on my desk chair and nodded toward the kitchen. "Do they know about us?" I sat on the bed facing her.

"They think I have a boyfriend in Paris. Except for Gerti, but I don't think she's told anybody."

"They'll figure it out, you know," she said.

"It's so unfair. Gerti's boyfriend is here and everybody thinks it's great."

"Get used to it. This is the cost of illicit love." She grinned.

"Well, I'm *not* used to it. That's why I was afraid to say anything to the others. I have no experience with this."

"Well, I have experience, and I think you were right to be careful. You really just never know how people will react. Have you told anyone else besides the German girl?"

"Yeah, I told my friends at the fac. Two Americans named Carly and Rose, and my friend Bernard."

"Bernard?" She tensed. "Wasn't he one of those hippies...?"

"Yes," I quickly broke in. "They broke up. I've been helping Bernard. He got a job and maybe he'll attend school here next semester."

Bernard had just started working as a dishwasher at a restaurant in the old town. He did write for his test scores. This surprised me, given his dysfunctional working-class family and everything he'd been through lately. I was proud of him. I didn't ask where he'd been sleeping, but I knew he was looking for a room of his own.

"Yes, and maybe he'll go back to his boyfriend," she said bitterly.

"I really don't think so. Anyway, Jean-Luc's in Aix now."

"Good. How do you feel about all that?"

I swallowed. "It doesn't just go away," I said slowly. "But I like it here. I'm busy. I'm making friends. I'm going to start taking a mime class next week."

"Sophie the mime?" she teased. "Sophie who likes to talk so much?"

"I don't talk so much. Come here," I said, patting the space beside me on the bed. I didn't need to ask twice. I took her face in my hands and kissed her. "I've really missed you, you know."

"Yes, I do know." I leaned back on the pillows and Geneviève lay down beside me. I touched her muscled arm but made no move to embrace her. It had seemed so easy the last few weeks to make love to her in my imagination. Now that she was here, however, it was a different story. "Geneviève, I know you've had lots of lovers…"

"Oh, no, not that again." She put her finger lightly over my lips.

"No, listen," I said and she removed her finger. "I don't know anything. I feel like I should be a character from Flaubert's *Sentimental Education*. I need a lot of educating."

Geneviève smiled. "I am a good educator." When that didn't make me smile, she said, "Seriously, of course you have a lot to learn. Sophie, do you think I would be here if I had a problem with that?"

"No, but…"

Tears came to my eyes. Geneviève reached up and brushed them from my cheek. "What's wrong, *chérie*?"

"Nothing, nothing is wrong."

"I want to be with you," she said earnestly. "That's the main thing. The rest I'm not so worried about."

We stretched out on the narrow bed, kissing and holding each other. I pulled off my jeans and rolled onto Geneviève, feeling the intensity of my desire. I had been waiting for this moment for so long. Now that it was here I didn't know what to do. Last time in Paris, I hadn't worried about anything, and it had been fine.

I forgot my shyness, discarding it along with our clothes, which we removed, one item at a time between kisses that were getting deeper and deeper. I wanted to explore her body and to make love to her even if I didn't know how. Smiling tenderly, Geneviève kissed me and I felt again as I had in Paris, as though I were falling away from conscious thought into a place where feelings and sensations were all that mattered. I caught my breath as I felt my nipple responding to her touch. As she brought her lips down to mine, my hands reached out for her back, her hips, gripping them as our bodies moved in an undulating rhythm. I was hardly aware of what I was doing. I had forgotten all about wanting to please Geneviève in my urge for her to please me. Her fingers reached the sensitive area between my legs, and I heard my voice emit a moan that I muffled against her throat. I let myself lose control; my body burst into pleasure, and I collapsed in a happy heap beside her.

I sighed. "Now I want to do the same thing for you."

"Later, *chérie*."

I wouldn't be put off. Gently, I pushed Geneviève onto her back and began to kiss her neck and throat.

I rested my head on her belly and grazed her thighs with my fingertips. She moaned softly each time my fingers came close to where her thighs met. It seemed I was doing the right thing. She spread her legs apart. "Sophie…" I moved my body on top of hers so I could kiss her while trying to keep my hand moving, but something didn't feel right.

"What should I do?" I whispered, self-conscious.

"It's okay. You are doing fine." She took my hand and moved it. "Like that," Geneviève said, closing her eyes.

Whatever I did seemed to work all right. Geneviève panted and arched her head back as she clutched me, emitting a long moan as she climaxed. I wasn't surprised when she fell asleep in my arms after the long night she had spent on the train. I must have slept too because the next thing I knew, I was hanging half off the side of the bed. "Oops," I said in English, waking Geneviève. I often said slang like that in English, which made her laugh. I suppose in French I could say, *zut*, or something, but that just didn't come out naturally. My stomach growled. "We forgot to eat breakfast, and now it's lunchtime," I said. "Do you want to go to the fac, maybe meet some of my friends?"

"Uhhh, if you like."

I put one foot on the floor. "Well, we have to do something. I'm falling out of bed here. I wish I had a bigger bed." She started to pull me back, but I shook my head and stood on the rug by the bed. "Why don't we go to the restaurant where Bernard works? Maybe you could meet him."

"Sure. Is he a cook?"

I shook my head. "Dishwasher."

"Okay, if that's what you want to do, we'll go meet

this Bernard that you've saved from the streets."

"Well, I did clean him up and give him a haircut." I laughed. "He looked like a stray puppy."

"I think you are the kind of girl who likes stray puppies," Geneviève said, pulling on her jeans and reaching for her sturdy black shoes. "We have that in common. I like to rescue stray American girls."

"Hey, careful. You know I have a thing about making it on my own," I said, teasing back.

"Oh, yes. I know all about that. It's why I am lonely every night and why I can't see any of my little Parisian lovebirds." She smiled at the look on my face. "I've been good, don't worry. The only one I've seen, I ran into at Monoprix. I told her I am out of circulation. She took it very well. She said she was seeing her dentist. A man! That's what I'm worried about, by the way. I'm worried you'll decide you want to be with men."

"What? Men? No way. Aren't you worried I might meet some cute girl, though?"

"That too. So that's why I'm afraid to meet your friends at the fac—I might get jealous." She smiled as she said all this, but I thought she partly meant it.

"Who are your lovebirds?" I asked. "Are they any of the ones I met that night?"

"Oh, no, those are just friends. Although, at one time, Colette and I—"

I put up my hand. "I don't want to hear about it." We stepped out into the corridor and ran into Gerti and Wolfie just as they were leaving Gerti's room.

"We're going to eat at the fac. You coming?" Gerti said.

"No, we're going into town," I said.

"Someplace more private?" she said good-naturedly.

"Yeah," I said. "It's not often that you have your girlfriend visit for the weekend, right?"

"Or your boyfriend," Gerti chimed in.

"Have you told any of the others?"

"No, it's none of my business. But I wouldn't worry about it if I were you. They're not stupid. They'll figure it out. Who cares, anyway?" She lowered her voice. "I'd be more concerned about 'you-know-who' upstairs."

"Uhh, yeah. See you later," I said as we went out the front door.

It was about a twenty-minute walk to the center of town. We arrived on the busy rue Saint-Guilhem where Bernard worked at a *crêperie*. They wouldn't let us go back in the kitchen, but Bernard came out for a moment, his hands in wet gloves, grinning like his old self.

"Enchanteé," Geneviève said, starting to shake hands then pretending she'd just noticed dish suds on his glove and pulling away. This sent Bernard into delighted peals of laughter.

When we sat down, she said, "I remember him from that day. He seems very sweet."

We walked all over the old town as we'd done in Paris. We stopped in a couple of antique stores around rue Foch.

"Sorry, I can't resist," said Geneviève. "And I might see something one of our clients is looking for."

"I think it's more that you can't resist."

"It's in my blood," she said.

❧❧❧❧

That evening, we decided to eat at the university because I wanted her to meet some of my new friends. I was glad to find most of them sitting around our usual table, avidly watching us come in the door. I loved the feeling of entering the cafeteria with my girlfriend. We loaded our trays and walked together toward the table as my friends watched.

"This is Geneviève," I said when we'd set down our trays. "See? She's real. I didn't make her up."

Daniel stood up and carefully took Geneviève's hand, bowing. "*Avec grand plaisir, mademoiselle.*" He exaggerated his syllables, which only made his antics more hilarious as he bent and kissed Geneviève's hand.

This broke the ice as they tittered. We sat down and Geneviève put her arm around me. "By the way, she's taken," she said.

Everyone watched us more closely than they would have if she'd been just my boyfriend. But after a few minutes, they forgot about the novelty. I felt accepted.

"We're going to a movie at the fac," Carly said. "It's in that hall where we have art history. They show second-run films there. Do you guys want to come?"

"What film?" I asked.

"*Butterflies Are Free.*"

"Oh, Goldie Hawn, right? Sure." I turned to Geneviève. "Do you want to? Have you seen it?"

"No, that would be great," she said.

The movie was about a young blind man who has been sheltered by his overprotective mother until a free-spirited young woman helps him to break free and have his own life. The title is from Dickens's *Bleak House*: "I only ask to be free. Butterflies are free."

"That was good," I said afterward as we exited the hall into the windy campus. Geneviève and I were a little ahead of the others. "It was about love and freedom. Is it possible to have both?"

"Oh yes," said Geneviève. "You have to have both or it's no good."

"But how do you figure out how much of each you need?" I said.

Geneviève squeezed me around the waist. "You'll know. Don't worry."

Carly caught up with us. "That film makes me want to dance!" She spread out her arms and whirled, her long strawberry-blond hair flying.

I raised my arms. "I'm a butterfly," I said, jumping onto one of the low brick walls around the shrubbery and leaping off, flapping my arms. The others followed my lead. Geneviève just watched, laughing at us. "I pretended I was a drunken bee a couple of weeks ago," I said. "Like this." I showed them how I had run zigzagging around in the orchard.

Geneviève and I said good night and began the trek back to my place.

"You know, the girl in the film," she said, "she reminded me of you."

"She did?"

"Yes, it's part of why I like you. You're free-spirited like her. I stand back and wait and analyze before I do anything. But being with you makes me feel more spontaneous."

"You didn't exactly stand back and analyze when you asked me to dance at the club."

"No, that was an easy decision. You didn't notice me leaping around back there, though, did you?"

"No, you just watched. But I like the way you are. You stay in one place and I can lean on you. I like that feeling," I said.

We could hear the music as we got near the house. Voices and laughter pierced the hallway as we hurried toward my room and closed the door. I pulled out my chair, and Geneviève sat on the bed, listening. The party was in Lee's room across the hall and movement from there rattled the door.

"Sorry," I said. "I hope it doesn't go too late like last time."

By the time we went to bed, although things had quieted down a bit across the hall, it was still impossible to sleep with the music playing. Reluctantly, I stood, put on my fuzzy robe, and knocked on Lee's door. He opened it, his eyes, without the usual dark glasses, were small and glazed from alcohol.

"*Excuse-moi*," I began. The room had several Chinese students of both sexes, as well as Charles and Françoise. "We want to sleep. It's midnight. Could you turn down the music?"

"You and your petite amie are welcome to join us," said Lee in a nasty tone.

"Listen," said Charles, "don't speak to her like that."

"But I thought he was a boy," said his girlfriend, who looked confused

"Sorry," I told her, my face growing hot with embarrassment.

"Mais, non, *ça va.*" She spread her hands graciously.

Charles continued, "Lee, she said she wants to sleep. And we have to go now, *n'est çe pas, chérie?*"

"*Oui,*" said Françoise and they stood, shook everyone's hand, and backed out of the room. "Merci, Lee," she said politely. "Bonsoir." Lee shut the door after them without a further word to me, but the music stopped.

"Whew," said Geneviève, when I closed my door and locked it for good measure. "You see the way things can be?"

Chapter Twenty-Eight

New Digs

W hen will I see you again?" I asked. Geneviève and I strolled along the Promenade du Peyrou. We leaned over the same railing where Jade and I had caught a glimpse of the sea that first day.

She snuggled closer beside me. "How about next weekend?"

I jumped and my voice squeaked, "What? Really?"

"Yes. I wanted to surprise you. I have to go to Lyon for work. It's in the middle between our two cities. Can you meet me there?"

"Of course!" I threw my arms around her.

"I will write down the details of trains and my hotel before I leave," she said.

I beamed at her. "No wonder you were so happy on this trip and didn't complain that I lived so far away. You knew you would see me again in a week."

"If you agreed, that is."

"You knew I would agree."

"Or maybe I am always happy when I am with you," she said and pulled me closer into her arms.

Did I dare kiss in public in a bourgeois town like Montpellier? I did dare.

※ ※ ※ ※

The day after Geneviève left, M. Nguyen stopped
me in the hallway and said he wanted to talk. We went
upstairs and sat at his kitchen table. I had a feeling I
knew what it was about; either Lee had complained, or
my landlord's kids had mentioned something.

"Sophie, you are a nice girl, but I'm worried
about some of the friends you bring here. I don't want
hippies here." *Oh, is this about Bernard?* "This is a good
house. I have to be very careful about who is allowed in.
Remember this is my home too, and my friends come
here."

"My friend doesn't look like a hippie anymore,
actually." I tried to smile. "He got a job in a restaurant."

M. Nguyen smiled. "That is good. But also the
friend you had here last weekend."

"*Oui?*"

"My kids said she was nice—that is not the
problem. And you are a good tenant. I am not prejudiced
toward homosexuals. But I don't want a reputation for
that here. This is not that kind of house. Will she come
here again?"

"Yes, but she lives in Paris. Maybe once a month?"

"I guess that would be all right. But you may not
have other gay people here. You may not have parties
like that here."

"Okay, I won't," I mumbled. I walked slowly down
the stairs to my room and lay facedown on the bed. I
supposed that in his terms my landlord was being fair.
He had to keep up the reputation of his house. But
it didn't feel very fair to me. I felt more like he was
putting me in a box. Why was I different from Gerti
and Wolfie who often came from Stuttgart to stay the
weekend in Gerti's room? Just because Geneviève was
a woman? Who cared about that stuff anymore? I knew

lots of people did. But I wanted to scream, "Everything's changing! Don't you all get it? This is not the same world it used to be. We've had Stonewall. Gay liberation movements are making the news around the world. We have civil rights for blacks in the US and socialism in Europe. People, get your heads out of the sand!"

But Friday was drawing closer and I soon forgot about everything but my rendezvous with Geneviève.

The weekend in Lyon turned out to be an intoxication of happiness. Everything seemed so easy. No metros. No buses. It almost seemed like Lyon the city was nothing but a backdrop for our love affair, as though we had our own magic carpet to take us around so our feet hardly needed to touch the ground. Maybe it was because we were both away from home, but it felt like a carefree holiday, despite the fact that Geneviève was there on business.

Geneviève met my train and we took a taxi to the hotel where she was already installed. Our newish hotel was in a northern suburb that had no quaint little streets like in Paris, no friendly old restaurants down the block. Instead it had imposing apartment buildings and a supermarket on the corner. We could have been in any modern French city. Except for the train station, we were never near the center of town where the old buildings were. We took no long meandering walks as we did in Paris, but we didn't want to explore the city anyway. We wanted to explore each other instead, making use of room service when we weren't out on business. I went along on her work excursion to the big auction house on Saturday, and I also went with her to supervise loading her purchases into the van on Sunday. We were never apart.

On Friday, the night of my arrival, we silently

exchanged bright-eyed glances in the elevator on the way up, standing beside two dark-suited businessmen. Once inside our room, I dropped my little bag on the floor, a canvas one I'd picked up at the market especially for this trip. Then we fell into each other's arms.

That first evening we mostly spoke just to praise each other and to say, "I love you." Geneviève said it in English, and I laughed because the first time I'd said that to her in Paris, my words had been in French.

"What is funny?" she asked. I reminded her of our visit to the Catacombs, after which, sitting in the café outside, I'd suddenly said "Je t'aime."

"I didn't know I was going to say it until it was out," I said. "It was like the words jumped out of my mouth. I was as surprised as you probably were."

"Ah, I was not surprised," she answered, her gray eyes flickering happily on mine. "I was thinking the same thing."

"That is the difference between you and me, then," I said. "You think about what you will say before you say it and I just hope that what I say makes any sense at all when it comes out of my mouth."

It seemed that my study of mime got put to good use that weekend. We didn't talk very much. It was as though too many words might break the spell. Nor did I worry any more about lovemaking techniques as I had the last time. I just let myself be pulled into the current on a river of love.

At the auction house, I sat next to her in the audience, tense with excitement, listening to the unintelligible roll of the auctioneer's French that echoed through the vast building. I never knew when Geneviève's deep voice would ring out, her finger raised, and sometimes she sat back and let the bidding roll on without her. I watched the stocky men in blue smocks and brown-gloved hands bring out the pieces to the stage, then come and remove them. I looked at the high warehouse windows that let slanting rays of sun into the room and onto the heads of the crowd that was as engrossed as we were.

When it was all over and the last table or commode was carried off the stage, we stood up and asked each other, "Are you hungry? What would you like to do now?" But all we really wanted to do was go back to our room. We did stand for a while talking to some people she knew after the auction. Geneviève introduced me as her friend. I am sure they knew I was her lover. We declined their invitation to dinner and walked in the brisk air until we found a cab. The driver knew a good restaurant in the district, so we had our dinner out.

The cuisine was French, but in a different style than I'd had before, more heavy with sauces. We sat idly talking about people and places, and the food we had eaten there. My experience of French food was limited; I couldn't afford to eat out much. There had been my cousin's hearty cooking on the farm, more French than Polish since she'd lived most of her life in France cooking for her French family members. And the student restaurant, of course, which emphasized starches and dairy. I was already gaining some weight. I needed to be careful or my clothes would no longer fit. I couldn't afford new ones. The few French restaurants I'd frequented were in Paris. A couple times I'd eaten out with my cousins three years ago. Twice with Kari and Annik: that time up on Montmartre, and the night before we left for England on the Champs Élysées. There was Sylvie's wine bar of course, and Bernard's crêperie.

"When I think of myself sitting with our Dutch

friends and Jade up on that hill the night I met you. What would I have thought if some angel or other had come in and whispered in my ear that I was about to meet the Woman from Montpellier."

"The who?" She laughed heartily. "You don't mean me?"

"Yes, you. Except I will always think of her as someone else, the mysterious woman who smiled at me and completely changed my life!"

"Oh, come on. How did I do that, *chérie?* Just by smiling at you?"

I nodded. "No French woman had ever smiled at me like that before. They all seemed so distant and unapproachable. And suddenly I realized that no woman at all had ever looked at me that way. If they had, who knows? Maybe my life would have changed much sooner. You see? It was all because of you that I realized I wanted to meet a woman, not a man. Except of course, I don't really think of the woman in Montpellier as you. I thought I might run into her again there. I hoped I would!"

She laughed softly. "And the gods brought us together just a few days later, in Paris."

"If you say so," I teased, "but you will never be the Woman from Montpellier. I'm sorry. You don't have her glamour, her special allure."

"But you like me anyway." She leaned forward and kissed me across the little table.

"Oh yes. I like your earthy charm. Just don't try to compete with *her* because you never can."

"I won't try as long as you like me the way I am."

That was the playful way we talked all weekend, if we talked at all. And when Monday morning came, we packed our few things in silence and headed in the blue van for the station.

"I will try to come down in November," she said as we waited for my train. "But the time before the holidays is very busy at work because we do many party decorations. So you must come to Paris at least once before your winter break, will you?"

"Yes. Will you spend Christmas with your family in Reims?"

"Yes, and with you too, I hope."

"Do they know about me?"

"No, but they know about me." She smiled wryly. "My mother is not totally comfortable with it, but she will make the best of it, and my father accepts me. It will be okay. You'll see. They're good people."

"You can meet my cousins too if you want," I offered. "I suppose I'll have to tell my cousin Anna about you. That'll be a treat," I added wryly.

❧ ❧ ❧ ❧

My Chinese housemate Lee was standing in the front hall peering through his smoky glasses at his mail when I opened the front door. He was the one who lived across the hall, the one who'd been rude to us at his noisy party. Lee stepped aside without a word to let me pass. He didn't greet me the way he used to. Last week I'd sensed an icy atmosphere between us, but I thought that would soon pass. Apparently not. During the week after Lyon, Lee continued to walk right by me in the hallway and avoided me in the kitchen. It spoiled the easy feeling I'd had before with the housemates.

One day I heard that Rick, one of the Americans I knew at Vert Bois, had a roommate who was quitting school and planning to go home. So I grabbed him when

I saw him leaving the student restaurant one evening.

"Rick, is your roommate really leaving?"

"Yes. He hates it here. He just hasn't been able to adjust."

"Well, I'm sort of looking for a place, actually. What kind of room is it?"

"Hey, it's a great setup. We have an addition on the side of this old house where Mme Chênier lives. She's in her sixties and really nice. She's a widow and lives all alone so she likes to have students. All she wants is that they be quiet, no parties. But you can have a friend over anytime. She doesn't care about that. And there's a big walled garden. Only it's kind of primitive. You have to use an outhouse in the garden."

"Sure, no problem."

"Also the only running water is downstairs, in my room. There's a little kitchen there. We have to share that, and there's no shower."

"Where do you shower?"

"I use the sink mostly. At least there's hot water. And I shower at the gym."

"Sure. I could do that too. When can I see this place?"

"How about right now?"

We walked into the old part of town, turning onto a cobblestoned street flanked by an ancient stone wall, called Impasse de Pierre Rouge. It was almost the same distance from the university as where I lived now, only in the other direction. Rick used a large key to unlock the gate, which creaked loudly as he opened it. "See, this is the chain that visitors pull." He pulled the chain on the door to show me and a little bell rang on the other side. "She wants us to keep the gate locked."

"That's safer for us, too," I said. The dark garden

had several trees surrounding a little patio in the middle with a table and chairs.

"This is where Madame sits," Rick said. He led me to the side, where we crossed a smaller patio by some French doors. "This is our place."

I already wanted to move in before I even saw the inside. The privacy, the sense of beauty and freedom—it was just what I wanted. Inside was a little kitchen built under the stairway, with folding wooden doors to close it off.

"This is my room," he said. "You'll have plenty of privacy because I'm not here that much. I have a girlfriend."

Then we climbed the stairs. The upper room had a double bed with a high wooden headboard. The bed was unmade and a lot of clothes and books were strewn about, but I tried to imagine it empty. A wardrobe and a table flanked the tall curtained window that looked out on the garden.

"This is great! It's charming. Perfect." I said. "Is your roommate leaving for sure?"

"Yep. He's got his ticket home already. Come on, we'll talk to Mme Chênier right now."

So that's how I suddenly found myself packing to move in the first week of November. Daniel, my mime friend, was going to move me in his car. It was sad in a way; I had become fond of my old room and my housemates. Except for Lee, of course. And M. Nguyen was not thrilled with the news either. At least he got to keep my last month's deposit. But the rent on the new place was a bit less, which helped.

꙳ ꙳ ꙳ ꙳

Bernard's restaurant was a quick walk from my new place. We already had formed the habit of meeting up sometimes after his shift. We would go somewhere to have a glass of wine. He often walked me home through the dark, shuttered streets, our arms around each other. When I lived on on rue des Tourterelles, the walk was longer. Sometimes we sang old French songs as we walked through the dark, narrow streets: like "Sur le Pont d'Avignon" and "Aupres de ma Blonde."

I met him one night at Café Tout Va Bien soon after I moved to my new room. I'd hung out in that café so much that the memory of meeting him and Jean-Luc there had been all but erased. That was partly because I'd met Geneviève there too; the aura of the "Woman of Montpellier" still shimmered in the air, which was why I went there so often. But now as I approached the table where he was sitting, the picture of the two hippies came back. After I sat down and ordered, I asked Bernard about how he and Jean-Luc had met.

"Oh, it was a bad day. And a good day too, I guess. I was hitching out of Nice. I needed to get out of town. I'd gotten into a fight with some guys and they were looking for me. Anyway, Jean-Luc picked me up. I was eighteen and I'd only been away from home for a few months."

"Where are you from?" Bernard never liked to talk about his family. I only knew that he was from somewhere in the south.

"I grew up in Marseille. Anyway, I had a job washing dishes in Nice in a pretty good restaurant, a fish place. I was living on the streets, but I almost had enough for rent when I had to leave town."

"And you stayed with Jean-Luc?"

"Yes. He became like an older brother to me. He

taught me about stones. I was really happy. He's not so bad, you know."

"Where's he from?" I asked.

"Marseille also. His dad worked on the docks. Jean-Luc didn't have the happiest childhood either. His dad was an alcoholic. He was like me—he left home early, after high school.'"

"You wouldn't go back to him, would you?"

"No way," Bernard said vehemently.

❧❧❧❧

I went by my old house to collect my mail a few days later and left happily with a stack of letters, including one from Geneviève. On my bed at Impasse de Pierre Rouge, I sat facing the window overlooking the garden as I opened them with great relish, saving Geneviève's for last. The one from Jade said she was definitely planning to come to France next semester. The news made me whoop with joy. I also got a letter from my sister, which I set aside. Instead I picked up the one with a small British stamp with a cameo of the queen. Natalie wrote rhapsodically about Max coming to England to see her for Christmas. I rolled my eyes. After the way she had treated me in September during my time of need, the news made little impression. I remembered at one point when she first arrived in the summer we had talked about getting together for winter break. No talk about that now. I really didn't care.

I couldn't wait any longer to open Geneviève's letter. She got her phone! There at the bottom of the page was her phone number.

It wasn't very private standing in Vert Bois as streams of students went by, but hearing Geneviève's rich, husky voice on the phone made me forget the crowds.

"Geneviève, remember I told you how my landlord talked to me and how Lee's been treating me? Well, I moved. I found a new place! It's really private."

Her voice cracked. "You moved? You didn't tell me you were thinking of moving."

"Well, it just came up. A guy I know from the fac had a roommate who left. It's cheaper and it has a garden wall around it. You will love it. It even has a little patio with a table and chairs. It's kind of cold now, but when it gets warmer I can eat my breakfast out there."

There was a pause. "Well, I'm sure it is very nice," she said stiffly. "I will see it when I come. Excuse me, *chérie,* I have to go. Sylvie is expecting me. I will see you soon."

Chapter Twenty-nine

A Visit to Sète

Geneviève and I held hands as we walked along the ancient stone wall of Impasse Pierre Rouge, now plastered over with peeling film posters. The wooden gate creaked as I pushed it open and she looked around the garden. "So this is your new digs."

"Do you like it, *chérie*? It is a real hideaway. We can be private here. Not like the old place."

"Of course I like it," she said, following me across our patio to the French doors of our apartment.

"Although, I have to warn you," I continued, "there's no shower. And we have to share a sink with Rick downstairs. But he's hardly ever here. He's with his girlfriend most of the time."

I opened the double doors with my key and we passed through Rick's empty room. After climbing single file up the narrow staircase, I shut my bedroom door behind us. Geneviève dropped her duffel bag with a thud and turned to put her arms around me.

"I missed you," I said fitting my head under her chin.

"Mais, oui," she breathed, turning the word, "oui" into a drawn-out, wistful sigh. "Seeing you two weekends in a row and then not at all for three weeks!"

I murmured, "Except for a phone call. I'm so happy you got your phone." I pointed to the big bed.

"That's another thing that is better. No more single mattress."

We fell onto it and kissed hungrily. But the abandon we'd felt in Lyon was missing. I felt a heaviness in her. I didn't want to ask her about it. Not yet. I snuggled up to her and pulled the big, old-fashioned, embroidered spread over us. She started snoring softly. Geneviève was always tired when she got off the night train from Paris. She never slept well in the sleeper car. I dozed off too while listening to the wind in the trees.

When she awoke, Geneviève sat up abruptly and glanced around as though she didn't know where she was. When she looked over at me, relief softened her features. "I had a bad dream," she said. "I was a prisoner in a ship going out to sea. Some of my brother's friends kidnapped me. They were thugs. They tied me up and put me on the ship." She grimaced. "I thought it was real. I think I dreamed this because when we were little, I used to wrestle with my brother and his friends. They used to pile on top of me and they wouldn't let me up. Sometimes I could hardly breathe."

I hugged her. I was getting to know her ups and downs. "Of course it's not real," I said softly, brushing my face through the dark waves of her hair. "Mmmm, your hair is so soft." I breathed deeply. "You smell good." She leaned into me, stroking my arm.

I could hear her stomach rumble. I asked, "Want to get some lunch?"

"Yes. I'd like to go down to the sea. We are so close. Have you ever been to Sète?"

"No, I've heard it's very pretty."

"It's one of my favorite places around here. There is a good restaurant there on the quay. When I was a child we always used to go to the southern coast for our vacations. The seaside is a good place for me."

"I love it too. That's why I came here." I laughed. "That was a joke on me, because Montpellier is nine kilometers away. But still, it's close. Shall we take the bus?"

"Yes. They go by the central square."

"I've seen them. In fact, I've always wanted to jump on one of the buses marked Sète and see where I ended up."

We waited for the bus in the cool sunshine of the Place de la Comédie.

"Did you know that the poet Paul Valérie was born there?" she asked as we rolled out of the city.

"No. That must be why they named my university after him."

She nodded. "I know how much you like poetry. There is a Paul Valérie museum we could visit."

"And I know how much you like history. And museums about anything dead and gone."

"You are right, but perhaps today I would prefer to just sit by the sea."

The town was crisscrossed by canals like in Venice. On our walk to the quayside restaurant, we passed colorful old buildings. Then, closer to the sea, sailboats bobbed, their masts clustered liked reeds. We ordered mussels and swordfish. The mussels came from the lagoon behind us, the fish from the sea in front of us. We had white wine and watched the November sun move in a gray arc over the horizon, talking lazily about many things. She told me more about her family and growing up. I did the same. Boats bobbed in the wharf as gulls screamed, hustling up their own fish dinner.

Geneviève's idea to come here had been a good one. The whole place was serene and timeless, far from the bustle of the city. Here we were safely cocooned, nestled below a small mountain that cut down to the water on one side and a network of canals and boats on the other. I felt more the way I did in Lyon that afternoon, maybe because we were again away from where either of us lived, away from each of our individual lives and concerns. It would have been nice to just stay there all night in one of the hotels on the hill, falling asleep to the sound of the waves lapping against the cliffs. But I couldn't afford it and I couldn't ask her to pay. After dinner, we walked among the canals until lights started to wink on in the houses. We watched the fishing trawlers come in with their catch, one by one docking and unloading baskets onto dockside trolleys that the fishermen pushed and pulled skillfully away toward sheds, followed by gangs of screaming gulls.

Geneviève and I slept soundly in the big bed on Impasse Piere-Rouge that night, worn out by exercise and sea air.

In the morning, I slipped out of bed and went out to the nearby bakery for croissants. I made coffee by pouring water through a filter. Rick hadn't come home that night, so we sat at the small table downstairs by the French doors. We didn't talk much. Afterward we put on our coats and explored the garden and let ourselves out the creaky gate. The day was warmer and sunnier than yesterday. We passed down the silent, sleeping lane, as church bells announced that at least some of its inhabitants were on their way to mass. We walked side by side, swinging our arms, until we had passed through the narrow streets of the old town and had climbed the steps to the park above the city.

This was where she'd asked me to meet her in Lyon last time. I felt disconnected from both of those two last visits; I didn't know why. Something was different this time. I wondered how to ask Geneviève about it. We walked in silence, admiring the view from the hill. No one was around.

Finally, I asked, "Is something wrong, Geneviève?"

We stood at the parapet looking out. Misty clouds blocked our view of the sea. All we could see were the red-roofed houses below and gray high-rises receding into the distance.

She gripped the cement railing with one hand and turned her head toward me. "I didn't want to talk about it right away," she said quickly. "I didn't want to spoil our visit. I had a nice time with you in Sète yesterday, Sophie. I always do." Her voice dropped. "But not as nice as it could have been."

"What's wrong?"

"Well, when you talked to me on the phone the other day and told me you had moved…it was a shock for me. You did it without telling me."

"But I had to move! Things weren't going well at the other house. I told you. I thought you'd be pleased that we have a private place almost to ourselves."

"Yes, but you said you would think about moving to Paris. Then I find out that you have gone to the trouble of moving, but not to Paris—to another place in Montpellier. Can you see how I felt?"

"Well, yes but…" I looked into her steely gray eyes.

"What hurt me the most was when you talked about your little patio. Remember that?"

"My patio?"

"*Mais, oui.* You said, 'when it gets warmer I can sit out and have my breakfast on the patio.' Remember that?" I sucked in my breath and nodded. I did remember saying that. "That's when I thought—she has no intention of ever moving to Paris. She is talking about spring, about still being here when the weather warms up."

"I was just *talking*. It didn't mean anything."

"Have you thought about Paris at all?"

"Of course I have. But I am not ready. I told you."

"Yes, I know that. You have been here for, what, about six weeks? You have made friends. You have a little life of your own, just as you wanted. But what about me? What about how I feel? Do you ever think about that? Is everything to be on your terms?"

A sharp pang of guilt seared through me. I was a selfish, immature twit. As she said, my plans were all about me. I'd been afraid all along that I wasn't ready to handle a relationship. Well, I didn't know how to handle this one right now. Fortunately, my emergency self spoke up. *She's talking about how she feels. Ask her how she feels, you idiot!* "Tell me how you feel," I said.

"How I feel? Sophie, you are here in France for such a short time. It would be different if you lived here. Then we would have years for a long-distance relationship. But as it is? Before I know it, you will return to the US."

"But we still have lots of time left. I told you I would let you know when I was ready."

"My question is, will you ever be ready?"

The question slammed against me with its implicit lack of trust. Her eyes were now shielded by a hard veneer. "Of course I will."

"When?"

"I can't tell you that!" I said, angry now. "Geneviève, it doesn't help when you pressure me."

"You wanted to know how I feel. I would feel

better if I knew what your plans were."

"I don't have any plans. Not exactly. I will tell you when I do."

She stood up. "That is not good enough. To have no plans. Am I not worth making a plan for?"

"That's not fair," I murmured. I looked up to where she towered over me. Tears trickled down my face. "Of course you are worth it. You don't understand." I paused to gather my thoughts, wiping my tears with my fist. "I like my life here. I love our weekends together too. If I tell you a definite date that I will move to Paris, it's like I am already packing up my life here. I am already saying good-bye. It ruins everything. Don't you see that?"

"I see that you don't want to change anything."

I swallowed. "We are different, Geneviève. You like things to be all set and decided, and I like things to be up in the air sometimes. Because that way I feel free. I can breathe. Otherwise it's like I am in a box."

"You and your freedom! What about love? I thought you loved me."

"I do love you. You know I do."

She stood with her arms crossed, her heavy brows furrowed. "I love you too, Sophie." Her voice had softened a bit, but still, there was a tension in it. "I don't think there is any point in continuing this discussion right now."

I looked at her face and her rigid stance. I wanted to give her what she wanted, but if I did, it seemed like I would be robbing myself. I didn't know what I could do or say to make things better. I stood up from the bench. We walked slowly back to my place. The day was ruined. She packed up her few things as I watched from the unmade bed.

"Good-bye, Sophie," she said after zipping up her

overnight bag. Only, in French it was "au revoir," which means, until we see each other again. At least that didn't sound as final as it would have in English.

"When…when will I see you again?" My voice was shaky.

"We will talk on the phone," she said.

I followed her down the stairs and out the double door. On the patio, she bent to kiss me lightly on the lips, then turned briskly toward the gate. It was clear she didn't want my company on the walk to the station. I stood there with tears in my eyes long after the gate clanged and the bobbing of her head was no longer visible above the wall. The cold stone wall seemed to surround my heart, keeping me away from her, maybe forever.

Chapter Thirty

The Walled City

I have to get out of town," I told Denise on the phone that night. Traveling had become a habit. Going somewhere was a way to distance myself from my troubles, from the knifelike pain in my heart. "I can't bear it in Montpellier. Can't you get a few days off?"

"I think I could. They owe me some time off. Maybe closer to the weekend. I might be able to leave Thursday. Where would we go?" There was excitement in her voice. "Do you want to invite anybody else? We could get a group together. We could share rooms."

"Yeah, sure. I don't care."

"I'm sorry, Sophie. I know you're feeling bad. But still, it could be fun, take your mind off things. We could go to Nice or Italy even."

"We need more time for a trip like that, Denise. How about someplace close? I've heard that Nîmes is interesting with all the Roman ruins."

"Sure. Why don't you check with the others at Vert Bois and let me know? And I'll ask my employers."

I hung up the phone. I sat in a café in the central town, where I had downed an aperitif in an effort to numb the pain that seeped through my whole body. It hadn't worked. The shock of my fight with Geneviève shattered the feeling of love and safety I'd come to count on with her. The comfort I'd begun to take for granted was now hanging in shreds. I couldn't bear it.

Even if I'd known what to say to her, she was still on the train to Paris and couldn't be reached. But to be honest, I had no idea what to say. We'd reached an impasse. We needed different things. Maybe there was an answer, but I didn't know what it was. If I went away, something would come to me, or anyway, being with my friends for a few days would help me feel better.

The next day at lunch I asked them all about joining us. Carly was the only one with either the funds or the desire to get away on such short notice. "We could go to the Camargue and see the flamingos!" she said, her blue eyes sparkling. She was talking about a vast marshland to the east. Carly flipped her long, strawberry-blond hair excitedly over one shoulder.

"I don't think the flamingos are there this time of year," I answered. I remembered seeing a brochure for an ancient walled citadel to the south. "How about Carcassonne?" In the photo the place looked stark and majestic, standing above and apart from life. It fit my mood. And from what I remembered, the city went back to way before the Romans.

Geneviève would love it. For a second I almost sobbed at the thought that now we might never have the chance to go there together. But I managed to keep a tight hold on myself. I hadn't told Carly about our disagreement yet. I hoped it was only a disagreement and not a breakup. I kept reviewing the last scene with Geneviève when she was packing. She'd hardly looked at me. She seemed so brusque and businesslike. And when I asked her when we would see each other, she simply said that we would talk. Talk? What did that mean? We did need to talk. Only I didn't know what we were going to say. I didn't know how to begin. We were on opposite sides of a wall. Maybe it would come to me on this trip. She had kissed me good-bye at least. Although it hadn't been much of a kiss.

"Carcassonne sounds great," Carly said. "Are there cheap hotels there? There must be."

"I'm sure there must be something. It's off-season. I'll look into it."

"Okay. How are we going to get there?" Carly asked. "Hey, I'll ask Daniel if we can use his car."

"Okay. I hope it won't break down. It's at least an hour and a half drive."

"It won't break down. That way we can be more private, and we can stop along the way if we want."

Geneviève couldn't call me and I didn't call her. I don't know how I made it through the days until Thursday. I went to class. I caught up on my French homework. I visited the tourist office to get brochures on Carcassonne. I thought because it was November, we wouldn't need reservations for a hotel. It would be more fun to just show up, the way Jade and I used to do when we were backpacking.

We agreed that it would save money if we filled up on lunch at Vert Bois on Thursday before we left. We met there at eleven with Daniel, who told us about all the quirks of his old car. The three of us waved gaily good-bye to him and sped south out of Montpellier on the road to Sète. It's a short trip if you're not on a bus that keeps stopping and we were soon crossing the narrow passage over the lagoon. Denise had been there to dine with the family she lived with, but Carly had never seen the town, so we stopped and walked around a little.

The canals and bright boats reminded me of when I was last there with Geneviève, and a dull heaviness consumed my chest. But Carly's laughter pulled my spirits back. Denise and I darted after her as she ran out to the end of a pier. Running and acting frivolous were typical of how we behaved together, especially when Carly was along. We breathed the salty air and grinned at each other.

Afterward, we returned to the car and continued on the road through town, which turned into a larger highway heading toward the town of Béziers. The sun blazed down, warming us through the windows of Daniel's Citroën. When we stopped and emerged from the car to take in the view at Cap d'Agde, the wind from the sea blew right through us. The port town looked patchy, like islands and fingers of wharves reaching into the aquamarine water. Then the road climbed eastward away from the coast. We no longer passed flashes of water.

We'd been talking mostly about the scenery and not about me. I wasn't averse to talking about my problems though, not as I had been at the beginning of the week. So when Denise tentatively asked how I was feeling, I knew what she meant. "Better, I guess. Still mixed up."

"Okay," Carly said, "I don't want to pry or anything, but what happened exactly? I mean, if you want to talk about it at all," she added.

I explained what Denise already knew as best as I could. "I told her from the beginning that I was a bad risk for a relationship," I said. "It's not like she didn't know. I tried to warn her when we first met that I was not ready for much. She's been around the block a few times and I haven't. Not on the lesbian scene. But it wasn't just that. It was everything. She said she didn't mind. She said I could do my own thing. But now, she's mad that I haven't been making plans to move to Paris.

The fact that I moved in with Rick is what got her, I guess."

"Is she jealous of Rick?" Carly asked.

"No, no. Not at all. Just that I would move without her permission." I smiled wryly. "And not to Paris. I think she thinks I'm not taking her seriously enough. She thinks I'm some kind of a flake." It felt good to talk to my American friends in my own idiom.

"But you have a right to live your own life," said Carly.

"You do love her, don't you?" asked Denise.

"Yes, I do!"

"Or else it wouldn't bother you so much," said Carly. "You'd just let her go."

"I don't want to let her go." I turned to look out the window at the passing tangle of low, grayish-green Mediterranean shrubs. Their scent perfumed the air through a crack in the window. "Let's not talk about it anymore right now," I said, blinking back tears. And with that, we left the subject alone as the car slowed down through Béziers and Narbonne. We decided not to stop until we reached our destination.

After crossing the Aude river, we saw it—an impossibly long wall with turrets, imposing and medieval, blazing in the light and shadow of the setting sun. Beyond the walled city, a town spread, ending in vineyards and blue mountains that were the Pyrénées.

"Wow," Carly said it for us all. "What a setup. I feel like I'm in a movie."

"Yeah." Denise's voice was sharp with excitement. "What do we do now? Find the drawbridge?"

"I don't think we can afford the hotels inside the walls, Denise," I told her. "Better find one out here and drive in and explore the old town tomorrow. And let's get some dinner."

I was in the back seat and Denise was driving. We cruised along the streets under mottled plane trees that dangled half their leaves and stopped in front of a building marked: Hotel des Pyrénées.

"This looks open," I said, as I saw a laughing couple emerging from its door. We parked the car down the street and got out, to be met by a gust of cold air. "Christ, it feels like winter in Minnesota." My hip-length cotton jean jacket with the fake-fur lining had been fine for Montpellier, but here it was inadequate. It seemed like all the winds from four directions met here to buffet the unsuspecting tourist.

"We've got to go shopping before everything closes," Denise said, her long chestnut hair flying in her face. "For hats and gloves!" We grabbed our bags and hurried toward the ancient-looking hotel.

We got a room that looked up the hill toward the ancient wall. We could even see a cone-topped turret from our window. Our room had two double beds. I figured Carly would get the single bed, since Denise and I knew each other better. But the two of them quickly claimed the one by the window. I thought of Jade for a second with nostalgia. How long ago those travels seemed. How strange time was. It felt more like years rather than months since that hot morning when Jade and I first stepped off the plane.

I put on my heavy wool sweater under my boxy jacket, jammed my hands into my pockets, and joined the others as we returned to the narrow street.

"Jesus, it's the wind that makes it so cold," I said. "Doesn't matter what you put on."

We searched for the woolen shop the hotel clerk had told us about. "Just turn left and then the first right..." Of course we got lost but asked directions from people we passed and there it was: a shop with a pair of knitting needles dangling in the window. A young woman sat behind the counter, knitting some kind of thick, hairy wool into a scarf. We bought colorful hats and gloves and finally felt semiequipped to face the cold wind back in the street. After that we stopped in shops along the way and searched for a place to eat. We bought provisions for the next day: some local wine, a couple of warm baguettes, and sausage. The next stop was a little restaurant where we had a hearty dinner of crusty bread, wine, and a delicious local stew.

The early dark seeped quickly into the town as we turned back in the direction of our hotel. Suddenly we saw the citadel walls blaze into yellow light.

"Oh, my God!" said Carly, "Look at that." Someone had thrown the switch. We started to run toward the lighted city, as we had in Sète, out of sheer high spirits. The walls and towers rose and fell with the level of the hillside. Below, the street lights were dim and mellow over round-topped trees. We searched for a way in, but the place was too massive.

"Hey," said Denise, "let's go back to our room and warm up. We can see the castle tomorrow. Let's decide what we want to do tonight."

Carly seemed to be the one with the best sense of direction because we found the Hotel des Pyrénées within a few minutes even though I was completely turned around. Back in our room, I pulled out the sheaf of brochures I'd picked up in Montpellier and threw them at the girls who now sat on the other bed. "Here, there's some night life in the area. You two pick."

Carly opened a map that had attractions printed on it. "There is a disco not far from here." She placed her finger on the destination. "We could walk."

A night of mindless music and dancing was just what I needed. I wouldn't let it remind me of meeting Geneviève a thousand years ago in Paris. "Let's go," I said. So when nine o'clock came, we left the hotel in short dresses, makeup, and platform heels. We also put on our new hats and mittens against the cold and went stumbling and laughing through the streets, following our leader Carly to the club. Amazingly, the small place was already in full swing. We danced together in a threesome, jostled by the crowd, occasionally joined by young men. I threw my body into the dancing. Hours later, we walked back into the night, sweaty and a little drunk from wine, and managed to disengage ourselves from a couple of persistent guys who followed us out the door.

Carly grabbed my hand and I grabbed Denise's and off we went, the three of us weaving like a ribbon through the crowd and into the deserted streets.

That night I slept better than I had all week, despite the lumpy bed. The next morning when I looked out the window, the trees were not tossing as vigorously as yesterday. We took turns in the shower down the hall and had our coffee and croissants in a café down the street. It was a slightly warmer day than yesterday and the sun was shining. We drove slowly around the walled city until we found the main entrance to the citadel.

"There's your drawbridge," said Carly. A stone bridge spanned a dry moat and led into a giant arched doorway in a fat tower. We drove through and soon saw that we had to leave the car in the parking lot as no cars were allowed on the village streets.

Brilliant shafts of sun cut into cool, gray shadows. Under our feet, cobbled roads and walkways passed under dark stone archways. The city was built from all kinds of stones, round and rectangular, bald and mossy, smooth and pitted.

We learned that the place went back to 3500 BC. The fortified city was rebuilt during different eras, and that's why the stones looked so different from each other. It fell into ruin and was renovated in the mid-1800s. We paid our money and toured the castle then climbed the ramparts and walked near the top of the outer wall. After that we descended into the quiet passageway that ran between the city's double walls. Above, clouds of birds flew back and forth. Wind whistled through the slits and holes on the top but couldn't reach us down below.

I wondered what it would feel like to live in a walled city. Would you feel safe? Or cut off from the world? I tried to imagine myself walking with Geneviève there. But she was far away on the outside of the wall we had put up between ourselves and I was on the inside.

Suddenly, though, Geneviève was with me, inside me, walking with me as though we were one person— one glorious person who was bigger and more loving than either of us was on our own and who forgave us our folly and lack of understanding. This other person was trying to show us that nothing could stop us from being together and we were foolish not to see that we were meant for each other. But just as I understood the message and was rejoicing in it, the feeling slipped away from me, and I was again only Sophie trailing dejectedly along after Denise and Carly.

During our wanderings in the city, we acquired a young French medical student from Montpellier. As unlikely as it would have seemed had I but known, Rémy turned out to be the catalyst I'd been hoping for.

Once he began walking with us on the ramparts,

he stayed with us for the rest of the day. He was slender, with wiry brown hair, a wry smile, and snapping brown eyes. I liked his name. I liked him. I wasn't surprised when he showed up; I'd half expected someone like him to appear. It was clear to me that he was spending a few days on his own and wanted the company more than anything else. Denise and I engaged him in conversation throughout the day, but Carly hardly talked to him at all.

The four us had lunch together and continued wandering the village streets until the afternoon light waned and we realized we were exhausted. I wasn't a bit surprised when Rémy asked if we wanted to do something that evening. Maybe go to the cinema? I said, "Sure!" right away, but Carly said, "No, thanks."

"Come by our hotel after we get a chance to rest," Denise said. She supplied him with directions and the name of the hotel. He waved and disappeared around a corner. Then we drove back over the bridge.

"Why did you tell him yes, just like that?" Carly asked me. "Why didn't you ask us first?"

"I don't know," I replied. "Why not? You don't have to come if you don't want to."

Chapter Thirty-one

Questions of the Heart

I ended up going out alone with Rémy because Carly refused to come along and Denise didn't want to leave her alone. We went to see *Papillon* at the local cinema. The last movie I'd seen was about butterflies too. This one was actually about a man in prison, but his name meant butterfly. We sat afterward over pizzas and I told him he should ask Denise out instead of me if he was looking for a girlfriend. "I'm gay," I said, blushing.

"It's okay," he said, smiling to show it didn't matter. "Maybe I will ask her on a date when we get home. Do you think she would say yes?" he asked seriously.

"Yeah, she might."

He walked me back to the hotel and we said good night on the street with a sturdy handshake. As soon as I opened the door to our room, I knew something was wrong. Carly's anxious, accusing eyes met mine from across the room.

In a tight voice she cried, "God, Sophie, I was so worried about you. Why did you stay out so long? How could you do this to me?"

"Do what? I..." I looked from Carly to Denise.

"We just sat here waiting for you to get back, hoping you'd be okay," Carly said. "Why do you have to take such chances? You don't even know him!"

"He's a nice guy," I said. "What's your problem? It was fine."

"Yeah, well you were lucky, then. How did you know he was going to be so nice?"

"Because I knew. I trust my own judgment," I said firmly, realizing that it was true and I was proud of it. I switched my gaze to Denise. "Didn't you think he was okay?"

"He seemed okay, yeah." I felt bad for Denise being cooped up with Carly all evening if this was what she'd been like.

"But he's French," Carly said insistently.

"So?"

"So he could have raped you, Sophie!" Carly broke down then. She threw herself facedown on the mattress, which began to shake with her sobs. Denise and I looked helplessly at each other. This was not the happy-go-lucky Carly we thought we knew. Denise sat beside her on the bed and stroked her back. I sat on the other bed facing them.

Carly's sobs subsided after a while and she got up and went to the sink to wash her face. We waited in silence as she scrubbed it with a towel before she sat back down, her face pink. "When I first got to Montpellier last summer, I met this French guy and he seemed really nice," she said. "He told me there was a party he wanted to go to. We went up to this apartment but no one was there. He raped me." She covered her eyes with her hands.

"Oh Carly!" We both put our arms around the still, silent form. "We didn't know," Denise said.

"The same thing happened to me," I said. "When I first got to Montpellier."

Carly raised her head slowly. "Really? You too?"

"Yes." We gazed at each other as if we had just found the other half of ourselves.

"So I'm not the only one?" her voice squeaked.

"No."

Carly continued to stare at me. "But...then how could you...how could you go out with some strange guy like that? Weren't you afraid? I could never have done that."

I shrugged. We sat there awhile, digesting the news that we had this major thing in common.

"Did you know about this?" Carly finally asked Denise.

"Yeah. I met her back then. She had to go to England for an abortion."

"An abortion? Oh God, this gets worse and worse," Carly said. "I want a glass of wine."

We dragged the bedside stand a few feet down between the beds to serve as a table, lowering the lamp that had been sitting on it to the floor. It cast weird shadows on the opposite wall.

"Did you guys eat?" I asked, getting the bag with the bread and sausage and opening Carly's pocketknife which had been sitting beside it. The knife had a corkscrew.

"Kind of," said Denise. "We got some soup down in the café. But I'm hungry again."

I opened the bottle of wine and prepared our snack. We settled ourselves against pillows and the headboard and Denise filled our plastic glasses.

"So tell me what happened," said Carly, taking a gulp of wine

"I had to go to England for an abortion. It's not legal here. And I saw Denise in Vert Bois and I told her my sob story."

"That was during the strike," Denise added.

"Yeah, I had to borrow money from her to get to England."

"A sucker is born every minute," Denise said with a smile.

I related the rest of the story. "You actually got pregnant from just one time?" asked Carly.

"I actually did," I said. "That's my luck."

"Well, I don't consider myself lucky, but I guess it could have been worse," said Carly. "Although I couldn't have done what you did today. Aren't you scared it might happen again?"

"What? Getting raped? No, I guess not."

"But you like girls. You wouldn't be susceptible the way I would."

"No, you're right. I didn't even like the guy. His friend was nice, though. That was Bernard."

"Bernard? That's how you met him? Gosh, if it was me I could never become friends with someone who was there. I couldn't bear to be reminded of it. You see how different we are? You're so much braver than me, Sophie. You just forge ahead. I don't know how you do it. I'm such a coward. I don't even want to date anyone right now. I just couldn't. I'm not ready. But you went and started seeing someone right away." She paused thoughtfully. "She's a woman, though. Does that make it different?"

"Not really," I replied. "Not the way you mean. I was still scared out of my mind when I first met her. I mean, I knew I was too screwed up to start a relationship. I tried to explain it to her without telling her about getting raped. I said I was a giddy girl who'd just left home, whereas she was a sophisticated older woman who should leave me alone. I mean, my God, she's five years older! But she just smiled and said it was okay. She loaded me up with French compliments. Anyway, I was so gone on her right from the beginning, I didn't have a chance. I was putty in her hands."

Denise laughed. "You met her in Montpellier first, right?"

"Uh-huh. Kind of."

"I thought you met in Paris," said Carly.

"Kind of both. I met her and Jean-Luc and Bernard all in the same crazy moment at Café Tout Va Bien." *That's when everything began. It's like someone opened a Pandora's box and it all came busting out.* "But we didn't have a chance to speak. I saw her, though. Maybe that's why I felt so…I don't know, like I knew her already when we met again."

"So then what happened?" asked Carly, wide-eyed.

"Well, we started a long-distance relationship. Every time we got together it was like a five-star movie. But it felt real too, like we had something together. In my mixed-up way, it worked for me. When she wasn't around, it gave me time to get my head together. But for her…I guess she just wants a normal kind of life where we see each other every day. Which I don't know if I can handle."

"I get it," said Carly. "I couldn't handle it either."

I nodded glumly. "I mean, when I picture myself living up there…For one thing, I would miss my friends. I'd miss you two." I looked at Denise. "You showed up in a certain moment of my life, you know? And you too, Carly. You both know things about me that no one else will ever know."

Denise nodded. "We feel the same about you, Sophie." She glanced at Carly who was leaning back on a mound of pillows, smiling, her long hair tumbled over her shoulders. "Right, Carly?" Carly assented vigorously. "I was brand new here," Denise went on. "Because of you I got to meet people and go to mime class and everything. It means a lot to me having you as a friend."

"Aw, shucks," I said.

Carly spoke up. "I don't want you to go either, Sophie. But I also don't want you to lose your girlfriend. She seems like a good person. I met her, you know, Denise?" Denise nodded. "So if she really wants you to move up there, maybe you should."

"But if I was in Paris, all I'd be able to think about would be her. I feel like I'd lose myself in the process. That's what scares me. Because at least now I think about other things besides her every day. Does that make any sense?"

Carly said firmly, "That does make sense. I get it."

"She thinks I'm a flake," I continued bitterly. "But I'm not! She says I'm always disappearing. She's afraid one day I won't come back. But she's wrong. I'm not going anywhere. Why can't she trust me? Why make me move when I'm not ready to? She's putting pressure on me. I'll go when I'm ready," I cried.

"So you are sure you want to go?" Denise asked.

My feelings of indignation deflated like a pinpricked balloon into something closer to despair. I sighed deeply. "I don't know. To be honest, I'm scared. I mean, I can't stay in France. I have another year left of school, Denise. What about my degree? I have to go back and finish it. Maybe I could stay for part of the summer, but then it's good-bye. When I leave, Geneviève will move on. She'll find other lovers. She's French. That's what they do. It's not like she is going to wait for me for a year. I'm trying to be realistic here. Maybe it's better just to end it now."

Carly disentangled herself from her pillows and came over to put her arm around me. "Or maybe not, Sophie. Look at the other side. Maybe she really loves you. Maybe she would wait for you, huh?"

I shook my head to try to clear it and looked at her. "I think she truly does love me, but we haven't known each other that long. What if it doesn't last? What if I move up there and we find out we aren't that crazy about each other after all? Then where would I be?"

"You'd be in the same place as everybody else who falls in love, Sophie," Carly replied sagely.

I nodded, giving in to my tears. "Oh God," I blubbered. "I'm a total basket case. I really don't know what to do."

"You asking for our advice?" asked Denise with a smile.

"I guess I am." I blotted my tears on the edge of the sheet. Even though we were the same age, Denise seemed to have been born older than me. She had the ability to understand other people's problems in a way that was harder for me because I was so wrapped up in my own head.

"Well," she said, "what occurs to me is, every time you talk about moving to Paris, I get the impression that the problem is not so much about moving per se, but about not being ready. Am I right?"

"Well, I guess so."

"So it's not so much about 'if' as about 'when.'"

"I guess. Logically, I know it would make sense to go at the start of next semester, but right now, I can't say for sure that's what I'm going to do."

Denise said, "You're not getting credit from the French university, are you?"

"No, I'll get credit from my own university when I get back. I'll have to take some equivalency exams."

"Right, so even if you go in the middle of next semester, it wouldn't matter, would it? You could just sit in on lectures and stuff."

"Well, yeah, but I prefer to be registered, so I can hand in homework and take the exams." I paused to think about it. "But, I guess you're right. I could switch in the middle if I wanted to, as long as I kept doing the work. Or I could wait till the end of next semester and just go up in the summer."

"So you could go anytime," Denise said."

"I guess so. But Geneviève..."

Carly said, "You said you're sure about moving, right?" I nodded. "So wouldn't it help if you told her that?"

"Yeah, that would help. That way I don't look like a total loser."

"Aren't you going up there for Christmas break?" Carly asked.

"Yeah. I mean, I was."

"Well, I was thinking, couldn't you just promise that you'll give her an answer then? As a sort of deadline?"

"But I don't know if I'll know by then."

"So what? Just tell her that anyway," Carly said. "It'll make her happy. Then at Christmas, if you're still not sure, you could say you needed more time."

I nodded. "I could do that. If I still go up there for Christmas. If she'll even talk to me again. I'm just so afraid she's given up on me. I haven't called her all week." I yawned. "Oh God. I can't think about it anymore. But thanks, guys. I do feel a lot better. Thank you for helping me figure this stuff out."

"No problem," said Carly. "I feel better too." She stood up and stretched. "Finding out we both had the same disaster happen to us kind of blew my mind at first. But it really helps to know I'm not the only one." She went over to her bag and pulled out her pajamas.

"I know, me too," I replied. "All this time and we didn't even know. We could have talked about it before."

Carly made a face. "I don't know if I would have wanted to before."

"Me neither, I guess."

"Well, the wine's all gone," said Denise. "Guess that means we'd better go to bed."

Chapter Thirty-two

Broken Plans

On Saturday morning, I dialed Geneviève's number from Vert Bois. My hand trembled on the receiver as the phone went on ringing. *Damn! I wanted to get this over with, but now I'll have to wait some more.* She was probably out with friends or shopping.

I tried after lunch again, but as I expected, she was still out. Before dinner, I called a third time, and she answered.

"*Allo?*" She sounded breathless.

"It's Sophie." My heart was pounding.

"Ah, Sophie."

"I'm sorry I didn't call all week," I said in a rush. "I was in Carcassonne with my friends. That's why I didn't call."

"Don't worry. I didn't sit by the phone all week." Her tone stung a little.

"I...I didn't think you did."

"Did you enjoy Carcassonne? I've heard it is very beautiful."

"It is!" I was close to tears. "Geneviève, I've felt so awful. Please don't be angry."

"I'm not angry." Again that neutral tone. "And you?"

"I was a little. You should have trusted me."

"Ah, *oui?*"

"Of course," I said. "I'm going to move to Paris!"

"Really?" Her voice brightened a little.

"It makes sense to move at the new semester."

"*Oui?*"

"So probably that is what I will do."

"Probably?"

"Yes. I..." I sucked in my breath. This was the hard part because it was almost a lie. Not actually a lie, but I had no idea whether it was true either. "I will tell you for sure when I come up for Christmas break," I finished. "Okay?"

"Okay. *C'est bien.*" She sounded so matter-of-fact. Didn't she care? Wasn't she even excited?

"So that's okay?"

"Of course. It's great," she added.

"And you're not breaking up with me?"

"No..." I could feel her smiling slightly when she said it with those cupid-bow lips.

"Geneviève, do you still want me to come up and visit this month?"

"Sure. Come next weekend if you can." Her tone was warming up a bit.

"Okay, I will."

"And call me more often. I can't call you, you know. Call me every day if you want."

"I will."

"So. Until next weekend."

"Until next weekend," I repeated and hung up. I dropped down on a chair near the phone and put my head in my hands as chattering students passed by. I didn't know whether I wanted to laugh or cry. She had sounded so distant for most of the phone call. But she accepted my promise. And she didn't seem to be angry anymore; a little remote maybe, but not upset like last

time. Even though things didn't feel as good as they used
to be, we hadn't broken up. And she wanted me to call
her every day. That was something.

By the time I talked to her on Thursday, the Paris
weekend was off. She had to go to Dijon again. The high
hopes that had been fueling my heart for the past week
deflated. I had been looking forward to the weekend to
try to reestablish things with her. But now that would
have to wait. She didn't ask me to meet her in Dijon as
she did with Lyon. But then Dijon was too far away to
meet. After that it would be December—a busy month
for her at work because they would be staging parties.
Then in three weeks it would be time for me to come
up for winter break. Neither of us said anything about
rescheduling my weekend visit. But I wished that she
had at least asked.

❧ ❧ ❧ ❧

Bernard finally found a room in the old city near
the restaurant. He'd obtained his test information
and applied to the university for spring semester. One
morning, I stopped by his new digs. After climbing past
dusty stairs dank with cooking smells, I knocked on his
door on the second floor, hoping he'd be home since
he worked nights. It was nearly 10:00 a.m., but he took
so long to come to the door, I was sure I'd gotten him
out of bed.

His curly hair was matted and he was still in his
pajamas. He kissed me with a welcoming smile. "*Salut*,
Sophie. Come in."

"How's it going?" I said, looking around. I'd
walked him home once before but had never been inside.
The room was minuscule, with a bed, a dresser, and a

table with a hot plate on one end and a sink and a tiny fridge on the other. There was a view of the street two stories down where a café and a tabac stood side by side.

"Well, I've been better," he said, yawning. "Do you like my place?"

"I love it," I said. "So what's wrong?"

"Do you want some coffee?" He filled a pan with water and turned on the hot plate. Then he sat on a chair at the table and gestured for me to sit down. "Jean-Luc came to the crêperie two nights ago. He waited for me to get off, sitting in the restaurant. I knew he was there—they told me. I was scared I'd do something crazy. Sophie, I was so happy to see him. We went out for a drink. He said he missed me. He said he loved me. He wanted me to come back. He's going to Paris in two weeks and he wants me to go with him."

"What did you say?" I asked tensely.

"I said no way. I said I want someone who would be just with me, like I told him before. He said he loved me, but he just needed to be with a woman from time to time. 'It's just the way I am,' he said."

"Well, at least he's not pretending he's going to change."

Bernard poured the water through the filter filled with coffee grounds. "I said no. We got into a little fight and I ended up crying. He asked me to think it over. I'm afraid I'll go back to him, Sophie. It was so nice to see him again. I remembered all the good times…and now he knows where I live. He was waiting for me in front of my building last night."

"Really? That's kind of creepy, isn't it? How'd he find out where you live?"

"Friends, I guess. I've told a few people."

"Sounds like the wrong people."

"He was crying. I've never seen him cry before, Sophie. He's always so tough. He asked if he could come up. I was tempted. I mean, I do care about him."

"He's just trying to manipulate you, Bernard. Remember this is the man who raped me."

"Well, I did say no. I ran upstairs. He didn't try to follow me or anything. Sophie, I'm afraid. Could I stay with you for a few days until he leaves?"

"Are you kidding? Do you think I want Jean-Luc coming to my house?"

"He wouldn't find out."

"He could follow you there! No way, Bernard. I don't want to see him. You keep him away from me! And keep telling him no, just like you did."

"I just don't trust myself. What if I say yes?"

"You have to be strong. Do you remember what he said to you? That you are completely lost? Anyone who would say that…"

"Oh. *Oui*, you're right."

I gave him a long, hard look when I left and said, "Remember, you can't come to my place, Bernard, while Jean-Luc's in town. Not even once. Do you understand me?"

"Sure, I understand."

"You have to be strong. Do you want to go back to your old life? Do you want to cry again the next time you break up? He's not going to change. He told you so."

"No, I know. I'll be strong," he promised me, draining his coffee cup. "So what about you? How's the girlfriend? Didn't you go out of town?"

I told him about Carcassonne and explained to him what was going on with Geneviève. "I have to decide what to do," I said.

"So? Just follow your heart." He made it sound so

simple. But he knew as well as I did that the heart was not a simple organ.

❧❧❧❧

"Are you going to come stay with us during winter break?" my cousin Anna asked me over the phone.

"No, I'm staying with a friend in Paris. I'm going to her parents' house in Reims for Christmas."

Anna digested this information. "So, come for Sunday dinner after you arrive."

"Can I bring my friend?"

"Sure."

I asked her for Jean-Pierre's number at school in Paris. She dictated it to me. "I'll call you as soon as I arrive in Paris, around the twentieth," I said. "Au revoir."

"Hey, Jean-Pierre," I said when I got him on the phone. "I want to bring Geneviève to the farm and I was wondering if you would talk to your mom about her, kind of explain the situation?" A sudden suspicion darted into my head. "You haven't already told her, have you? You and your brothers?"

"No, no. We promised we wouldn't. So you don't want to tell her yourself, eh?"

"I can't. I just can't say the word 'lesbian' to her. It would be so much easier if you told her. I know she'll still ask me about it, but...would you mind? You could get Casimir or Claude to help."

"Uh, okay, but there will be paybacks."

"Oh, come on, how hard is it? It'll be like gossip. Sophie has a lesbian girlfriend. I bet you've been dying to tell anyway. What kind of payback?"

"Oh, I don't know. You could go to bed with me,

or...take me out to dinner with your *amoureuse*."

"Make that coffee. Okay, you're on. Will you let me know, please, when you do it? I'll give you Geneviève's number. She'll give me the message."

The message came through the next time I talked to Geneviève. She sounded annoyed. "Your cousin said to tell you that his mom knows what we do in bed. He was laughing, and he said just to tell you that. What the hell does he mean? What have you told him?"

"Relax, he's crazy." I explained that Jean-Pierre had actually done us a favor.

Chapter Thirty-three

Christmas Break

I filled my backpack with clothes for Paris, and as I did so, I also mentally packed the day I'd danced with the bees, the wine festival, the mime classes, the meals at the restau-U with my friends, along with my private room. I needed to weigh all that I would lose against what I would gain if I decided to move to Paris next semester. Even though I'd told Geneviève I would decide for sure by winter break, I had only told her "probably," about next semester, which allowed me the space in the past four weeks to keep my sense of freedom and independence. I was grateful for that.

On the train ride Thursday night, I lay awake as Carly and Rose slept in bunks across from me. They were going to visit friends from Antioch College on rue Mouffetard. I listened to the roar of the wheels on the rails while watching a new moon rise out the window. In my mind, I saw Bernard with his bright, childlike eyes, telling me to do what my heart said was right. My breath kept catching in my throat. I had to remind myself to breathe.

Then she was there, her two feet planted on the platform, a smile on her face. Poor, fickle, contrary creature that I was, I threw myself at her like a lost child.

"Sophie," she said, laughing, "are you all right?"

"Yes, I'm fine. I missed you!"

At rue Vivienne, the first thing I did was look at Geneviève's little sculpture of Les Innocents. It was just as she'd described it that day after the Catacombs, with a trench full of tiny skulls circling the fountain.

"I like it," I told her.

That weekend had been so strange and contradictory. Back then I was still in traveling mode. But I lived somewhere now. I could feel Montpellier claiming me, pulling against the joy of our reunion like a tug-of-war. I sighed and clutched the back of my neck, trying to ease the tension there. My life was still a contradiction.

"You're tired," Geneviève said. "Take a nap. I've got things to do."

I nodded and turned toward the bedroom, dropping my outer clothes one by one on the floor. Instead of leaving, Geneviève climbed into bed with me. She held me from behind, her hands warm against my skin.

"Are you really moving up here?" she whispered.

"Yes." I was no longer sleepy. Her hands began to roam and soon we were locked in an embrace from which it took three-quarters of an hour to loosen.

Later, she left to do errands, and I slept most of the day, nestled happily under the down comforter. In the late afternoon, I awoke and took a bath, then dressed in the long, paisley wool dress I'd bought recently with my latest check from home. I pulled on leggings and warm socks under it, then poured myself a glass of wine and nestled into the sofa with a book of Rimbaud's poetry I'd found on her shelf. But before I had gotten more than a couple of pages into it, I dropped the book to the floor at the sound of her key in the lock.

We had dinner that night in a cheerful restaurant

on the Champs Élysées. I loved the fairy Christmas lights strung all over the trees, the bustle of Parisian life on the sidewalk out front. I got pretty tipsy as I chattered to Geneviève about all the details of the last few weeks in Montpellier, about Bernard's situation with Jean-Luc, about my visit to Carcassonne, and about Rémy, who was now dating Denise.

It was hard to understand that we wouldn't have to say good-bye after the usual two days. We normally had to pack so much into our short visits, but now we had two weeks to relax. I was in no hurry to talk about the future. I knew the subject would come up. But for now, I was just going to kick back and enjoy myself.

The next day, Saturday, I jumped at the sound of the phone ringing in the kitchen. I was not yet used to that sound. Her employer was calling to ask her to pick up some paintings. Geneviève had taken time off work for the holidays but with the agreement that she would run a few errands when they needed her. I went along with her to the art gallery. I loved looking at art, especially modern. I found it odd that Geneviève would mix antiques with abstract art, but she had an eye for harmony. She went by color, weight, and shape, not time periods. I watched as she carefully carried the wrapped paintings and stacked them in the back of the blue van.

Sunday, we would visit my cousins. Monday, we were going to shop at the flea market for some upholstery fabric. While we were there, we'd do some Christmas shopping.

❧❧❧❧

I snuggled closer to the warm body beside me and tried to go back to sleep but couldn't, remembering it was Sunday and we were going to the farm to have lunch with my cousins.

"Sophie? Are you awake?"

"Yes," I said, stretching luxuriously.

"Are you nervous about my meeting your cousins?"

"A little."

"I'll win over your battle-ax of a cousin with my charm, you know."

"She's a tough one. But, yes, you have plenty of charm, so you probably will."

"I bet my family will love you, too."

"I can't believe you never brought any of your girlfriends home before," I said.

"Did I say that? Actually, I did bring someone once, the first one, Brigitte. I was all excited and in love. I thought my parents would be so happy for me. That was while I was still naïve."

"What happened?"

"Everyone acted fine except *Maman*. She was just kind of cold and distant. Didn't talk to Brigitte except to say hello. Stayed on the other side of the room whenever possible. Brigitte was hurt. I never did it again. That's all."

"Wow. What makes you think it will be any different now?"

"She's had a lot of time to get used to the way I am. I certainly talked about the women I was dating around her. I made a point of it. Anyway, I want to give her a chance. And if she still acts that way, well, I think you can handle it."

"I hope so."

She looked at me. "*Chérie*, do we have to go to Amsterdam? I'll hardly have any time to be alone with you. Why can't we just stay here after Christmas?"

"But I've been looking forward to it! Kari and Annik have a guest bedroom, so we can be alone." I paused to think about why I wanted to go so much. Maybe it was the chance to be around a lesbian couple so I could see what it might be like with Geneviève.

She took me in her arms. "It's just that this is the first visit we've had more than two days together. And we're going to go stay with my family on the twenty-fourth, and we're seeing your cousins today. My pals want to see you. Sylvie has invited us for dinner. I'm just afraid that I'll blink my eyes and you'll be gone again."

I kissed her arm, which was next to my face. "Well, I guess we do have a lot going on. We could postpone that trip, I don't mind."

We stopped at a flower shop on the way to the garage to get Geneviève's van, coming out with a mixture of daisies, chrysanthemums, and tiger lilies that took up half the back seat.

"You couldn't have gotten something smaller?" I asked as we drove away. "I don't know if these will even fit in the dining room at my cousin Anna's house."

"Ha. Your cousin will love them," Geneviève replied, turning onto the long road flanked by poplar trees that led to the farm courtyard.

I got out and opened the gate. We parked near a pile of what looked like a hay stack, but was actually a mix of straw, manure, and compost, steaming in the cool air. The smell reminded me of the farm. A cow mooed from the barn.

I smiled as Geneviève walked a stride ahead carrying the huge bouquet. She was wearing her charcoal-gray wool pants and baby-blue wool turtleneck under the leather jacket. On her ears was a pair of small silver earrings. I was dressed in my long dress again.

Anna took the flowers with a big smile lifting her pink cheeks and causing her eyes to squint into slits. "*Bonjour, mademoiselle,*" she said.

"She's called Geneviève," I said.

Anna continued to smile, searching in the cupboard for a vase to put the flowers in. I heard voices in the other room and my three younger cousins emerged to greet us, devouring Geneviève with their eyes. Yvonne came out too and hugged me, carrying Claudine on her hip.

The three men shook hands in turn with the guest then came to give me their kisses. "Come and sit down," Casimir said to Geneviève, gesturing toward the living room adjacent to the dining room. The branches of a Christmas tree showed from the doorway.

"Can I help you, Anna?" She nodded and handed me the flowers to put on the table. I could hide behind them if need be. Geneviève was already taking part in a lively conversation. The flowers did seem too big for the table, so I put them on the sideboard. When I went back to Anna she looked grim now that the guest was in the other room.

"Sophie," she whispered fiercely. "It's not possible! You are not lesbienne. I don't believe it."

"I think I am." I shifted my feet nervously.

She sighed and handed me some lettuce to wash and shred. At the stove, she stirred the soup vigorously for a few minutes. "Do your parents know about this?"

"No."

"But, what about marriage? Children, eh?"

A good question. I decided not to go into the reproduction issue; it was still a raw one for me. Anna took the pile of lettuce from me, dropped it into a salad bowl, and began tossing it with dressing. I could hear laughter from the other room.

"You can set the table," Anna said. As I trooped back and forth to the dining room I heard rapid French. Geneviève was talking about a film she'd seen, a comedy with Jacques Tati. I entered with a stack of plates to see Jean-Pierre leap up and imitate the tall, ungainly comedian.

"No, no, it was like this," said Casimir, getting up to join Jean-Pierre. Now there were two Tatis wobbling around the room. I retreated, laughing.

Georges came in from the dairy and we all sat down around the table. The courses slowly followed each other, Anna leaving the table to bring the next one. Sunday dinner often took three hours, especially when there was a new addition to the table. Georges watched everything with his usual amused smile. I kept glancing at Anna. She didn't say much but sat stolidly eating and regarding Geneviève, who included her in the conversation.

"What do you think, Anna, about the direction France is going? Casimir thinks we will be Socialist by this time next year."

"I hope not. I supported de Gaulle! Look what socialism is like in Poland," she said angrily. "Do we want to be controlled by the government?"

"It won't be like that here, Maman," said Casimir. "We'll have a good life: free medicine, good wages, more vacation, and paid maternity leave."

She frowned. "My life is about hard work. Do you think I'll get a vacation under socialism? If so, I'll vote for Mitterrand."

The chicken, which I knew Anna had killed, scorched, and plucked herself, was superb. The wine kept flowing, and we paused between courses. Geneviève asked to hold Claudine and was now bending down, talking baby talk, her hair falling forward over her eyes. *She really does love children.* It was still hard for me to think about that evening when Geneviève had reacted so strongly to the news of my abortion. But the sharp pain and joy of that time had smoothed over like the stitches in knitting a few rows back.

We followed the younger cousins outdoors to take a tour of the farm. I took Geneviève's hand as we paraded past the fields, the vegetable patch, the strawberry patch, the dairy, the cheese shop, and the chickens.

"You must come again, Geneviève," Anna said genuinely as we were leaving the house. I looked at her with surprise. Then she turned a sour look on me. "Don't forget to write your parents."

Chapter Thirty-four

Christmas Market

The next day at the Paris flea market, shoppers swarmed through stalls that sold everything from clothing and jewelry to pots and pans. I clung to Geneviève's hand.

"This place is like a maze, eh?" she said. "So don't wander off. We'll have time to do some Christmas shopping after I finish my work stuff, okay?"

At the fabric stall, the dealer asked a neighbor to keep an eye on his counter, and we followed him into a warehouse across the alley, climbing a dusty wooden stairway to a large chilly room with bolts of cloth on floor-to-ceiling shelves. Geneviève pointed and the dealer climbed nimbly up a ladder to fetch the bolt she wanted. She fingered different fabrics, comparing them with swatches she'd taken from her black leather shoulder bag. Even with those for reference, I marveled at how she could carry the memory of some Parisian apartment in her mind. She had told me that one of her assets as a buyer was her near-perfect visual memory. When she had decided on a bolt in nubby tangerine, the man cut it for her, wrapped it, and carried her selection back to the booth for us to pick it up on our way out.

Afterward, we went from stall to stall, browsing through china. Her mother collected antique *faience*. Geneviève finally selected a delicate hand-painted teacup and saucer with a gold handle from about 1920. The clerk handed her the package, which she put in a string bag.

We rounded the corner to another row of booths displaying leather bags and continued on to where the jewelry stalls began. Suddenly I stopped.

"What's wrong?" Geneviève paused beside me.

A cold chill ran through my body. I was sure it was him! Stringy brown hair falling over his face—who else could that be? Jean-Luc! His narrow back was bent to select something from the case for a customer.

"What's wrong, *chérie*?" Geneviève took my arm.

My heart hammered wildly. "It's Jean-Luc!" I whispered, ducking behind a man with broad shoulders.

She followed my eyes through the crowd. "Bernard is there too," she said. I peeked around the man. Bernard sat placidly beside Jean-Luc.

"I have to get out of here!" I hissed.

"I think we should go say hello," Geneviève said calmly. "Why not? You have no reason to be afraid of him. Come on. Let's go find out what's going on."

I followed her on shaking legs, holding tightly to her hand. Bernard smiled in happy surprise when he saw us. Jean-Luc looked up. His blue eyes flared in shock, but he didn't move a muscle in his face.

"Bonjour, Sophie." He didn't extend his hand. "*Ça va?*" His eyes flicked down to our joined hands.

I looked at him with contempt, saying nothing. Bernard must have told him about the pregnancy and abortion. I don't know what I wanted him to say, but a casual "How's it going" was not it. I felt my stomach rise toward my throat. Afraid of vomiting, I pulled on Geneviève's hand. "Come for a walk with us, Bernard," I said. As we moved away, I looked back. Jean-Luc held up two fingers in a peace sign before the crowd closed around him.

I was too shaken to speak. "What are you doing here?" Geneviève asked Bernard. "Are you back with Jean-Luc?"

"*Mais, non.* We're friends now."

"Friends? How can you be friends with a rapist?" I said.

Looking abashed, Bernard said, "I don't know..."

"You better figure out your priorities," I said, still trembling inside. "You didn't tell him where I live, did you?"

"No, of course not." Bernard said, his brown eyes wide with indignation.

"I just wanted to make sure." My voice softened. "So what are you going to do for Christmas?" After all, I reasoned, I shouldn't blame Bernard for what Jean-Luc did.

A lost-puppy look appeared on his face, and he answered, "Maybe I'll be with friends in Montpellier. I've had a couple invitations."

I hoped it was true. But I knew his friends in Montpellier were also friends of Jean-Luc's and might feel awkward about inviting them both even if they were friends now.

"I'm going back," said Bernard, leaning to kiss me. "*Bonne Noël.* See you soon."

≈≈≈≈

For the first part of the trip to Reims the next day, we were quiet as Geneviève drove the van out of the city. The back seat was filled with presents. Geneviève had on a repeat of what she'd worn to my cousins' farm. I made an effort to dress up too in a red-and-green tartan skirt, a dark green sweater, and tights. My hoop earrings from England completed the ensemble. The navy wool coat I'd bought at the flea market in hopes of impressing her family was in the back seat. I didn't want to wear my tatty fake-fur-lined jacket to Reims.

"Geneviève," I said suddenly, "I'm glad we ran into Jean-Luc yesterday."

"You are? I thought you said you never wanted to see him again."

"I know. I didn't. But I was going around all the time afraid of bumping into him, you know? I mean, it was always in the back of my mind in Montpellier, and even here, because I knew he was in Paris. And now I don't care. It doesn't matter anymore."

"Doesn't it? So you're free."

"*Oui.*"

We drove along in silence for a while, Geneviève staring at the road. She turned on the radio, which played Christmas music. I watched the procession of snow-covered fields go by, one after another. We could have been in Minnesota, except the carols were in French. What was my mother doing now? Maybe cooking Christmas eve dinner with my little brother under foot? I could picture her keeping him busy putting sprinkles and chocolate stars on the doughy cutouts. Suddenly, I wanted desperately to be home with my family, sitting around the tree, singing carols, opening presents, not in this strange country. I wanted everything to be safe, comfortable, and familiar, the way Christmas ought to be.

Geneviève's voice interrupted my thoughts. "Sophie, do you really think you will transfer to Paris at the end of the semester? My family is going to ask me a lot of questions about you, and I don't know the answers. Come on, please tell me."

Here it was. For some reason my mouth wasn't working. I sucked in my breath and felt cold. *What is going on, Sophie? Why don't you say yes and get it over with?* I had thought the decision was made. It was fun feeling like a couple the last few days. I felt like I belonged in the environment here with her. I was going to say yes; I would move up here to be with her at the end of the semester. Denise said you can't count on this kind of love happening twice. You have to grab it while you can and hold on tight, and I agreed with her.

My eyes filled with tears. I struggled to speak, but Geneviève beat me to it. "Don't you love me?" she asked tersely. "Don't you want to be with me?"

"Of course I do."

"But?" she prompted me.

"Well…" I said the first thing that popped into my head. "What about Jade? She's coming in a few weeks. I can't just abandon her. She's all signed up for classes!"

"Invite her to move up here too. You two could get a room together."

"Yes. I could do that," I said hesitantly.

Geneviève sighed with frustration. "Do you just want to continue visiting each other like this? Before you know it, the school year will be over, and you will go back to the US. I'll never see you again!"

I struggled to make sense of this conversation, one that I hadn't expected to be having. "I guess I need a little more time," I said. "I'm sorry." She stared at the road and didn't answer, her hands tight on the wheel. "I told you I'd move up and I will!" I said with a little more heat. "Who cares when?" She stared at the road still without answering. "Look," I said, "I'll talk to Jade about it, okay?"

"Fine." We drove along in silence for about half an hour. I kept stealing glances at Geneviève. Finally, I noticed that she looked more relaxed, humming along with the radio. Maybe things would be okay. After all, she had a way of being able to handle situations in a way that I couldn't. For example, last September after her anger about the abortion, she pulled herself together, hadn't she? She worked it out through her artwork that night and by tramping around Paris with me. And after our fight in November she accepted my decision. Maybe it was because she was older and more mature. Or maybe it was because she was French. It seemed to me that the French didn't take things as seriously as we Americans did. But that probably wasn't right. They'd perfected the art of living more than we had, that was it. They called it "*savoir vivre*"—knowing how to live. Akin to "*savoir faire*," knowing what to do. Maybe just being in France, I'd eventually pick up one or the other.

Twin square cathedral towers showed gray against the overcast sky as we approached. In Reims, we made a detour through the center of town. Geneviève showed me the cathedral and basilica, and we passed along a square with a tall fountain, shops, and cafés. There was a busy market on one side. For an instant, I remembered Jean-Luc's hard eyes.

"That's the Christmas market," she said. "Lots of last-minute shoppers. Hold on." She made a turn. "I want to show you my favorite place." We drove for a few minutes and stopped at another square. A statue of a soldier in armor on horseback stood in the middle. "Who's that?" I asked.

"That's Saint Joan of Arc!" she exclaimed. "You thought it was a man, didn't you?"

I nodded. "You can't tell it's a woman until you get close up."

"She's here because Reims is where the kings were always crowned and she got the throne back for Charles VII. His coronation was here in 1430."

We pulled up next in front of the Fournier family home. It was a two-story house with a garden, a red-tile roof, and an iron fence in the front. As soon as we opened the gate, a small girl wearing red tights and a full skirted red dress emerged from the front door. "*Tante* Genny!" She skipped down the walk toward us then stopped short to stare at me with huge gray eyes.

"Minette! This is my friend Sophie. Come kiss me!" Minette came, forgetting about me for the moment, and Geneviève picked her up, lifted her in the air squealing, and held her in a hug. Others were coming out of the house now. I watched, fascinated as people of different shapes and sizes approached. Holding the little girl, Geneviève said, "*Maman, c'est Sophie.*" A small woman took my hand and shook it. Her eyes were dark and narrow as she scrutinized me. Her mouth was like Geneviève's, the way the lips curved up at the corners.

A large man stepped up. "*Bonjour*, Sophie. I am Geneviève's *papa*." His eyes twinkled and I saw he was an older, male version of his daughter. Geneviève put Minette down and hugged her parents.

"Where is Gabriel?"

"He'll be here soon," said her mother.

Behind her parents stood a pretty young woman whose bleached blond hair jarred with her dark eyes and brows. A tall, serious-looking young man stood behind her. "*Salut,*" she said, taking Minette's hand and, shielding her eyes with her other hand, she smiled shyly at me.

"Sophie, this is my sister Vivienne. My brother-in-law, François."

"Bonjour." Looking around at all the strange faces, I tried to imagine the possibility of coming here for Sunday dinners. Something began to quiver inside me. I knew I wasn't ready for it. I didn't feel prepared to meet Geneviève's family either, but, too late, that's what I was doing. I let myself be swept into the crowd and into the house. I was going to practice my savoir vivre if it killed me.

Chapter Thirty-five

Jade Comes Back

Geneviève and I spent the rest of my break roaming Paris, sometimes meeting one or more of her friends at cafés. We hung out with Carly and Rose on rue Mouffetard, and one night we had dinner in the city with my male cousins.

We bickered from time to time about my moving to Paris, but nothing that counted as a full-out fight. The visit lacked the five-star quality of some of the others, but we still managed to have fun. The night before I left, I lay awake while she slept, wondering what was so different this time. We still loved each other, but... maybe it was that all the time I'd known Geneviève, we had been on an upward trajectory, climbing toward some climax, and now...it was like we'd passed it by. Somehow, we were standing still, and this was my fault. My feelings were locked up inside me, no longer moving and living as they had been, no longer sending out rays of possibility and hope.

Finally, as the dim light started creeping in under the bamboo blinds, I let go. The French didn't lie awake and worry all night. Or maybe they did for part of the night, but when the time came to sleep, they slept. They shrugged their shoulders in that special way they have and let it go. Hardly anything mattered enough to make you lose a night's sleep or miss a meal. Maybe a revolution did or if your house burned down, but even then, at some point, you still shrugged and moved on.

The next day at the train station, Geneviève and I hugged good-bye. "Thank you," I said into her neck. "I had a good time. You've been very patient with me." My eyes filled with tears.

"Talk to Jade," she replied.

"Yes, I will! *Oui!*" We kissed, and I stepped onto the train, only able to find a seat on the opposite side. So I didn't wave good-bye but sat morosely in my seat all the way south.

❧❧❧❧

I spent an intense few weeks going to classes, finishing essays, and taking exams, which I was pretty sure I failed. At least I'd tried my best. Within the general whirlwind of finals, I talked to my friends one by one, and they all tried to counsel me.

I ran into Bernard at Vert Bois the first day I was back. Shrugging in a typically French fashion, he smiled his toothy smile. "So, you can't decide? But you love her." I nodded. "So go to her. What is the problem?"

I just shook my head and shrugged, imitating his own gesture.

Talking to Denise wasn't much better. She said, "Remember the story about my parents?"

"Of course I remember," I replied irritably. "They broke up because of going away to different colleges and they were lucky to get back together a hundred years later. I know. If I mess things up with Geneviève, I'll be like them."

"So don't let that happen," she instructed me. But all I could do was shrug.

The next day Jade stepped off the train. Her familiar grin lit me up inside. We hugged by the side of the train as memories of our travels buzzed through me. Life was new and exciting then. We were so innocent, getting on trains, checking into youth hostels, meeting new people, traveling with Natalie. We didn't have any real sense of responsibility.

Jade and I walked companionably from the station toward my house, she with her backpack and me carrying her suitcase. I realized we hadn't been together in Montpellier since those first days that had so changed my life.

"Oh God, Jade. Remember when we were here last? We were so stupid!"

"Yeah, I guess we were," she said reflectively. "But...we were on an adventure, Sophie. The biggest one of our lives. We didn't want to say no to anything, did we? Can you imagine if we'd done the smart thing and had Jean-Luc take us back?"

"Yeah, I wouldn't have gotten pregnant!"

"But we wouldn't have known that. We would have been just sitting there in the dorm regretting the decision, I bet. We would have felt like we were missing out. So maybe we did the right thing by staying with them."

I looked at her in surprise. "The right thing? Are you kidding me?"

"Yes! No! I mean, we learned a lot from the experience, right?"

"Of course, but..."

"Well, that's life, isn't it, Sophie? Doing things, not knowing how they will turn out?"

I didn't know how to answer her. I took out my key and opened the little gate in the wall and waved to Madame, who was crossing the garden. As we approached my door, I said, "It wasn't like sleeping out in the Black Forest, Jade. There are certain things in life you don't ever want to do again. So yeah, you learn from the experience. You learn that even if you have to become a completely different person, it's worth it so you don't ever do anything like that again."

Jade said, "Right on! That's what I meant. Sorry if I sounded kind of flip. I didn't mean to."

I smiled at her. It was good to have her back. I opened the door with my other key, and Jade scrambled up and down the stairs exploring everything. "Wow, this is a great place, Sophie!"

I made us cheese omelets for dinner and we carried the food out to the table on the little terrace outside the double-glass doors. It was cool, but with our coats and hats on we were able to enjoy the last of the sun as it crept behind the garden wall.

I looked at her fondly as she pushed her glasses up with one hand and ate with the other. I said, "Jade, Geneviève wants me to move to Paris."

Before I could finish, she cried out, "Sophie! I come all this way to see you and you're just going to run out on me!" She peered at me accusingly.

"No, no, Jade. I'm not going to run out on you. I...I was going to ask if you want to come with me. Geneviève said she'd help us find a room." I squinted at her. I couldn't tell how she was taking this idea. I wasn't even sure yet what I thought of it. "But you're all signed up for classes here. And anyway..."

"So what?" she interrupted me sharply. She put down her fork. A very Jade-like glint had appeared in her eyes. It was just the way she'd looked when we talked about leaving for Paris so many months ago.

"What do you mean, so what?"

"I only came here because of you, Sophie! I never liked Montpellier that much. I can find the same course up there. I'd much rather be in Paris."

"But Jade, if I go up to be with Geneviève I…I just feel like I'll lose everything that we had when we were traveling last summer. You know? If I move to Paris, I'll have to be an adult!" I struggled between the urge to cry and to laugh at myself. "I don't know if I am ready to grow up. I'm not even twenty-one yet!"

"You're almost twenty-one, Sophie. Come on. Let's do it!"

I should have known. I'd forgotten about Jade's infatuation with Paris. Maybe deep down I hadn't forgotten and was just waiting for her to help me with a decision I was too scared to make on my own. Now Jade's enthusiasm swept it all away. I stood up and went inside to get my purse.

"Where are you going?"

"I have to call Geneviève."

"Okay. Go. I'll get unpacked."

I ran all the way to Vert Bois. "*Chérie,*" I began breathlessly.

She could tell by my voice. "You are coming?"

"Yes! *Oui!*" I did my best to kiss her through the telephone line.

꧁꧂

Jade and I pushed a luggage trolley away from the train at Gare Saint-Lazare when we caught sight of Geneviève. I was startled by her face. It was the same face I knew, and yet very different, almost like a stranger's—brighter and happier than I had ever seen it. I thought of the Winged Victory statue at the Louvre. This was it. Geneviève was the goddess Victory; we both were, winged and triumphant. She quickened her steps and grabbed me under the arms, whirling me around. I laughed. We forgot about Jade and all the other people surging around us.

After loading my boxes and backpack along with Jade's suitcases into the blue van, Geneviève maneuvered through the traffic toward rue Vivienne. She glanced back at Jade. "Jade, how would you like to go with Sylvie to a dinner with her friends? She has invited you. You would meet a real French family."

"Oh! Sure." Jade seemed to understand that we wanted to be alone and that Geneviève had anticipated and planned for this. "That would be nice. But can I wear this?" She glanced down at her jeans.

"Of course. It is casual. You look very nice."

We dropped Jade off at Sylvie's and ended up sitting on the sofa smiling at each other.

"Geneviève, I don't have to go back south again. No more trains!"

She squeezed my hand. "Not unless we are going somewhere together."

"Right, or…unless one of us is going alone but planning to come back."

"Back home." She smiled into my eyes.

"Home! Paris is home. I just can't believe it!" I crowed.

"Believe it, ma *chérie*. We are home together."

I sucked in my breath with sudden worry. "But Jade and I were planning to look for a room together."

"You will be here in my city. That is enough for me."

"Although maybe…" I grinned coyly. "Who

knows, Jade may find something small that she likes."

"Whatever." She stretched out her neck and kissed me tenderly. "You are here, my love, and that is all that matters to me."

❧❧❧❧

Jade and I tramped through the streets looking for a room. Back on rue Vivienne each night, Jade slept on the couch and I shared Geneviève's bed.

One morning, during our second week in Paris, I realized that I considered this apartment home and didn't want to leave. When I told Jade this, she didn't mind. In fact, she seemed to have expected it. Sylvie soon found her a little garret at the top of an old building down rue Vivienne from Geneviève's that had surely once been a maid's room. It reminded me of Bernard's with its tiny table, hot plate, and narrow bed.

After the first joy of moving to Paris, I had to start all over at the university, making friends, finding out where everything was. I had just done that in Montpellier and now I had to do it all again. I registered for a Realism class. I'd soon be reading Zola and Stendhal.

During those first few weeks, I spent a lot of time walking the streets by myself. Geneviève was probably glad to see me go out the door on my solitary tramps. I was not always good company in those days. I half expected her to change her mind about having me live with her, but she didn't.

I thought about the friends I'd left behind, especially Denise, Bernard, and Carly. In my mind, I examined how each of those three had helped me in different ways.

Denise had trusted me from the beginning. That

had given me a huge boost.

And Bernard. I didn't see it before, but because of him, I couldn't completely vilify Jean-Luc. I had to step back and deal with him as a real person who was closely connected to Bernard.

I'd gotten to know Carly a lot better since she'd revealed that she too had been raped when she first came to Montpellier. Talking about it had helped both of us.

One night I climbed all the way up to the top of Montagne Saint-Geneviève. I had tea in the same little café where she and I had sat and talked that balmy September evening. It was too cold to sit outside now, but from the window, I saw the same view down the shadowy street.

It was as though my young self from all those months ago was sitting with me at that table now, trying to explain her fears to Geneviève. And I was a slightly older cousin or something, patting her hand and telling her it was going to be all right.

I remembered how the Louvre had looked that night as we crossed the bridge to the Left Bank, how I had taken one step after another that deviated from the plan I'd mapped out for myself.

And Montpellier was not after all where I was going to spend this school year, not the whole year anyway. The southern city had taken up a good chunk of my time, though, filled with people and experiences I would never forget. Maybe I had sensed from the beginning that I would not stay, but it wasn't until I'd seen Jade's bright, hopeful face that I knew. I could see the future then.

I started inviting Geneviève along on my walks after that. We both had this mania for dragging the streets of Paris at night, but so did half the city.

As for my parents, it took them awhile to get comfortable with the idea that their daughter had moved in with a lover and that the lover was a woman. I tried to explain, but I don't know if they understood. They wanted to know whether I was still planning to come back and finish my degree in the fall. I replied that I was returning in August as planned. I also told my family that they should expect a certain French visitor during winter break.

Dad wrote and said he was proud of me. It gave me a little thrill to read the words although I wasn't sure what he meant exactly. I'd flunked my exams and switched schools. Maybe it was just that I sounded happy and had made a big decision on my own. I didn't tell them that it was, in fact, Jade who had made it for me.

Jade seemed to adjust quickly to her new environment, bubbling over with enthusiasm most of the time. She was busy with new friends. She'd even started seeing an American guy she met in her classes.

We celebrated my twenty-first birthday at the end of February. Denise, Carly, and Rose came up for spring break. Denise slept on our couch and Carly and Rose stayed with their friends on rue Mouffetard. After that, the three of them went to visit Gerti and Wolfie in Stuttgart and they all went down to Italy together.

Jade and I decided we would visit Kari and Annik in Amsterdam in the summer.

Bernard never did go back to Jean-Luc. Now he was a student in *Sciences*, studying mineralogy. I was proud of him.

≈≈≈≈

One spring evening, Geneviève made me put down my book because we were meeting her friends Katrine, Dany, and Colette, along with Jade. She wouldn't tell me any more than that. We ended up standing in a small crowd on rue Bonaparte near her old school with our friends nearby, jostling each other, and laughing as the Beaux-Arts students paraded by on their way to the Bal des Quat'z Arts end-of-year bash. Most of them were wearing not much of anything, their undulating bodies painted. Some of the girls wore grass skirts; the boys had on helmets, Roman style, their faces blacked so their teeth and eyes flashed in the lamplight.

"I told you I read about this, remember?" I said.

"Of course. That is why I brought you here."

"I was jealous thinking of you dancing half naked."

"I did dance topless once," she admitted, "but only after I was pretty drunk. I don't think you would have wanted to see it."

"Oh, yes, I would." I came up behind her and put my arms around her. We fit. The feel of her plush stomach, the muscles of her arms as I ran my hands over them evoked fragments of memories. It seemed when I closed my eyes that we existed both in the present and together in a deeper dimension.

Geneviève turned to face me. Her curvy lips touched my ear as she murmured, "*Je t'aime*, Sophie."

"*Moi aussi.*" I touched my cheek to hers. "So, will you marry me?"

After a quick intake of breath, Geneviève said teasingly, "I can't marry you! You're a woman!"

"Oh yes, you can," I said, "but if you insist, we can wait until it becomes legal."

"No, no, let's do it," Geneviève said as the others converged around us.

"What were you two talking about?" demanded Jade in French, looping her arm through mine.

I just grinned and shook my head, shouting above the din of the crowd, "Come on, let's go to Deux Magots and celebrate!"

"What are we celebrating?" Katrine asked as Colette gave Dany a passionate kiss.

"*L'amour*," Geneviève cried while Jade shouted at the same time, "France!" They laughed as the others chimed in. "Springtime! Freedom! *La Liberte!*"

The six of us linked arms and paraded up rue Napoleon toward Boulevard Saint-Germain.

About the Author

Mary M. Wright lives in Minneapolis with her wife Layne, a large cat and a small dog. She is a painter as well as a writer, and teaches both. This is her first novel.

9 781943 353835